D1149498

GHOSTS
of the
DESERT

Withdrawn from Stock
Dublin City Public Libraries

GHOSTS
of the
DESERT

Ryan Ireland

A Point Blank Book

First published in North America, Great Britain and Australia
by Point Blank, an imprint of Oneworld Publications, 2016

Copyright © Ryan Ireland 2016

The moral right of Ryan Ireland to be identified as the
Author of this work has been asserted by him in accordance
with the Copyright, Designs, and Patents Act 1988

All rights reserved
Copyright under Berne Convention
A CIP record for this title is available from the British Library

ISBN 978-1-78074-820-7
ISBN 978-1-78074-821-4 (eBook)

Text designed and typeset by Tetragon, London
Printed and bound in Great Britain by Clays Ltd, St Ives plc

This book is a work of fiction. Names, characters, businesses,
organisations, places and events are either the product of the author's
imagination or are used fictitiously. Any resemblance to actual
persons, living or dead, events of locales is entirely coincidental.

Oneworld Publications
10 Bloomsbury Street
London WC1B 3SR
England

Stay up to date with the latest books,
special offers, and exclusive content from
Oneworld with our monthly newsletter

Sign up on our website
www.oneworld-publications.com

For Tara and Steve
and memories of Frisco

ONE

Jacobyville

I.

The world went blank, awash in white. For many this is how the world ends. A flash of white and then a silence. For Norman the flash of white and the silence were consequences of his hasty retreat. A single strand of barbwire caught him in the side and dragged its rusty metal length through the flesh of his underarm, rubbing a wound more than cutting it. He had cursed and stumbled forward when a second shot rang out, the sound of the ricochet at his feet whining long across the desertscape.

He lost his footing and toppled to the ground. His shoulder glanced off a rock. His leg twisted. His ankle throbbed from where he sprained it on a low-laying gravemarker. As he skidded to the flat bottom arroyo his ear grated on the hardpacked soil. The force of the final impact thumped the air from his lungs, leaving his jaw yawping at nothing, his neck straining upward and his teeth opening and shutting, biting at the sky above him. Dust blinded him and he blinked rapidly. Yet, the wound under his arm occupied his mind—it burned as if the wire still dragged long and slow through the skin.

He used his good arm to prop himself up. Blinking some more, he cleared the dust from his eyes and looked up the bank at the driftwood and barbwire fence. The desert plays tricks on

Leabharlanna Poibli Chathair Bhaile Átha Cliath
Dublin City Public Libraries

the mind and the trick it played now made the wire look like a crack across the clear blue of the sky.

From the opposite bank of the arroyo, the distinct sound of gravel crunching under boot, heel to toe. Norman turned his head almost imperceptibly to the side, as if by not looking at this figure on nether bank, it would simply disappear. But this is a child's game.

'Run, if you got the mind to,' an old man's voice said. There was a timbre in the voice that shattered the silence like the gunshots.

He dropped the charade of not looking at the old man. He started to his feet and pivoted, still in a stoop, to look at his assailant.

'Go on.' The old man used his free hand to make a shooing motion. His other arm cradled a rifle. His voice crackled a little, wizened, kindly. Ruts in his face, his filthy clothes, white windblown hair—had this been another time and place he might be viewed as a sage or a saint.

'Didnt mean to trespass,' Norman finally said.

At first the old man nodded, then he said yup. After a few more seconds he seemed to think better of his answer. 'This land aint mine,' he said. 'An you know it.'

For a moment they both nodded in agreement, one convincing the other, but neither knew which one. 'You know good an true this land here belongs to the Bureau of Land Management. Thats why youre here.'

'Yessir.'

Again, the old man nodded. Pulling at his pant legs he squatted on the bank, the rifle still cradled in his arm. Though he whispered as if speaking to a child, his voice amplified as all things do in the desertscape, voxed in the space of nothing. 'I coulda hit you with the first shot,' he said. 'That woulda been the last thing you ever read.' He nodded up the slope at the headstone. Then the old man chuckled and for a moment both parties seemed to be at ease. 'Figured I should scare you down here into this ditch before I cut you down.'

Twice now the breath had been forced from Norman's lungs. He lay half-propped in the dirt while the old man stood back up, the bones in his back audibly cracking into place. He groaned. Norman took in his surroundings once more. Down here in the dirt wash nothing offered shelter; up above, the desert stretched out without respite. Aside from the few gravemarkers in the wayward cemetery, there was also nothing. Running would be futile.

The old man reached into the breast pocket on his shirt and fished out a bullet. Casually he loaded it into the rifle, the parts clicking and sliding into place. He squinted at his target for a few seconds, both men staring and breathing at each other. The younger man held up a hand as if to make a pledge. Instead his words came out only as a series of pleadings punctuated with the word please. The old man hefted the butt of the gun to his shoulder and peered down the length of the barrel.

'I didnt have anything to do with that graverobbing,' Norman said. 'I'm a scholar. I'm just here to study ghost towns.'

For a long time neither of the men moved, each of their bodies held in poses designed to fatigue—the older man holding his breath with the rifle raised, the younger man's hand held up like a proselytizing beggar. Finally the old man gasped and in doing so caused the younger man to gasp.

'Scholar,' the old man said.

'Yessir,' Norman said. 'Like an academic type from a university.'

'I know.' The old man smiled wryly, licked his lips and cleared his throat. 'And what do you study, scholarman?'

'Anthropology.'

'Anthro…'

'Anthropology,' Norman repeated.

'The study of man, I know.'

Finally, the old man's poise with the gun grew completely lax and he leaned on it like a walking stick. He looked past Norman, toward the opposite bank of the arroyo and nodded. Norman craned his head around, following the old man's line of sight. Three figures dressed in rags descended on him, whooping as they came.

He'd driven across the United States on the interstate. For weeks his home had been his station wagon—a wood paneled tank with an extra large cabin. In the flatlands of Kansas he stopped for the night by simply pulling to the side of the road. Stink from the cattle farms permeated everything and he woke to the occasional roar of the passing tractortrailers. He continued on, stopping for fuel at two-pump gas stations and eating a late dinner at a Ground Round.

A middle-aged man with meaty hands sat three seats down the counter from Norman at the Ground Round. As he used his thumb to hold the hashbrowns to the fork and lifted them to his mouth, a blurry tattoo of the eagle, globe and anchor became visible on his forearm, indicating he served as a marine once upon a time. As he ate, dabs of ketchup hung from his mustache.

'Tell you what, missy,' the marine said to the waitress. 'Gonna have to order me up another plate of these hashbrowns.' He slugged back the last of his coffee and said to make sure the cook knew this was the best hash and scramble he ever done tasted.

'Sure will,' the girl cooed. She smiled and winked at the man. When she strolled down to ask Norman if everything was alright, the marine watched her walk away.

'Everythings good,' Norman said. 'Like he said, best hash an scram I ever had.'

He stopped, like he said too much—he tried to decide if he should say something else, but the marine decided for him.

'Where you from, stranger?'

The waitress cocked her head to the side as if she had just posed the question herself. Norman looked down at his plate, the smears of ketchup and strings of fried potato when he said Indiana. Then he looked up at the waitress, her face a painted mystery—either she was young and the late nights and hard work aged her prematurely or she was older and tried to look younger.

'You a long pull from Indy-ana,' the marine said. He rotated on his stool, slowly and forcefully in tectonic motion. There was a question left unstated.

'Driving out to Utah,' Norman said.

'Salt Lake?'

'Farther south.'

'Provo?'

'Going out to desert country.'

The marine's eyes narrowed. He glanced at the waitress and she shrugged.

'What kind of business could a boy from Indy-ana way have out in the deserts of godforsaken Utah?' Before Norman could answer, the marine looked at the waitress and said he'd been out to south Utah before. 'Aint nothing there but dirt, wind, few hippies, and villages of polygamists.' There was a rejoinder of laughter.

'I'm doing some research,' Norman said. 'I'm an instructor at a university.'

'Research?' The marine snorted with laughter.

'You a little young to be a professor, aint you?' the waitress asked. She leaned on the counter feigning interest.

Norman stammered. 'I, well, I'm not a professor. I'm an instructor. And I'm old enough, I guess. I got my masters degree.'

The marine guffawed and slapped his hand on the counter.

'I'm sorry,' Norman said. 'I'm not sure what the—whats so funny.'

'Nothing,' the waitress said. She straightened back up and cocked her head to the side again. 'Nothings funny.'

'Desert will eat a straight lace like you alive,' the marine said. 'Stationed out in the Mojave just after Korea ended. Goddamnedest place I ever been.'

Norman looked back at the waitress, hoping for some sort of kindness, some type of pleasantry. But she forced a smile and the ruts around her eyes were wrinkled with age, not laughter. And Norman knew this job had aged her prematurely. She began to wipe at the countertop again and said she had a sister out in Indy.

'You aint never mentioned that,' the marine said.

Norman acknowledged the remark with a single nod.

'Yeah,' she sighed. She glanced up at Norman, then at the marine; said her sister met a man and they ran off to Indy. 'Havent heard from her in years.'

'Like she got kidnapped,' the marine said.

'Well, she was in love with him,' the waitress said.

'But he made it so she never talked to her family again—that sounds like a kidnapper. How you know she isnt in some sort of trouble?'

'I guess I dont know,' the waitress said, her voice small.

The man turned back to Norman. 'Guess we cant trust you Indy-ana types. You aint here to steal our women, is you?'

With a surge of confidence, Norman faked a smile, winked at the waitress and said he had already kidnapped one, years ago. 'Came back when I realized I got the wrong sister,' he said. He laughed at his own joke, then stopped when he realized no one else laughed with him.

The waitress shrank back from the counter and the marine sat sideways, watching Norman's every move until she gave him the bill. He paid in cash, counting out single dollars silently. And without waiting for change, he slipped out of the glass doors into the parking lot.

From the station wagon in the parking lot, Norman watched through the flat-paned windows of the diner as the woman and the marine chatted. He watched other customers come and go, some sitting and smoking, talking with the waitress and the marine, the tables cluttering with dishes and food and then cleared and wiped clean again. On the corner of the counter the pie rack spun around. When the waitress and the marine left the diner together, the marine noticed Norman sitting in the station wagon. He leaned in to whisper something to the woman, guiding her by the elbow toward his pickup truck. They parted and the marine strode over to Norman's car and motioned with his forefinger for Norman to roll down the window.

Norman cranked the window down.

'Parking lot aint no motel.'

'Just sitting here,' Norman said. He placed his hands where the marine could see them, then dropped them to his lap. For a second he made eye contact, but quickly looked away.

'Aint a place for just sittin,' the marine said. 'Best if you just roll outta here.'

'I'm not looking to make any trouble,' Norman began.

'You done made it already,' the marine said. 'Just by comin here and being like you are, you done made trouble.' The man struggled to keep his voice at an even keel and his hands were balled up in fists. He glanced across the parking lot where the waitress watched through the back pane of the pickup. Taking a deep breath, the marine continued, 'I dont want to make no more trouble here, so I'll tell you what.'

Norman raised his eyebrows in feigned interest. But the marine didn't notice; he looked out over the roof of the station wagon as he spoke. 'We're both gonna pull outta this lot. I'm gonna go thataway'—he pointed his finger one direction— 'an youre gonna go thisaway'—and he used his thumb like a hitchhiker to indicate the opposite direction. 'Give that little lady another scare, foller us outta here an I'll make sure you meet your maker.'

Norman nodded and the marine finally made eye contact.

'Go on now,' he said and Norman shifted the car into reverse, the taillights behind him lighting up the otherwise vacant lot. The marine stepped back and watched him idle away. In the mirror Norman watched the man grow distant and then vanish altogether.

Time blended into a phantasma of transit—the blaring sun, snippets of the men's voices, yuccas and scrub and grass and dirt and sky. No clouds or water. Some broken bottles and a pile of rusty cans. Later he opened his eyes to look up at the sky stretched plaintive and blue and even in all directions. It seemed to pulsate. The mountains on the horizon looked to be no more than scraps of torn paper fluttering in a non-existent breeze.

'Pa,' one of the voices called.

The old man walked over and looked down on Norman. 'It's alright, son,' he said. 'We got a ways to go yet. You just get some rest.' He patted Norman's chest.

And with the old man's permission Norman collapsed back into an exhausted slumber where his dreams were illusion and his dreams were real—a nexus where all things meet and we believe we see with divine eyes. Some of the images presented themselves as mere images—a toilet full of bloody condoms in a truck stop bathroom, the floor of the stall sticky with piss. Others were fledged past imagery alone and unfolded across an artificial timeline. In these visions he saw people he knew. Dusty, his colleague from the university, stood in his office doorway, a paper cone full of water in his hand.

He said, 'Forget it, man.'

And though the conversation did not exist outside this moment, somewhere in Norman's brain the comment found a context.

'I wasnt going to act on it or anything,' he heard himself say. In this dream—like the dreams of those in comas or who lapse into hypnotic spells they attribute to some distant god—Norman did not see with his own eyes. Rather he looked down on the figure of himself, small and weak.

Dusty nodded, looked past Norman and around the half-empty room. 'She's married. She's way the hell outta your league.' He sipped at the water. 'And in case youve forgotten, she's also our boss.'

'I was just saying,' Norman began, but Dusty walked away from the door and Norman could see her from straight down the hallway. In the real world—in the waking life—there was no such geography. Her office sat at a sharp right angle to his. But the reality of dreams is a fickle thing.

Doctor Blanche looked up from her desk. The distance between them shortened and she asked Norman where he was going.

He said he would head west, the grant for the ghost town study came through.

'You better take it,' she said. Then she stood and unbuttoned her jacket, exposing her bare chest. Her breasts were full and firm, the nipples slightly oval shaped. Teeth marks rankled around the left areola. Bruises, purple and jaundiced, spotted her ribs. The jacket dropped to the floor and her bare arm showed four little fingerprint bruises.

'Signs of life here!' one yelled.

The dream vanished into mystery. Doctor Blanche and her bruised body became not even a thing of memory. A hand grabbed at Norman's crotch and jostled his erection. He swatted clumsily and laughter bellowed out around him.

He did not allow himself to recede back into dreams this time. Instead he propped himself up on his side but a hand pressed against his chest and flattened him back out on the makeshift gurney. It must have been noon, for the sun hovered directly overhead and the heat spread out hot and even and unforgiving. The old man leaned over him, his face mostly a shadow. 'Got a couple miles yet,' he said. 'Take a nap, rest your eyes and I'll show you the place I made for us.'

Out on the plains, the towns spaced out farther and fewer. In the early morning haze, the lamplights of the farmhouses set back from the road appeared as fallen stars, burning white with celestial heat. Once the daylight came on in full, after the sun rose up over the horizon, each homestead became visible—most of them white and mottled with age and weather. Barns with roofs of flapping husks of tarpaper, moldered straw floors and slatwood walls littered the sideroads. Some barns still had peeling advertisements for Mail Pouch Tobacco, some with forty-eight star flags on their broadsides. These structures served little purpose other than housing strays and feral creatures, the occasional drifter.

He slept more than a couple times in the shadows of places like this. The vacant and vast landscape drifted on forever, hypnotizing him with the rhythm of the road: the tick of one dashed yellow line after another, the dipping and swooping of telephone wires spaced at regular intervals on wooden poles. The vibrations of the steering wheel pulsating in his hands and arms. He had to sleep.

He found a barn huddled next to a curve in the road, the morning sun casting its shadow askew, blotting a patch of asphalt with shade. He pulled onto the shoulder and into the shadowed spot and parked the car. He figured he could rest here a while, and when the sun rose a bit further the sudden brightness would wake him.

In Provo he had stopped at a Laundromat to make a few phone calls. He took some change from the ashtray in the wagon and went to the payphone on the side of the building. Exhaust fans from the dryers vented nearby, blowing steady gusts of gas-fired air and cinders of lint. First he dialed his parents' house. After the fifth ring he hung up and retrieved his quarter. He contemplated the coin for a moment before redepositing it. He waited for the dial tone and punched in the number for the university Anthropology department. In his head, he calculated the time difference and doubted anyone would be in this early.

'Hello?' a voice said. Then she corrected herself. 'I mean Anthropology and Human Sciences department.' It was Doctor Blanche. A heat that felt like pin pricks spread across the back of Norman's neck.

'Uh, is Dusty in?'

There was a pause and Norman figured Doctor Blanche had no idea who this was. He imagined her looking at the in-and-out board. 'I havent seen him, Norman.'

On the last word, his name, Norman broke into a sweat. He started to respond, but she interrupted. 'When are you coming back?' Then, more professionally, she restated the question, asking how long the grant let him stay out in the field.

'Few weeks,' Norman said. He looked at the laundry exhaust fans as he spoke, the jets of lint and dust cascading into the air. He had to shout his answer into the phone. 'Figure it might be midsummer.'

He imagined Doctor Blanche playing with her necklace charm that rested at the top of her cleavage. She often did this inadvertently while talking on the phone.

'I'd like to hear about it,' she said.

'My grant?'

'Your whole trip,' she said. 'I mean, the whole department is talking about it.'

Norman laughed, said it was summertime. 'The whole department is you and Dusty and the secretaries,' he said.

At first it seemed like the line had gone dead, then Doctor Blanche said, 'Well, we're all talking about it—about you.'

'Is this the drug cartel thing again?' Norman asked.

Ever since he had applied for the grant, his colleagues kept dropping by his half-empty office to warn him about the latest news article concerning the drug cartels in the southwest.

'No,' Doctor Blanche said. 'We just all want you to come back and tell us what you did out there all by your lonesome.'

'Research.'

'You are out there by yourself, right?'

'Only wrote the grant for me.'

The phone beeped in his ear and Norman told her so. They paid each other hasty farewells and Norman hung up only after hearing the phone click and the line went dead.

At first Norman couldnt keep track of how many there were. Sometimes when he awoke a small crowd had gathered around him, staring. Other times, in bouts of fitful waking, he saw but only one or two men. Always the old man stayed close. Jacoby, they called him. This much Norman could remember. The others seemed interchangeable at first—as if they could number just a couple or as many as a score. But in each subsequent waking Norman came to recognize the individual men as distinctly their own beings and counted them to be four or five.

A hand rested on his forehead. In his confusion, Norman did not know if the hand had been there or if someone had just now placed it there. He opened his eyes.

'Hi there,' a man said. His face was darkly bearded, streaks of white running from the corners of his mouth and down his chin. Equally dark were his eyes. Through the thick facial hair he smiled, turning the lighter stripes of hair into bowed lines.

Norman tried to formulate a question, but his mind seemed muddy, slow. He tried to speak, struggling to make any sort of articulation. The bearded man called for his pa and looked back down at Norman.

The place where Norman now found himself was of another time. Even in his foggy state, he could guess the structure to be from the late eighteen hundreds. The floors where he lay were rough hewn planks, the walls much the same. He stared up at the tresses of the ceiling, the missing slats revealing patches of sky.

The old man Jacoby entered through a doorway, devoid of any door. A short, curly-haired man followed him, clapping.

'Get him some drink,' Jacoby said and the two other men left together.

For a long time, Jacoby and Norman stared at one another.

'You cant figure if youre mad at me or not,' Jacoby finally said.

Norman didnt answer. He felt dizzy and the nausea left little time for emotions or controlled thought.

'Your...' Jacoby searched his mind for the right word— 'dilemma goes like this: I was gonna kill you and that is upsetting.' He shrugged as if casting his own judgments to mirror those passed by Norman. 'But then—an act of kindness. I spared your life.'

'You abducted me,' Norman said.

Jacoby nodded in agreement. 'Yes,' he said. 'Part of letting you live meant taking you with us.'

The two men came back into the house with a stoneware cup, proffering it to their father.

'Mix it up right?'

'Did, yeah.'

Jacoby eyed the cup and sniffed it. 'Put in more of one than the other, huh?'

The bearded man's head bobbed side to side before he said yeah.

When Jacoby thanked the bearded man, he called him Oz. Then he blew on the liquid and lowered the cup to Norman's mouth. At first Norman resisted the supposed act of kindness. But the thought of moisture in his mouth won out and his lips pursed out to the edge of the cup in an effort to consume as much as possible. The drink tasted like a thin mud, a sort of tepid tea.

'Easy now,' Jacoby said. He tilted the cup back and pulled it from Norman's lips. The same conundrum of gratefulness and bitterness consumed Norman. He wanted more of the liquid, but couldnt bring himself to ask for it.

'Where am I?' he asked.

'Youre in my town,' Jacoby said.

'Your town.'

'Thats right. Call it Jacobyville. Little place. Once you get up the strength I'll show you around, get you used to it.'

'I'm not staying,' Norman said. It was a child's defiance.

'Sorry to hear that,' Jacoby said. He frowned and studied the stoneware cup he held with both hands. In a slow and deliberate motion, he poured the contents out on the floor. The wizened slats soaked in the tea until the liquid existed as no more than a stain.

'Here.' He extended one hand to help Norman stand. Reluctantly, Norman took it and they stood together. They walked together, unsteady, to the door of the house. Though the sun set behind them, casting the shadow of the house long and shadowed out into space, Norman squinted.

The house sat halfway up a craggy slope. Other houses constructed from grayed timbers lay scattered in the folds of the mountainside. From here on this barren slope, Norman could spy a number of structures. Some had skeleton roofs, others had sheets of reddened tin peeled back to expose the beams beneath. At the base of the mountain the land became less rocky and stretched into a pan of tanned dust. The dust turned to haze, then to nothing. At the edge of nothing, the faint outlines of mountains blurred in and out of vision.

For a time both men looked out over the whole of Jacobyville, the land surrounding it. Jacoby sighed wistfully. 'Strike out on your own and you'll die alone,' he said. 'Aint nothing round for miles. Not a goddamned thing.'

Norman scanned the skyline, the nearer landmarks of buildings and boulders. Then, cropped up from the ground like a matchstick, a post stood. Another one stood out a ways from it. Strings stretched between them and the posts continued on in both directions until they looked no more than a filament.

'Youre not going to tell me where we are.'

'Done told you, son. We're in Jacobyville. You want to leave, go on.'

'You think I wont make it.'

'Nope,' Jacoby said. 'I know you wont make it.'

Suddenly Norman felt weak, hollow. He leaned against the doorframe.

'See, I know the land here. Grew up here. Father was a miner before the town went bust. Family stayed on workin the mines even after most all the town done shuttered up. I knowed this place when it was livin and I know it now.'

'So you renamed the town,' Norman said. 'What'd you call it originally?'

Jacoby clucked his tongue and wagged his finger. 'We only call it Jacobyville.'

Pressure began mounting in Norman's chest, like he was building up the energy to scream. Meanwhile, the old man seemed so serene, staring calmly out over his ghost town. With eyes roving restlessly over the desertscape, Jacoby spoke again, his voice resounding more harshly than before. 'This town here is what remains when you wake up from a good dream. Most everyones dreamt of something they wanted only to wake and find themselves alone and disappointed. In one moment youre—how will it be said?—living the dream. Then you wake and—' He turned his whole body to look at Norman, made a magician's hand gesture and mouthed the word poof. 'This place here, my Jacobyville, it's an in-between.'

Norman spat. 'I never had any dreams like this.'

Jacoby sighed and rested one hand on his hip. With his other arm he took Norman by the elbow and led him from the house. 'I'll show you around,' Jacoby said. 'Walk with me a ways and I'll show you how we live.'

Norman considered running away. It was as the old man had said, no one in the village would try to stop him. There were no constraints. He weighed the foreboding words of Jacoby about not making it through the desert and matched those against what he knew of the geography. Some ghost towns could be as many as a hundred miles from a town—a thought that only became daunting if one forgot about the roadways connecting the towns. Finding any mark of the contemporary world would save him; he simply needed to pick a vector and hold to it.

After a few days' recuperation, when Norman regained his sense of balance, he tried to leave. Dawn broke and Norman woke. He lay on the floor of Oz's cabin. The early morning sun shone through the missing patches in the ceiling, throwing lopsided squares of light on the slatted floor. Before bed Norman had positioned himself where the first patches of light would appear, hoping to create a natural alarm clock. It worked.

He took nothing with him. Perhaps he realized it was not his time to go; that time would come much later. He walked. Out in the distance he studied the line of telephone poles, marking this as a path to civilization. The poles ran southwest to northeast. In the southwest, the poles became swallowed in the slopes of Jacobyville. In the opposite direction the poles disappeared into oblivion. Behind him the sun rose rapidly. He walked faster.

The poles—the first destination in his journey—stayed distant things, his goal being the place beyond what he could see.

As he walked the remnants of Jacobyville populated the land around him. Posts—little more than dry-rot wood with tangles of wire spindled from the top—stood erect, marking the boundaries of properties long since dissolute. A collapsed hovel, a pile of sheet metal and timbers, lay farther out. To his left the land became cultivated into a strange shape he recognized as a dike wall to an earthen reservoir. And indeed he proved himself correct as he stumbled over a pipe running half above the ground. He shook his head, refocused his gaze on the posts and continued onward.

In the classes he taught at the university, he would have considered Jacobyville a classic example of a boom ghost town. Its mines, the epicenter, were located in the steppes of the small mountain range. Out of the main shaft came the bulk of production. Norman could tell this much from a single glance: an enormous wash had been set up for the workers to separate silver and copper, zinc—whatever material was common in this region—from the lesser elements.

The lecture itself became a thing of second nature to Norman. He often took slides of ghost towns from his library research and showed them in class. With the lights off and one responsive student ready to turn the carousel on cue, Norman would stand at the back of the lecture hall and describe to the class what they saw and how to really see it.

'The ghost town seems pretty empty, right?'

One or two students might dutifully nod their heads. Norman continued on. 'As an anthropologist you have to be able to see what was there. In this regard, our friends over in Archeology can be invaluable.' He exchanged glances with the student at the projector and the next slide appeared on the pull-down projector screen. The picture showed the inside of a stone building, thousands of cylindrical stones scattered across the floor. 'Anyone want to take a guess as to what this is?'

The fan inside the projector hummed. The students stared at the screen intently, avoiding any eye contact as he prowled between the rows of tables. A single pupil ventured a guess, saying it must have been some sort of surveyor's office and the stones were samples.

'Thats right,' Norman said. 'Typically all mining ghost towns have a similar anatomy and the surveyors office is a staple. Being one of the wealthiest and most important men in the town, it wouldnt be unusual for the surveyor to have his dwelling constructed out of stone. The windows might even be glass, which we all know was a major luxury.'

The next slide showed the entirety of the ghost town from above. The shadow of the airplane remained visible in the slide. Norman approached the front of the room, stepping before the screen. The image of the slide warped across his body. He pointed to a building. 'This is the office,' he said. 'See its close proximity to the main mining operation?' The students nodded. Toward the back of the room a pencil scratched away on loose leaf paper. 'We know from historical documents—a census and some manifests—that this town in particular, New Daisy, had a population of three thousand at one point. Yet, aside from the surveyors office and a few shacks, we see very little in the way of residences. Why is that?'

No one answered. Norman sighed and pointed to the barren lands surrounding the mines in the photo. 'See this area? This gap between the mines and the smelters, the kilns?' he asked. 'This is where the miners lived. In tents. Some might construct shanties, but there were very few permanent structures for residences.'

Three bumps cropped up on the horizon, near the telephone poles. Norman narrowed his eyes, trying to discern their shape and purpose. He quickened his step until he trotted along at a light jog. Sweat beaded at his hairline. He looked over his shoulder. Jacobyville—the structures remaining from a much older town without name—looked distant now. The bumps became more distinct and Norman recognized them as kilns—configurations made from brick and used to melt down the mined minerals. This marked the beginning of the edge of Jacobyville. Kilns and smelters and any other industrial facility usually sat outside of town and downwind to reduce the risk of fire. Because of their shape, these sorts of kilns were called beehives. The opening in the sidewall was large enough for a man to walk through upright and the domed inside was considerably bigger.

In any other situation Norman would have stopped to examine the structures—an inspection of the kilns would reveal the materials wrought from these furnaces. He kept going.

'Best to slow down some,' a voice said.

Norman stopped and all lay silent. Voices carry in the desert. He turned. The town grew evermore distant. Now the flat bake of the sun washed it out. From out here, there appeared no signs of life.

'Just cause you aint sweatin dont mean you aint dehydrated.'

No doubt the voice belonged to Jacoby. It seemed to project from the beehive kiln. For a while Norman stood like an animal half-poised for flight. Then he resigned. He traipsed toward the kiln. As he drew closer, he saw Jacoby sitting cross-legged in the aperture. 'Sweat'll dry up soon as it leaves your body out here. Sticks in the hair, true enough, but the rest of your body, it just dries on up—evaporates. Can be confusing for a man whos used to soakin through a shirt on a hot day.' He licked his lips. 'Goin out to cross the desert means takin in little bits of water, keepin a steady pace—a slow pace.'

Norman looked at the ground, chewed on the inside of his cheek. Jacoby continued talking. 'Some folk'll say the winter is a better time to leave, but it's just as dry then. Cooler, but just as dry. The dryness is what kills a man.'

Norman's nose itched and he used his thumbnail to scratch at it.

'Now followin the lectric lines outta here—now thats clever.'

Like a child embarrassed by his transgression, Norman looked up at Jacoby and said he was sorry. On the ground before Jacoby lay a dismantled pistol.

The old man chuckled. 'You aint got to say sorry. You did like most everone else would do.' He picked up the butt and forestock of the gun and clamped them back together. Using his thumb, he rotated the chamber. As it spun around, it clicked like the gears of some immortal clock.

'You knew I'd be coming out this way,' Norman said.

'People have a limited range of reactions,' Jacoby said. 'Put a man in a place like this—a place that limits his choices—an you'll be able to predict what he's gonna do.'

'You going to let me go?'

'No. Dont figure I should.' Jacoby reached in his shirt pocket and pulled out a few bullets. He plopped them into the chambers, one by one, leaving the last chamber vacant.

'Youre gonna shoot me then.' Norman tried to stand straighter when he said it, but the defeat resounded in his voice.

Again, Jacoby chuckled. 'You an your limited mind,' he chided. 'Live out here for a time an you'll learn theres no bottom, no limit to what you can do, what youre capable of. Theres more to this life than life an death.' He patted the ground next to him as if beckoning Norman to hear a bedtime story. At first Norman resisted; then he shrugged and sauntered over and sat next to the old man and they looked out over the creation laying before them—the barren stretch of dirt and dust and sky and wind and nothing.

'Youre eventually gonna kill me, right?' Norman asked. He stared out into the expanse, doing his best just to ask the question, not look at the man next to him.

But Jacoby cackled and rubbed his palms together. 'No,' he said. 'I'll tell you right now, I'm no danger to you.' He sighed, spat and stared with Norman out into the desert.

'Youre going to tell me that I'm the biggest danger to myself,' Norman said.

Jacoby's head bobbed up and down in agreement, though his sights remained set on the horizon. 'Youre smart,' he said. 'No denyin that. But this place, it's the stuff you cant think of—thats the stuff thatll kill you.'

'I'm willing to take my chances.'

'Just know theres nothing out there for you,' Jacoby said.

Norman disagreed, telling the old man he had a life—a job, an apartment, friends, family, the usual trappings of existence.

'But theyre gone,' Jacoby said. 'Youre here an all that you had is gone.'

'No,' Norman said. 'I'm going back.'

He feinted like he was going to stand up. But something in Jacoby's stare out into the desert gave Norman pause. The old man cleared his throat, swallowed and cleared his throat again.

'While you were asleep, the world ended.' He said it blank—blank as the space they inhabited.

It took a few moments for Norman to digest the words. He let out a bark of laughter and began to stand up. Jacoby grabbed the waist of Norman's pants and pulled him back to the earth. 'I'm serious—deadly serious. The world you know is gone.'

'This'—Norman pointed back and forth between their faces with his index finger—'this crazy talk might work with your sons, but it wont work with me. The world isnt over. Youre crazy if you think I'll buy it. If the world was over, we'd know it. Fallout would be snowing down on us. Heat waves and glowing skies, explosions.' He squinted at Jacoby and said he was leaving. 'Shoot me in the back because I'm walking away now.'

He stood and took a few steps, until he emerged from the growing shadow of the kiln. With each footfall he expected to hear the click of the pistol, but a half dozen steps later only Jacoby's voice filled the air.

'It started in California,' he said. 'The end of the world. The end of society anyway. It started with a loaf of bread.'

Norman's steps slowed.

'Everyone thinks the end of civilization will be this great event, that everyone will know about it. An explosion, as you say. An asteroid. A war or famine or disease. There'll be a war, jets screeching overhead. Tanks in the streets. But the truth is that the places we build are so delicate it'd hardly take some cataclysm to destroy them. The threat—the rumor—of destruction is enough to bankrupt us of our humanity. Thought alone can bring us to our knees.'

Norman had stopped his walking, but he did not turn around. Instead he looked at the rocky soil beneath his feet. The old man's voice changed as he spoke—the timbre growing less gruff, more poetic like a man practiced in the art of storytelling.

'Theres a neighborhood where people cant get out. Theyre so poor they cant gather up their belongings and shove on. Rundown houses—shacks really—boarded up Methodist church where they used to hold elections. The streets are cracked and gravelly, trash tumbling down them like bramble. A convenience store run by an Iranian man might just be the only surviving business.'

He did not know when, but Norman had turned to look at the old man. With the sun past its apex in the sky and the shadow of the kiln stretched out before him like a dakhma woven from shadow and darkness, Norman could no longer see into the void of the kiln, the man contained within. From the darkness, Jacoby's voice continued telling of how the world collapsed.

'Like so many businesses, this Iranians goods arrived through a complex system of transportation—rails an trucks, warehouses an boats. The toils of some slave labor factored by some accountant into the cost of a box of cereal or a pair of jeans. The folks in this neighborhood hate the Iranian. They hate his success; they hate that he does not give his goods away in charity. They hate his skin color and they hate his accent. The people in this neighborhood look at his storefront with the wrought iron bars across the windows an his tricolor banner with suspicion. The only reason he is allowed to exist is that he has bread.

'And one day this bread does not come. Maybe the bread provider stopped distributing to this neighborhood because the cost of gasoline climbed to nearly three dollars a gallon and it was no longer economic to deliver goods to this place. Maybe the truck had a flat or the driver quit. Maybe the driver died of a heart attack while sittin at a stoplight. No one really knows. Whats important is that the bread did not come and a small congress of families became upset. They pointed at the Iranian an accused him of withholdin products so he could gouge them on the price. Simple words escalated into shoutin an passers-by stopped outside the storefront. The Iranian pushed people from his store, condemning them in his tongue. A blow was struck somewhere in the midst of the commotion, then another and another.

'But lockin the neighborhood people out of his store did nothing to stop the torrent of madness already unleashed on this world. The neighborhood in some collective madness began assaulting the storefront—bottles an cans, rocks, a hammer. Then, of course, fire.'

The old man made a guttural noise and shook his head.

'By the time anyone responded the entire neighborhood had become a place of rioting an what men in skyscrapers—the types who wear suits an drive shiny cars—what they would call senseless violence. What those men dont realize is that violence is the only thing that makes any sense in this godforsaken world. When everything else falls apart—your government or the church or family—violence becomes the only natural conclusion. It is who we are at our base.'

'The store,' Norman prompted. 'What happened with the store?'

From the shadows Norman could hear Jacoby's laughter rumbling again. 'You want me to tell you—or do you want to wander off into the desert an find out for yourself?'

Norman stepped closer, into the veil of shadow from the kiln. The sun became obscured and it took a moment for his eyes to adjust.

'Tell me,' Norman said.

Jacoby obliged. 'Like plucking the keystone out of an arch, the whole thing collapsed in on itself. The poor in this neighborhood rioted an the riots spread into the business district where men in suits worked. Some of these men were killed and it outraged their families and they demanded retribution. By the time the police stepped in, they did not know how to control the mob and they resorted to violence. News of the police actions spread an the National Guard was called in to restore peace. But there was no peace to restore—just a system to return to. A system where the poor depended on the Iranian. Across the towns of California folks became enraged. Some saw the Iranian as a symbol of greed and they attacked anyone with skin of that color. Bread trucks became targets for the rioters and soon bread delivery ceased along certain routes. Others saw the police an military as the enemy. The governor tried to say something, hopin the words might help, but they went unnoticed, the violence spreadin across the country incited by headlines an folk stories.

'It didnt take a bomb. It didnt take a plague or something born of revelation an scripture. Death is rarely so glorious as we make it in the mind. Centuries of city buildin an law-makin—then it's gone.'

The men stared at each other in measured silence. Norman tried to read the expression on the old man's face, to see if he hid some guile. But he found none.

'I dont believe you,' Norman said.

'Dont you?' Jacoby asked in return. 'What dont you believe?'

'Any of it.'

'As I told you how these events came to pass you thought of the times you saw your father grow angry with a store for not stockin a product, of the times your mother muttered something under her breath about the country lettin their kind—whoever that was—in. Youve seen the news an watched, some part of you secretly envious of the rioters settin fire to cars and throwin bricks at the police officers.'

Norman felt light-headed. He shifted his weight from one foot to the other and ran his fingers through his hair. 'I think if I walked through the desert and reached a town, I'll find out that the story you just told me is completely bogus. I think youre a—a man who needs someone to lie to.'

Jacoby grinned, amused at this prospect. 'Perhaps,' he said. 'You could very well hoof it through the desert an reach a town in a few days time. The townsfolk will talk to you, tell you the world kept truckin along. But the reality is still there. The world will have ended for you.' He leaned forward and dropped his voice as if there were prying ears about. 'The worlds we live in are fragile, son. They are held together by what we cannot see. And now youve seen.'

2.

When the desert heat intensified to a blistering constant burn, Jacoby announced they would leave on an excursion.

'Take us a week in all,' he said.

The entirety of the village gathered in the barn. The building itself sat in the fold where two slopes ran together. Some years ago a rockslide knocked in the rear supports of the structure, filling the back end of it with rubble and sagging the roof. Even with these deficits, the barn remained the largest of the buildings in Jacobyville and became, by default, the meeting hall for their settlement. Because of its location, the barn received little in the way of sunlight and little in the way of wind. Norman surmised that the more perishable goods might have been stored here once upon a time.

Norman took a seat on the dirt floor, picking at shafts of straw scattered around him. He nodded at Oz who returned the gesture. Since he had stayed, this had become their way of silently greeting each other. His brother, the curly-haired son, was never so quiet. All called him Gay Jim—never just Jim. As Norman made eye contact with him, Gay Jim began with the whooping. The sounds were almost canine—a yowling and yipping punctuated by stutters of idiotic argot. He stank of sweat and moldered clothing. Sometimes the intensity of his stench in the desert heat caused Norman to gag.

'Whatre we talkin bout here?' Raybur asked. How a man like Raybur managed to keep any fat on his frame in a place like this bewildered Norman. His eyes glinted deep in their pudgy sockets. He spoke like he moved—slow and deliberate.

'Run down to Clarks Crick, get some supplies, freshen up.'

Raybur's wife, Martha, asked the next question. 'Doin any dealings while you down yonder?'

'Figured I would.'

Raybur and Martha whispered in each other's ear. Meanwhile, Gay Jim worked himself up, whooping and clapping, forcing Jacoby to acknowledge the racket. 'Oz,' Jacoby said. 'Take your brother out of here. Walk him round.'

The two children who played in the corner followed the brothers out of the building. Gay Jim whooped and they heard him take off into a sprint, the gravel crunching under foot until the sound faded into nothing. Oz called after him, to no avail, and he began to swear and the children giggled in return until he told them to go on and git.

Jacoby smiled at those few left in the barn. 'My boys,' he said. He shook his head, then refocused on the matter at hand. 'Trips gonna be a hard one. Wont deny that. The salt licks are bound to be hotter than a skillet.' Everyone nodded in agreement. Since the days had grown into this furnace heat, Norman had become more aware of how long he had been gone. The grant he drafted allowed him to stay out in the desert until mid-June. After mid-June the desert became unbearable, too dangerous to survive. Though he never counted the days, he figured it to be July by now.

'It'll be a tough one an we'll have to go light,' Jacoby said. 'Thats why I'm only takin my boys an Norman here.'

Norman heard his name and looked up. All the villagers looked at him.

Raybur shifted on his rump and said he wasnt certain if that was a good idea.

'Shit, you done take dead weight with you.' The statement came from the corner where Lucas Brown stood. He spat on the ground and glowered at Norman. 'You headin to Clarks Crick, you dont need no cityboy.'

Norman tried to find a place to interject, but Jacoby spoke first.

'He's got to see how we make a livin at some point,' Jacoby said. 'Me an my boys'll give him a good introduction.'

'Lemme go long,' Raybur said. 'Been a spell since I been down Clarks Crick way.' He waited, knowing he needed more justification, then added he could carry Norman if he passed out from exhaustion.

Jacoby mulled the proposition, then advised them all to pack light. 'Leave the shotguns an rifles. Be a pistol only show.' He directed his attention to Martha. 'You be alright without Raybur?'

'I'll make it just fine,' she said.

'You'll care for our Madonna then?'

Lucas Brown forced a cough and Raybur's gaze shot over at Norman.

'Of course I will,' Martha said. When she said it, she also fixed Norman with a look.

'Good.' Jacoby clapped his hands. 'We'll leave just after midnight.'

The mention of an excursion sent Jacobyville into a bustle. Each man went to his respective house and readied his gear. Across the gulf of graveled railings the denizens of this place called back and forth to one another.

'Rope?' Oz yelled out from the door of his house.

Down the slope, in the shack perched on a stone shelf, Raybur yawped back, saying he had rope.

'Shells?' he called back up the slope.

'Damn it,' Oz sighed. He began looking through some crates, cursing as he went when Jacoby's voice cracked out across the chasm. 'No shotgun, no shells. Pack light.'

Packing light came as second nature to Norman. When he left Indiana for the desert, he only filled half of the back of the station wagon. Dusty had stopped by the apartment with a six pack of beers.

He opened the fridge. 'You should toss out that milk before you go,' he said. 'Turn to cheese by the time you get back.'

Norman sat on the arm of the couch in the living room. The only divider between the kitchen and the living room was a waist-high counter, which often served as a bar. Dusty leaned on it and used a bottle opener he kept as a keychain to open the beverages.

'Youre sure you want to do this?'

Norman leaned over and took the beer from the counter. 'What? Have a drink with the likes of you? I guess I can stomach it.' He took a long sip of beer.

Dusty paid Norman a courtesy laugh. 'I mean heading out into the damned desert for a month.'

'Why not?'

'Yeah,' Dusty said.

'Whats the problem then?'

'The timing I guess.'

They both took long drinks this time.

'It'll help to get away from here,' Norman said. 'When I

get back I'm gonna sign a lease over at Oakdale Apartments. Get a smaller place.'

Dusty nodded. 'Probably best to get out of this place,' he said. Then he asked where Norman had been sleeping.

'On the couch,' Norman said and they both looked at the door to the bedroom.

Dusty brought the bottle most of the way to his lips then asked if Norman would have to repaint the walls.

'Yeah. Landlord said we'd have to when we first began painting the walls. Told us we'd have to put a coat of primer back over it.'

They quieted themselves for a long while before Dusty spoke again. 'Hey, man, no one thought Grace was, uh, that she was doing all the things she was doing. We were all as surprised as you were.'

Norman traced his finger around the lip of the bottle and said no one was as surprised as he was.

'True,' Dusty said. 'Lot about folks we dont know.'

Norman drained the last of his beer and sat cradling the bottle in his hands. 'Whatre you getting at?'

'I understand wanting to get away because of everything that happened with Grace, but then theres this whole thing with Doctor Blanche.'

'Yeah,' Norman said. 'That thing.'

'Man, listen—no one actually thinks anything happened.'

'People are talking then?'

Dusty bobbed his head side to side. 'Well, yeah, of course everyones talking. I mean—'

'These fucking women.' Norman swigged his beer. 'What am I supposed to do about it?'

Dusty wedged his empty bottle between the couch cushions. 'Stay here,' he said. 'Defend yourself. Running out into the middle of the desert country where a bunch of crazies and drug-fueled communes are looks like youre running away.'

'Like admitting I'm guilty.'

'Just say it, man—one way or the other.' Dusty's eyes connected with Norman's and his jaw tightened. 'Shit,' he said. 'You did do it. Doctor Blanche didnt imagine anything. You did it for real.'

For a moment Norman seemed to contemplate an answer by looking at the label on his empty bottle. Then he swung it in a single arcing motion until it exploded on the side of Dusty's head.

'You ready?' Oz asked.

Norman took a moment to process the question. 'Dont really have anything to get ready.'

Oz scoped out the living quarters Norman claimed as his—a few rags of clothing and a three-legged stool he'd salvaged from somewhere.

'Right,' Oz said. 'We'll take care of you then.'

Gay Jim hooted in agreement and slung a knapsack across his chest.

'Here.' Oz pulled a pistol from his belt and handed it to Gay Jim who stuffed it into the pocket of his trousers.

'That a good idea?' Norman asked.

'Why wouldnt it be?'

—

Much of a fire wasnt needed. The night still burned with the heat of the day, the ground radiating warmth, the air still ablaze. A full moon cast the space aglow so all appeared as bone and ice. Still, the villagers gathered around the flames Lucas Brown fanned into existence.

'What kind of business you up to?' he asked.

Jacoby sighed, said business was business. 'Errands.'

'Gonna give the greenhorn a gun?' Lucas Brown asked and he nodded toward Norman.

Jacoby spat into the fire and craned his neck back to examine the starfield above. A few embers fluttered up and disappeared into the celestial menagerie. 'Time for us to be gettin.'

'Youre not gonna give me a gun,' Norman said.

'No,' Jacoby said. He looked at the people gathered around the fire. 'Dont think it's prudent to—not just yet anyways.'

'Pa—' Oz began.

Jacoby held up a hand to silence his son. He directed his words at Norman. 'You done chose to walk with us,' he said. 'But before I give you the power that comes along with totin a gun around, I want you to see exactly what it is we do.'

'I never chose this,' Norman said.

'You what?'

'You all kidnapped me,' Norman said. 'I never chose this.'

Lucas Brown flapped his arms in exasperation as if to say Norman's statement proved his point.

'You did choose,' Jacoby said. He leaned forward so his elbow rested on his knee. The fire cast the white of his beard into a furious oranged glow. 'You begged me not to shoot you. You chose. You drove out here in your station wagon, supplies in the trunk. You drove out here with a plan. You chose alright.'

Norman opened his mouth to speak, but no words formulated. Jacoby spoke for him. 'Youre gonna say you would never choose this. But you are wrong. Whatever happened in your previous life—your time before this time—is gone and you wanted it that way. You chose to leave an you had no intention of returnin.'

Norman looked at the faces studying him: Oz and Jacoby, both by the fireside; Martha and her husband stalking off into the shadows; Lucas Brown standing smugly outside the circle. Somewhere the children laughed and a part of Norman's mind wondered who watched over them.

'You will love us,' Jacoby said.

Norman shook his head imperceptibly. 'No,' he said. 'I cant think of anything less likely.'

'I knowed we shouldve put him in the mine with his car,' Lucas Brown said. 'First chance he gets, he'll run.'

'Already tried to,' Oz said. 'Pa caught him trying to foller those lectric lines outta here.'

'Fuckin fool thing to do,' Lucas Brown said.

Jacoby stood up, the bones in his back cracking. The orange left his beard and now he appeared as a frosted figure, his face coated in a shade of winter. He kicked the logs of the fire until the flames subsided and only the coals glowed red and orange. He made a pouring motion and Martha came from the shadows and picked up a tin percolator and dumped it on the fire. Hissing plumes of steam rose up in the air. With the toe of his boot, Jacoby mixed the water into ash until it formed a paste. Then he stooped and dipped his hands in it and implored his sons to do likewise. They rubbed the mixture on their faces and forearms, behind their ears and down their shins.

Norman felt a hand heavy on his shoulder and the deep voice of Raybur buzzed in his ear. 'Better rub yourself down,' he said. 'Less you wanna fry come sunup.'

They walked for several hours, guided by constellations before the sash of sunrise unfurled behind them and chased the luminary vessels from their heaven homes. Hunger gnawed in the pit of Norman's stomach, but he dared not speak—for none had spoken since leaving Jacobyville. They continued on like silent pilgrims who undertook some sacred march. Even Gay Jim did not whoop or holler—only the occasional discordant noise echoing in his throat. The paste of mud and ash dried on Norman's face and arms and began cracking. Flakes fallen from his neck itched down inside his shirt. The men walked in single file, Jacoby leading the way. Twice they passed a waterbag up and down the line. Norman barely gulped a mouthful of water before having it snatched from his hands by Raybur.

'Days breakin,' Jacoby said. And already a sliver of sun crested the horizon. When they looked back, the outcropping of mountains they set out from could be witnessed in their full range—and the whole of the range appeared as an island with the plaintive stretch of dirt on all sides.

Oz caught Norman looking back at Jacobyville, at the mountains.

'Never in a million years would somebody guess we got a town there,' he said.

Gay Jim, who followed Oz, laughed and slapped his leg.

Jacoby called from the front of the line. 'Keep it down, boys. We got a piece to go yet. We'll rest up here in a few hours.'

By midmorning the full fury of the sun blasted down on the itinerants. Sweat soaked into the mud and ash compound turning it back into a paste. Drops of the protective coating rolled down into Norman's eyes. He could not use his fingers to wipe away the grime as they too were coated. He blinked, trying to clear his vision, but it was no use. Tears welled up and irrigated the dirt.

She had told him to keep blinking; he shouldnt be splashing water around inside the dig. 'It might contaminate the findings,' she said.

'Problem is I got too much natural irrigation,' Norman replied.

Even when they stood still, they would sweat. Up in the mountains, in this part of Appalachia, the summers became a sweltering sauna. But the opportunity to jointly excavate an early settlement with other universities over the break was simply too good to refuse.

Norman blinked few more times, used the back of his wrist to rub his eyes clear of moisture and looked at Grace. Her skin was shiny with perspiration, the fabric of her shirt stuck to her body. Smudges of dirt marked her face and her hands.

They stood knee-deep in a dig, carefully stepping around the skeletons. Two weeks before, they had stumbled across this place while looking for any peripheral sites of interest. Grace found a slice of stone embedded in the ground. She had correctly guessed it to be the foot of a gravemarker, broken years ago.

The professors overseeing the excavation of Whitetail Pass deemed the small graveyard to be less important than the other digs. The bulk of the settlement lay two miles farther up the valley, the site of a winter avalanche that buried the entire population over one hundred and fifty years ago. Grace had insisted on excavating her find and Norman had offered to help. Together they uncovered what now appeared to be a mass grave. The skeletons lay entangled and twisted, thrown into the shallow grave without ceremony.

'Diseased or criminals,' Norman had speculated.

But it was Grace who said, no, this was something else. She stooped, picked a leg bone—a fibula—from the ossuary and held it into the sun. Notches, like tallies cut to mark the passage of days, adorned the bone.

'Knife marks,' she said.

The skeletons they pulled from the grave all had these markings.

They squatted together in the grave over a ribcage.

'Female,' Norman said and he patted the pelvis bone as evidence. His hand drifted up the naked form to the broken sternum, the stubs of rib there. He picked up a chunk of bone and saw it had broken along a scored line. 'They cut her chest,' he said. Then he said they filleted her breasts.

'Cannibalism?' Grace said.

Norman stood, looked up the valley toward the settlement, then back down into the grave, the few skeletons laying within.

'If the entire village is destroyed, it doesnt mean everyone had to die. These might have been the survivors of the avalanche.'

'And because the village and the pass were sealed off, the food was buried, they had to eat each other.'

'The proof is in the bones,' Norman said. 'The cut marks are evidence of taking the most flesh, of carving meat.'

Grace stood, taking a careful step around the skeleton. She kissed Norman on the cheek. 'You Indiana boys know your way around a graveyard,' she said.

Gay Jim let out a whoop that jarred Norman back to reality. Behind him Raybur laughed. 'He takes some gettin used to,' he said. 'Hes just excited cause he can see the rest spot up ahead.'

Again, Norman blinked, trying to see what lay ahead, but to no avail. Not until they drew closer could he see the source of jubilation. A small outcropping of rocks, alien in form, bubbled from the earth. They hued the same bleached and sickly color as the land around them. Almost as inexplicable was the presence of a broke down pickup truck. Without wheels or glass or doors, only the rusted metal body betrayed its original identity as a vehicle.

'Alright,' Jacoby said. He set his knapsack on the ground beside the biggest rock. 'Lets set her up, then we'll eat.'

The boys and Raybur took a stretch of tarpaulin and unfolded it. Each corner of the tarpaulin was grommeted and threaded with a short piece of rope. The brothers used the ropes to tie it to the truck frame. Raybur tugged on his edge, pulling Norman along with him, and they secured their end to the rocks.

When all was secure, they crawled under the tarpaulin and the sun's rays dampened somewhat. Heat, however, still seemed to radiate from the earth itself. Norman propped himself against one of the boulders, but leaned forward when it scorched his back through the fabric of his shirt.

'Get some shuteye,' Jacoby said. 'We'll eat here in a little bit—once the sun passes overhead.'

Already Gay Jim and Oz snored. Raybur took off his shirt and folded it to use as a pillow. Jacoby did not settle in, though; he peered out across the desert, as if he could see his village from here, as if he could see across time—what lay behind them and what still lay ahead.

Breaking the bottle on Dusty's head didnt render him unconscious like Norman thought it might. He'd seen a lot of westerns where a damsel would sneak up on a man—usually a man with his gun drawn—the music heightened, and she'd smash the bottle over his head. Depending on the actor, his eyes might roll backward before falling to the floor. In Dusty's case, he clutched his temple, where blood already started matting down his hair. Norman dropped the broken remainder of the bottle and moved from the couch. In other movies, the jagged neck of glass proved to be a lethal weapon. Dusty threw his bottle at Norman and missed. It exploded against the wall and one of the resulting shards caught Norman in the cheek, drawing a thin line of blood.

'Youre a goddamned lunatic,' Dusty said, still holding his head.

For a moment, Norman stood dumbfounded—not just by his own actions, but by the accusation that precipitated the outburst. 'I—I thought that maybe—'

Dusty took a dishtowel from the bar and pressed it to his wound. Bloodstains soaked it red immediately. 'You know what? Run the fuck away. Run away and when you come back, we're gonna crucify you.'

Norman's mouth moved, but it formed no speech. Dusty shoved past Norman, walking through the beer-soaked carpet and flecks of colored glass. 'You know what?' he said. 'I dont feel bad for Grace,' he said. The door to the apartment opened and slammed and Norman was alone.

Their meal consisted of meager portions of jerky and a handful of oat bran.

'Better goin down if you take a swaller of water with it,' Oz said.

Norman heeded the advice and funneled the handful of bran into his mouth then chased it with water from the bag. He took a hard swallow and the bran hit the bottom of his stomach like a rock.

'You piss yet?' Jacoby asked.

'What?'

Jacoby asked again if Norman had pissed any since leaving Jacobyville.

'No.'

'Give him another few swigs,' Jacoby said. Raybur sighed and passed the waterbag back over to Norman.

'Pissin is a sign of life,' Jacoby said. 'You stop pissin, you stop livin.'

Norman tipped the bag up and let the water drain into his mouth.

'Easy now,' Raybur said. He pulled the bag back. 'Dont want to drink too much either. Flood your system.'

Gay Jim chewed his strip of jerky with his mouth open, flecks of bran on his lips. He nodded in agreement.

Norman's mouth felt caked and dry, his legs too weak to stand. 'Why dont you just leave me here?' he asked.

Neither Oz nor Raybur seemed especially surprised by the request. Gay Jim paid the inquiry no mind. Norman asked again and the men turned to Jacoby. And when the old man answered that leaving Norman here would ultimately mean death, Norman said he would take his chances.

'I wont tell anyone about your village,' he said.

As he often did, Jacoby laughed at Norman's assumptions. 'You think thats why youre a captive? You think I'm afraid people will know about my village, how me and mine live?' He snorted, said to go on tell people about his village. 'See if they believe you—all those people who live in the world thats already over. They wont hear of it. They cant fathom someone like me. I'm a myth, a childhood story, a tall tale.'

'People know about desert hermits,' Norman said. 'Youre not as unique as you think you are. People are always talking about the hippies and the desert dwellers.'

Raybur laughed and shook his head, exchanging knowing glances with Jacoby.

'You really believe thats all there is to it, huh?' Oz asked.

Jacoby didnt wait for Norman's response. 'Your mind is small, professor boy. Your world limits you. Go ahead and run along.' He made a shooing motion and the other men chuckled. 'Done told you, I aint gonna harm you. I promise.'

Norman sat mutely.

'You stay because you want to understand us,' Jacoby said. 'It's your line of work, understandin people an how they live, yes?'

Norman nodded, said it was.

'But really, what you really want to know is how you work— what your limits are.' As he glanced at his comrades, they nodded in silent agreement, even Gay Jim. 'And the things you can do are astounding. Stayin alive is just the beginning.' He stopped to contemplate his next words, then said, 'I'll tell you what, you stick with us for a spell an you'll learn how to survive on your own. You could escape—but by then you wont want to.'

Norman looked out across the desert from under the tarpaulin. The land spanned out like skin stretched tight. The blue of the sky met the dust of the land in a violent contrast. It hurt his eyes.

From behind him, Jacoby's voice came low and soothing, nearly a whisper. 'Just say it, son. Admit that this is what you want. Admit that you know nothing and you want to learn.'

Above them, the tarpaulin rippled with a slight breeze. 'Yes,' Norman said. He closed his eyes. 'I'm yours.'

Norman and Grace had grown more secretive since their find. They left the home base of other archeologists and anthropologists, the jumble of cots and air mattresses assembled in the church basement of a nearby town, leaving before daylight. They hitched a ride with another field crew and asked to be dropped off a mile south of their site so they could walk in. Norman talked of their find, calling it Grace's discovery.

'What we uncovered wrecks the idea that early settlers in this valley were peaceful types—pioneers with brimmed hats and buckle shoes or whatever crap theyre telling them in school.' He slowed his pace to catch his breath. Already the mountain humidity labored his breathing. 'This shows they were a gruesome lot, that life was hard.'

Grace looked sidelong at Norman. 'Want to slow down?' she asked.

And they slowed their pace.

'Where you from again?' he asked. She had never said, but she played along.

'Saint George, out in Utah,' she said.

'Got folks from all over,' Norman said. 'See the guys from Massachusetts?'

'The ones doing the archival work in town?'

'Yeah, them.'

'Yeah, what about them?'

'Ever been out to Plymouth, the villages they reconstruct out there?'

Grace said she hadnt. 'This is the farthest Ive been from home. I got an older sister whos jealous of me right now.'

Norman debated how he wanted to answer, then he asked what her sister did for a living.

'Picks up truckers,' she said. 'Says she wants a man who can take her places.'

They rounded the bend in the gravel drive that led to their graveyard. The plastic sheet they staked over the dig still held in place, the morning condensation pooling on it. Together they loosed the stakes from the corners and pulled it back. The bones lay as they had the day before and before that and for a hundred years before that. Finally Grace asked why Norman was interested in the researchers from Massachusetts.

'That tourism shit is big business,' Norman said. 'Go to these historical reenactments and it's like visiting Coney Island. These guys from Massachusetts are employed by these folks.

Think there wasnt cannibalism and rape and terrible things happening in Jamestown or Roanoke or Williamsburg?'

Grace knelt next to a skeleton, the skull mostly free of the soil around it. 'So you think theres evidence of this sort of activity and they just cover it up?'

Norman set the supply cases of shovels and brushes down and put his hands on his hips. 'You think I'm a conspiracy theorist?'

Gently, Grace worked her fingers under the skull bones and began to work it free. Without needing to ask, Norman handed her a small shovel with a rounded end. She began to pry the bone loose. 'You are, arent you?'

He knelt next to her, using a metal rod with a plastic tip to leverage the bone. When it pulled free of the soil, it left an imprint. 'I guess I am as long as the conspiracy is true.'

They pondered the skull for a while, its chalked bone tincture matching the white haze of the mountain morning. Norman felt her hand rest on his leg then slide upward. He turned and kissed the corner of her mouth as she murmured, 'Tell me what you think is true.'

3.

Clarks Crick was a misnomer. Like most ghost towns, no source of water could be found. When these settlements were said to dry up, it happened on the most literal of levels. The ruts of the arroyos nearby posited some evidence of water flowing here occasionally, but nothing steady—nothing to live on.

The few buildings of the town stood as little more than skeletons, the only major structure being a long wooden wash. The men fanned out amongst the buildings, their guns drawn. Norman walked with Oz. Every few steps they paused and listened.

'Whats going on?' Norman whispered.

Oz shook his head, put his fingers to his mouth and unleashed a shrill whistle. On the other side of the small town, Jacoby did the same. Somewhere in between Raybur sounded off too. They reconvened near the wash.

'Nothin I could see,' Raybur said as he approached the group. The brothers agreed and Jacoby said this was good.

'Oz an Gay Jim'll take care of our water situation,' he said. 'Raybur, I want you to keep a lookout while Norm an me do a little diggin around.'

Typical for a town of the old west, the dead were buried outside of the town-proper and downwind. Most people who died here were put into the earth without regard—no grave, no marker; just buried in their underclothes. Should there be a marker, it consisted of a crude cross made of two waste pieces of lumber and a few misshapen nails. But if a child died, the rules changed. The headstone for a child's grave stood the tests of time—their names etched into granite or marble or limestone. Norman had been looking at one such headstone when his world changed some weeks before.

There had only been his breathing. And when he held his breath, the thundering of his heartbeat became audible. In the grave before him an aged wooden coffin, no longer than two-and-a-half-feet long, lay broken open. The delicate and sickly yellow bones of an infant were strewn about the site. The ribs reached up like slender ghostly fingers ready to clasp shut in a prayer of atonement. Tiny vertebrae segmented like a fossilized centipede, the skull smashed like pottery. He stood looking at the grave, his mind at a standstill. He had come upon it like this and knew from the cleaved heaps of soil that no animal could have done this. Turning around once, he examined the land about him, this patch of place they once called New Daisy. Not a soul in sight.

He approached the headstone, taking care to step around the disturbed skeleton, and examined the marker. Bits of lichen in the inscribed letters. The surface felt grainy, eaten away by sand and dust and age. He drew a pad of paper from his pocket and ripped out a sheet. Then, angling the pencil, he began to rub across the name on the stone, hoping to produce a legible rendering of the inscription. He leaned in close, rubbing vigorously up and down. Droplets of sweat sprouted on his scalp. Had it not been so dry, the beads might have rolled down. Instead they merely evaporated.

Then a chunk of the headstone exploded. Dust and splinters of stone pelted his face. The two-tone report of the gunshot disappeared as quickly as it resounded. Debris temporarily blinded him. He squinted and stumbled, taking refuge behind the headstone. He could hear nothing over his panting.

For a split second Norman thought the incident was a delusion. Then another gunshot glanced off the top of the headstone, making a long beaming sound and sending flakes of rock onto the top of his head. He pulled his legs up to his chest. Tears from the irritation in his eye cleared the dust. The arroyo ran just on the other side of the fence—that slackened strand of wire strung between driftwood posts. He could duck between headstones and lunge for it. From there he could make a run through the twisted route of the dry riverbed and make his way back to his station wagon.

He ran headlong like a sprinter stretching out his body to meet the finish line. Another gunshot and something jarred Norman's step—a low-lying gravemarker. He stumbled, blinded by a jumble of dust, sound, sun, pain. A burning raw and ragged pain laced under his arm where the wire caught him and his world went blank, washed over in white.

'Right here,' Jacoby said. He struck a shovel into the rocky soil and sliced through Norman's thoughts. The two of them began scooping dirt aside, each to an opposite bank. The tombstone read the girl's name and called her a child of God. She had lived for two days.

'A man like you spends a lot of time in his head,' Jacoby said between shovelfuls of dirt.

'Hows that?' Norman asked.

'Just now, you wasnt even really here,' Jacoby said. He worked more rapidly than Norman, yet never seemed out of breath. 'You were thinkin.'

'Rememberings more like it.'

'Same thing.'

'I wouldnt say that,' Norman said.

Jacoby stepped down into the oblong hole. Enough dirt had been shoveled out that he needed a better position to continue digging. 'You dont remember much from the time I took you til the time you done woke back up,' he said.

For a moment, Norman tried to recollect the shadowed figures who hovered over him, what the land in transit looked like—those passing images between then and now.

'No,' he admitted. 'I guess I dont.'

'Suppose I tell you Jacobyville is fifty miles south-southwest of New Daisy and if you did foller those lectric lines outta there, you'd hit a small town in two days time.'

Unsure if these words were truth or jape, Norman recounted their earlier conversation. 'You mean I would have found that town—before the world ended from lack of bread.'

Jacoby leaned, scooped another shovelful of dirt and tossed it onto the growing heap next to the open pit. He chuckled at the answer. 'Look at yourself, son. World ended or no, there'd still be buildings an such.'

'So I'd find another ghost town.'

'Sure, lets call it that.'

Norman inhaled sharply through his nose and changed the grip on his shovel. He studied Jacoby, looking down on the old man from the edge of the grave. Sun blazed through the hermit's threadbare shirt. Sweat peeled the caked dirt off his skin in curls of crust. He imagined swinging his shovel and splitting Jacoby's skull open. If he did it in a single blow, neither the brothers nor Raybur might hear it. He could even lay Jacoby in the hole and toss some dirt on him.

'There you go again,' Jacoby clucked. 'Always thinkin, aint you?' He tapped his forefinger against his temple. 'What was it this time? Were you free from here again? Were you second guessin those words you said when you said you would stay with us?'

'Whats the name of this abandoned town youre talking about?' Norman asked.

'Who said it was abandoned?'

Norman stomped on the edge of his shovel, said he always hated riddles.

'No riddles, son,' Jacoby said. He continued to dig as he spoke. 'Just common sense is all. Like I done said, your world is small. Your thoughts are small.'

Norman began to reject the old man's words, but Jacoby began to explain: 'When the world ends you people all think the same way. Buildings disappear. People turn into air. The idea that the world cant exist without us is small minded.' He shook his head as if in pity. 'When the world ends like it did—an you'll see well enough that it is gone, all of it—it's still the same place we left behind. People havent turned to dust. Buildings will still stand. But the thing, the unknowable thing that made that place an time a reality for you—that will be gone.'

The sudden knock of Jacoby's shovel on wood interrupted his explanation.

'Yee-haw, cowboy,' Jacoby said. He winked at Norman. Together they cleared the dirt from the coffin lid. Jacoby pulled a knife from his boot and used the broad edge of the blade to pull at the boards. The wood splintered as Jacoby lifted the top of the small coffin. He sheathed the knife, straddled the void and reached inside. Norman took a step back and Jacoby lifted the contents into the air. The small, ragged corpse of the infant toughened and held together by sinew and desiccated skin, the clothes like gauze and turned the color of the desert itself. The tiny mouth ayawp like it had been awakened from a hundred years' sleep. Jacoby held it in both hands, elevated above his head as if this child—this long dead baby—constituted a sacrifice to a droll god who is without pity, without humor, without impunity.

The noise of the coffin crackling open drew the attention of Raybur and the brothers. Gay Jim stumbled twice on his way to the grave. Oz toted several canvas bags, dripping their contents onto the bleached earth. Somewhere in this forsaken place, he found and collected water.

'Good find?' Raybur called from behind the boys.

'Aye,' Jacoby said. He lowered the child, looked into the tiny face where all the flesh disintegrated into a yellowed parchment pulled flat and tight across the bone. 'She's a beauty.'

Raybur walked to Jacoby's side and they traded the corpse. When he looked upon the dead child, Raybur did not coo or ogle the baby as Jacoby had. Instead, he used his free hand to pull a pocketknife from his belt. He opened it with one hand, then used the small blade to poke inside the mouth.

'Whatre you doing?' Norman asked.

'Checkin the merchandise,' Oz said.

'He's doing what now?'

Oz repeated himself, said this is part of living out in the desert.

'Youre a smart fella,' Jacoby said. Raybur probed the baby further with the knife. 'You tell me whats goin on here.'

Gay Jim plopped contentedly to the ground and crossed his legs.

'Well.' Norman crouched, resting his elbows on his knees. 'Youre graverobbers, right?'

Even Raybur smirked at the mention of graverobbing. The others simply laughed until Jacoby goaded him to go on, elaborate.

'People often buried tokens and souvenirs with their loved ones when they died. Things that might be worth something.'

Jacoby responded with an aye, saying this much was true. 'But the real treasure is the people themselves,' he said. He took the baby back from Raybur and cradled it against his breast. 'A hundred years ago soldiers bought an sold an traded for injun scalps. They wore injun teeth on strings like pearls. The injuns werent no better. They wore a soldiers peter on a chain, put a white mans heart in a pot an boiled it an drank it. The body is the treasure.'

Norman squinted at the men now gathered like mourners around a fresh grave. 'Doesnt make sense, what youre doing now.'

Jacoby turned to Oz, as if laying the office of explanation on him. Oz cleared his throat. 'Jacoby explained to us all how you study places—whats left of them anyhow—how you look at them an write about them, but what youre really tryin to figure out is how the people lived in these places, what they were like.' He caught Jacoby's eyes and they exchanged a discreet nod, before Oz continued. 'This heres the person. Most of them peoples gone an you aint never gonna get at them. It's like they never was. Nowadays everybody knows everyone—aint nobody disappearin.'

Jacoby forced a laugh and said that would suffice. 'Come on,' he said. 'We got more graves to see to.' And he stuffed the baby into a satchel.

Grace reached up from the dig site and felt for her pants on the grass nearby. Norman lay partially on the plastic sheet in an effort to avoid further dirtying himself. He watched Grace, naked from the waist down, dirt streaked on her legs, placing her feet carefully around the bones. He expected her to turn with her clothes in hand and start to dress. Instead, she held a small white object. She pinched it between her fingers and lit the end with a lighter. Bringing the joint to her mouth she sucked on it, held her breath, then exhaled. A sweet aroma filled the air around them.

'Smoke after you fuck?' she asked. Her voice was strained, trying to suppress a cough.

'No,' Norman said. 'Cant say Ive ever smoked a—one of those.'

She smiled serenely, said most everyone at this camp came to this part of Appalachia because of the weed. 'Some of the best stuff and cheap.' She drew on it again and the tip glowed orange. 'Want a hit?'

Norman declined, saying it messed with his head. 'Dont like my thoughts to get disorganized.'

Grace's free hand drifted toward her crotch, her fingertips grazing the swath of hair there. 'Youve never tried it,' she said.

She was right and Norman said so.

'Why not?' She sauntered to him, her disregard for keeping the site uncontaminated now completely abandoned.

The scent of the smoke wafted heavy in the air around her like a perfume, like incense. She seemed to tower over him and his eyes took in the whole of her. He felt blood returning to his penis and he shifted.

'Just not anything I want to get mixed up in,' he said.

Grace rolled her eyes and he tried again.

'Got scared of drugs,' he said.

She considered the answer, toeing at the soft dirt, before sitting on the plastic sheet next to him. 'You'll fuck me in a graveyard, but wont take a hit off a joint.' She smiled.

For a time they just sat there. She puffed lightly on the joint; he watched her.

'My brothers in Vietnam,' he said finally.

She looked down at him and said she was sorry.

'He signed up,' Norman said. 'Four years ago.'

Around them the woods had grown quiet. The shrills of insects and the calls of birds subsided and all seemed to bask in the midmorning sun. The foliage did not move and the trail of smoke from Grace's joint floated straight up in a line.

'He re-upped his tour,' Norman said. 'They offered him a month of leave anywhere he wanted between the six month tours and he chose to come back home to Indiana. I met up with him and he told me to stay out of drugs.'

'Probably saw some guys get killed while they were high,' Grace said.

'No, that wasnt it.' Any sexual excitement had left him now and his penis dangled shriveled and limp, the tip wet. But neither he nor Grace cared. 'When I saw him, he told me part of what keeps Vietnam going—what perpetuates the war—is the river of drugs being traded there.'

'Your brother is a conspiracy theorist.' Grace said it without accusation.

'He said protecting the drug trade was a duty of his, that drugs—heroin, powders, crystals—came across the borders in truckloads, that entire helicopters left with them as their cargo. He told me over coffee on our front porch at our parents house how kids—little kids like ten years old—are made to carry high-end shit; that if they get shot, theyre expendable. The army doesnt have to account for them.'

'You think thats true?' Grace asked. She stubbed the joint out in the soil.

'It was the way he said it,' Norman explained. 'He came back from that first tour and he was different. Like he knew something and didnt want to and couldnt shake it. He spent the whole month sitting on the porch, staring out into space.'

'Then he went back?'

Norman nodded. 'Last I saw of him. Listed as missing in action.'

They returned to Jacobyville several days later, haggard and staggering, the desert having wasted their energy into nothing. Lucas Brown greeted them in his usual gruff manner. Atop a piling, Martha looked down upon them, her hand shielding her eyes in a strange salute.

'Successful trip?' Lucas asked.

Raybur said it was by all accounts.

'Managed to bring this one back,' Lucas said, pointing at Norman.

'He did alright,' Oz said.

'Asked enough questions,' Raybur said. 'Thought my ears might fall off.'

Gay Jim began running through the village, tearing the clothes from his body. He reached the base of the tailing and started scrambling up the side, falling and bruising himself, yet undeterred and continued on.

'Back in the village for two minutes an already lookin to give Martha a poke,' Oz said.

The men shook their heads. Gay Jim made the summit and Martha took him by the hand, her other hand groping at his erection.

'Hows your, uh, wife gonna handle this?' Norman asked.

Raybur shrugged. 'Mens got needs,' he said. 'Looks to me like she's handlin it pretty well. Keep the peace for a while.'

'You wantin to give her a poke when Gay Jims done?' Jacoby asked.

'Shit.' Lucas Brown spat. 'Professor boy here probably thought Jimmy couldnt get it up.'

'Well,' Norman said. 'I did think... I mean I figured that Jim was gay.'

'Hows that?'

'Gay,' Norman repeated. 'That he preferred men over women. Thats why you call him Gay Jim.'

The men all looked confused. 'You mean like he's a queer,' Raybur said. 'A dandy.'

Norman said he'd heard it called that, sure.

'Gay means happy,' Jacoby said. The placid innocence on his face belied no guile. 'Jims a happy boy. Been happy since he nearly died.' With that, Jacoby turned, starting up the slope toward his house saying he needed to spend some time with the Madonna.

Norman turned to Raybur and Lucas Brown. 'You mean Gay Jims happy because he's got brain damage?'

'See?' Raybur said to Lucas. 'He never stops askin questions.'

Lucas just shook his head and smiled. 'Gay Jim makes bein half-crazed look like a damned holiday.'

From up on the slope, from inside the little shack beside the mineshaft, came groans and grunts—a discordant howling of pleasure.

She let out one last groan and sighed as Norman climaxed. They had gone back to the dig site several times, but never managed to make much progress. The skeletons still lay tangled in the grave, nubs of bone protruding from the earth, artifacts like brass buttons and belt buckles rusting in the soil. Unlike the first time, they were careful not to have sex in the grave itself for fear of destroying the site. Instead they spread their clothes on the grass to form a rudimentary bedding and fucked there. Afterward, Grace smoked a joint and talked about life in Utah—how there were only two choices for her: go to school and be something or waitress like her sister at the Ground Round.

'Sounds like a tough choice,' Norman said.

'Always wanted to get away and do something with my life,' she said.

They lay in the grass a long while—long enough for the clouds to billow and morph and clear, blotting the sun in and out. The day was cooler than it had been all week.

'Run away with me,' Norman said.

She laughed and pursed her lips on the joint, making the tip glow.

'Really,' Norman said. 'Come back to Indiana with me. We'll write about our findings here and get a grant to excavate more sites.'

The joint burned down to almost nothing between Grace's

fingertips and she flicked it into the open grave in her usual stupor of disregard.

'You think youre in love with me.' She said it not as a question.

The blankness in her voice caused Norman to fall silent and he nodded as if unsure of the answer himself.

'I cant go,' Grace said. 'I got to—'

'Doesnt matter,' Norman interrupted. 'We'll get grants to study some ghost towns or something. We'll find a way to get back here. But we should stick together. I could get you an adjunct position in the department. I'll share my office with you.'

'You think if I stick around we'll fall in love?' She smiled wryly and Norman said he hoped so.

In the evening, Lucas Brown and the children built a bonfire in the flat space outside the saloon. They gathered scrap wood and brush, a few timbers soaked with creosote, and lit them ablaze with a single match. Everyone, save Jacoby, gravitated toward the flame. Though the heat of the day remained even in this time of darkness, the wayward souls of the ghost town were drawn to the fire. If Norman tried, if he squinted, he could see out across the pan of the desert; he could see the pylons of the electric poles. Jacoby's directions echoed in his mind: two days of following those lines would land him in a small town, back in a civilization that never had known it ended.

'Here,' Oz said and handed Norman a crock with a tepid liquid in it. 'Put a fire in your belly.'

Taking a cautious sip, Norman tipped the crock to his lips. Alcohol denatured and raw caused his face to go numb.

It burned his lips and sweltered in his chest. 'Good stuff,' he said and passed the crock to Raybur who gulped the liquid and smacked his lips.

'Jacoby coming down anytime soon?' Norman asked.

'Sortin out the merchandise,' Oz said. They all looked farther up the slope, where Jacoby's residence sat cut into the cliffside. Originally the mine operations manager's office, the building's vista overlooked the entirety of the mines and their production lines—the washes, belts, the reservoir, and the cart tracks. Directly outside the front door was a vertical shaft—a square void in the ground close enough for the manager to stand on his porch and piss on the sumbitches down below. Oz told Norman the shaft sank fifteen hundred feet or thereabouts. A lucky man, he said, might fall onto the lift twenty feet down, the device still suspended from busted rigging. The back of the structure sat butted against the cliffside, its roof meeting the rock behind it. Smoke, a thin gray stream of it, drifted from the tin pipe sticking out of the roof. Several of the window frames still held glass intact—some were just square voids, like the one in front of the office.

The crock passed back into Norman's hand. And still feeling the fire set within him from imbibing he drank more deeply this time, smacking his lips in the same fashion as Raybur. He looked at his comrades around the bonfire. Lucas Brown sat with the children slumbering in his lap; Raybur and Oz conversed in muted tones with Gay Jim listening attentively and rocking back and forth. Across the flames, Martha stared at Norman. The firelight softened her features and she looked younger—forty perhaps.

'You a quiet one,' she said. 'Dont talk near as much as Raybur says.'

'It's my nature, I guess.' Norman wanted to stand up, walk over and sit next to her, but as he shifted in his seat, the effects of the grog made his legs go weak and he stayed where he was. 'I like to observe people. I'm a watcher.'

'But now you takin part.'

'Still observing.'

Martha smiled. 'Youre a part of our clan now.'

It took a moment for the gravity of the words to register with Norman and he voiced a small protest, asking how this came to pass.

Raybur interrupted. When he had ceased conversing with Lucas Brown and began eavesdropping, Norman couldnt tell. 'You done went on a mission with us,' he said.

'A mission?' Norman asked. The alcohol increased the amusement he derived from these people's choice of words.

'Mission,' Oz repeated.

'And that makes me one of you?'

'Makes you see us from the inside,' Martha said.

'Doesnt mean I got to be one of you,' Norman said.

An uneasiness passed around the fire, the crew looking one to another. Then Lucas Brown spoke. 'You got little choice,' he said. 'Once you done look from the inside, theres no unseein it.'

'Yall trying to convince me to stay?' Norman asked.

'Wont matter,' Raybur said. 'You'll run at some point.'

This statement was met with a solemn chorus of agreement.

'You'll either run or you'll die; theres no in between,' Lucas Brown said. 'The world out there'—and he pointed into the indigo horizon bathed with moonlight '—that fantasy place Jacoby talks about is the dream youre achin to fall asleep next to.'

'But it's not there,' Norman said, predicting the next line. 'Cause the world has ended, I know. Jacobys told me all about it.'

'But it's more than that.' Martha had an urgency in her voice as if startled by Norman's words. She cast her gaze to Lucas Brown, goading him with her eyes.

'The world,' he said wearily. 'It dont exist. Never has. People who think theyre livin is fools.' He grabbed for the crock and drank.

'Better pass that over here when youre done,' Norman said. Then he laughed and looked at his companions. No one, including Gay Jim, laughed.

'Aint a joke,' Raybur said. 'None of us believed it at first either.'

'Pa had to explain it once he finally understood it.'

Even with the alcohol, Norman became frustrated by the ambiguity of the conversation.

'I'm a dead man,' Lucas Brown said. 'Took me a while to realize I was dead. But you, me, the rest of us—Jacoby—we're all dead. Only difference is that Ive always been dead.'

'Jacoby tell you this?' Norman asked.

'I told Jacoby.' Lucas Brown said it with defiance. 'I come from the other side.'

Raybur slapped Norman across the back. 'Time to wake up an realize youre dead.'

TWO

Wyrick

I.

At first Dusty passed Norman in the hall, then stopped and turned.

'Hey, how was Appalachia?' he asked.

Norman nodded his head, trying to formulate an answer. 'Pretty good, I guess.'

'Havent talked to you since you been back. Every time I head to your office, youre out.'

'Been busy,' Norman said. From the work room the copy machine hummed and clicked as it spat out papers.

Dusty grinned. 'Yeah, heard about that.' His voice dropped. 'Got a publication out of your find—got some pussy too.'

A rush of heat spread across the back of Norman's neck. He stammered and Dusty slapped him on the shoulder.

'Relax, man. She's fitting in well with the rest of the department. Heard good things. Maybe they'll send you on more summer digs and you can find me a girlfriend.'

'Yeah.' Norman forced a smile. 'I was actually on my way back home.'

Dusty made a sweeping gesture as if sending Norman on his way and he continued down the corridor. As he passed Doctor Blanche's office, his eyes darted to the side. She sat at the desk, poring over some manuscript, her fingers playing with the charm around her throat.

Going home became harder for Norman. He sat in the station wagon in the apartment parking lot. On the radio some monotone commentators were yakking about a military coup in a South American country. Grace always left work earlier than him since she had fewer responsibilities. More often than not, he arrived to find her mostly naked and smoking a joint.

'Thought you saved those for, uh, afterward,' Norman said the first time he found her getting high.

Casually she replied that he was right. 'Fucked the landscaper,' she said. 'Think the neighbors saw.'

At first Norman thought she said this in jest. Then he looked at her—the tussled hair and tired eyes, the nipples showing between the gauzy T shirt. The realization must have been writ on his face; Grace arose from the couch, balancing her joint on the edge of an ashtray first and pulled the shirt over her head revealing her naked form. Her breasts hung firm and the pubis was still matted with moisture.

'Love is free, Norm.' The words came out hollow and she tried again. 'Just because I live here doesnt mean I pay the rent like a prostitute.'

Finally Norman spoke, saying he thought they were in a relationship. 'I thought we were being true, I mean, to each other.' His words sounded as hollow as her words.

She came close to Norman, took his hand and placed it around her waist. With her other hand she pulled at his belt. He did not resist. On her he could smell a scent that was not hers and he shut his eyes. She leaned in and whispered in his ear, saying, 'Being true means fucking whoever we want.'

Waterson, like most silver mining operations, dried up nearly as fast as it sprang to life. Though the weather cooled significantly since the clan's excursion to Clarks Crick two months ago, the walk south through the desert proved equally exhausting. When they arrived in the ghost town, the land had grown less rocky and now grass—beige and tan and dead—rustled in the wind. Only a small church and a graveyard stood as discernable structures.

'Careful now,' Jacoby said. 'We're in Buchanan boy territory here.'

'Damn fool mission,' Lucas Brown said. He had been opposed to the excursion from the start, but Jacoby had insisted, saying it came from a higher power. Lucas Brown relented, but only after insisting he bring his son along—a mop-haired boy no older than nine.

Both Jacoby and Lucas drew their guns and started for the building. Norman began to follow, shovel in hand.

'What should I do?' Norman asked.

Jacoby put his index finger to his lips, then pulled the pistol from his belt and began walking with his body turned diagonally, crossing his feet one over the other as if in some strange dance.

Norman stood back with the boy and watched as Lucas Brown pushed open the door of the church and it cried out a long and steady note. He stepped into the building and nothing moved, save the sweeping waves of grass. After a few seconds his face appeared where a window used to be in the rear of the church. 'All clear,' he called and Jacoby stuffed his pistol back in the waistband of his pants and waved for Norman to follow them.

'Not much of a town,' Norman said.

'Not much of a silver boom,' Jacoby said. 'Anybody'd tell you there aint silver out here, but a hundred years ago a couple of fellas by the name of Waterson went into the camp over by Jaundice Rock an told people they found a spot where silver flakes came up out of the ground.'

'And people believed this?'

'Like it was Gods own word.' Jacoby laughed. 'Helped that one of the Waterson boys was a preacher. Men got out here to mine an the only building was this church. Everything sold through the church too—clothes, food, plots of land, tools… The brothers is buried over yonder.' He pointed with a crooked finger to the graveyard beyond the building. 'Back then men'd tell you anything to get you to buy what they were sellin.'

As they excavated the grave of Emmanuel Waterson—the preacher brother—Norman asked about the Buchanan boys.

'Couple of ruffians,' Jacoby said. 'Maybe they think it's their legacy, bein in a place founded by brothers. They think they own this portion of the desert.'

'So theyre like us?'

First Jacoby said nobody was like them, then he said, 'Closer to bein like us. Dont know how many people there is like us, but we know of a few round here. Buchanan boys is one of the smaller clans.'

'And this is their territory?'

'Boundaries,' Jacoby explained, 'are just constructs of the mind.' He tapped his temple with his fingers. 'Borders give us something to fight about—the proverbial line in the sand.'

Lucas Brown and his son walked over from the church. The boy crawled down into the pit of the grave and pulled up handfuls of dirt. He sang quietly to himself—a tune Norman recognized from a life before this one.

'Done drained the cistern in there,' Lucas Brown said. 'Found a few tins of food, some jars too.'

Jacoby nodded. 'Give us a hand,' he said and he began dusting off the slatwood top of the coffin. 'Got a big boy in here.'

They exhumed the body by removing six of the slats near the top of the box. Lucas reached in and grabbed the corpse under the arms and pulled him out. His son squatted at the foot of the coffin, watching. Once they completely removed the body from the box, the boy scrambled into the hole and felt around for any miscellany of treasure, of which there was none.

The men stood over the body, a gray skeleton with paper thin skin adorned in rags. Jacoby knelt over the bones like a shriver who beckons one last confession beyond death. He leaned in close, inspecting the body.

'Well, I'll be damned,' he said. He pinched at something near the jawbone and held it up.

'What is it?' Lucas Brown asked.

'Some knotted up thread,' Jacoby said. 'Must be what they used to stitch the mouth shut.'

'No way,' Norman said. 'It wouldve disintegrated by now.'

But there, in the pinch of Jacoby's fingers, the frail stitching hung. A breeze blew and Jacoby sent the relic into the wind.

Like an apothecary of old, Jacoby probed the joints of the skeleton, leaned his ear down to the chest cavity and felt along the shrunken shaft of neck. Then, without ceremony, he pulled the knife from his boot and straddled the body. He cleaved the arms at the shoulders—the legs at the hip.

'Here,' he said and hefted the torso on end. 'Strap this fella to your knapsack.'

The truncated corpse seemed to stand at attention, waiting for Norman to do as he was told.

'What bout the legs an arms and such?' Lucas Brown asked. He kicked at one of the limbs. His boy picked up an arm and swung it. When it broke at the elbow he threw it to the ground and kicked it.

'Leave them,' Jacoby said.

'Be upsettin to the Buchanans,' Lucas Brown said.

'So be it,' Jacoby said. 'They'll figure someones been here soon enough. Aint nothing to hide from one clan to the next.'

When Grace had come back from the rally she'd immediately headed for the bathroom. The water turned on and he heard the shower curtain slide shut.

'Grace?' He emerged from the bedroom where he had been waiting.

The rally had lasted most of the day and he knew she would end up fucking someone she met there. Then she'd come home and tell him about it until he couldnt take it anymore. His stomach would turn and his eyes would glass up, then he'd undress and fuck her without regard. In some secret part of his mind, he had been looking forward to this.

'Grace?' he said again. He eased the bathroom door open where her form came like a shadow through the shower curtain. 'How was the rally?'

She sniffled and said it was a rally.

He pulled back the shower curtain and she tried futilely with her hands to cover her body. Her eyes were red—either from drugs or crying or both.

'Whats wrong?' he asked.

Her hair clumped together and water streamed from the ends and from her elbows and chin. Creases formed around her mouth and under her eyes when she said she was raped.

The words seemed empty to Norman and she said them louder and louder. 'I got raped,' she said. 'There were four of them and they called me a whore and they raped me. I was only interested in one guy there and these other four raped me. They held me down and they took their turns raping me.' Her voice had escalated to a scream. She stopped, heaving deep breaths, and her eyes connected with Norman's and grew wide. She tried to pull away, but by then Norman had already seized her by the wrist.

The torso and head of the corpse weighed much less than Norman expected. He secured the dismembered trunk of the body to his knapsack with some spare rope Jacoby carried around like a bandolier. When he hoisted the pack onto his back, the corpse faced the opposite direction as if keeping sentinel over the places Norman passed through. True enough, Norman had read about some Indians who viewed the trail laying ahead of the traveler as the past and what lay behind as the future—the logic stating that the past is visible to us while the future remains obscured.

If a wind breathed out across the flats, it whistled in the voided spaces of the cadaver and shook loose flakes of skin and wisps of hair. As the evening hours came on, Norman cast sideways glances at the strange, misshapen shadow trodding beside him—one face looking into the past, the other with his dead eyes set on the future.

At night they camped in a nowhere place—one of the salt flats where the smell of sulphur hung heavy and acrid in the air. They built not a fire nor a tent, nor a hovel, opting instead to lay their bodies out on the white crusted earth and letting their minds run into abandon.

Before setting his pack down, Jacoby studied Norman. The twilight hours cast them both in shadows that seemed to move like fog—as if they were amidst a cloud of light and dark and this very vapor carried the pungent smell of the desert land with it.

'Youre protectin the merchandise,' Jacoby said.

'Yessir,' Norman said.

'No,' Jacoby said. 'It wasnt a question. I'm tellin you, it's your job to protect my merchandise.'

Again Norman replied in the affirmative. Already Lucas Brown and his boy stretched out, using their arms to cradle their heads and fall to sleep. They snored.

'Even out this far in the desert, you can get a stray coyote.'

'Havent seen anything livin in the last day.'

'Except us.' Jacoby grinned.

The memory of the night when the villagers claimed the mantle of death as their existence had persisted in a hazy hungover spot in Norman's memory, but he dared not speak of it. The next morning no one spoke of the mission, the fireside conversation—nothing beyond the usual banter of the village.

'Youve got questions,' Jacoby said.

Norman unburdened himself of the knapsack and body, standing the load on end and letting it slump to the ground, the corpse's face turned toward the dusky sky. Jacoby pulled at the waistband of his pants and seated himself on the ground.

'You think I am a god,' Jacoby said.

Norman laughed; it was a true and genuine laugh and Jacoby began to chuckle with him.

'It's funny,' the old man said. 'I know. But you listen to my words like gospel an you read into them as if they are scripture. You think the people in my village are my holy followers—what do you call them, my acolytes?' He sighed. 'Truth is theyve got thoughts of their own. Maybe they havent spent the time thinkin as hard as me, but they got thoughts about what life is an isnt. Youre free to think what you want, Norman; I dont control your thoughts.'

Norman turned the words over in his mind. He had never thought of his thoughts as Jacoby had. Finally he said he heard coyotes in the desert were small creatures.

'Aye,' Jacoby said. He held his hands a foot apart. 'Some're not bigger than a farm cat. They only grow to the size they can survive.'

The conversation had gone as Norman anticipated and he asked if the same principle applied to the desert clans. The darkness of night came on quickly now and with it a host of stars twinkled into existence above them.

'Youre a smart boy,' Jacoby said. 'Theres a desert way of life an it takes a while to learn. Me an my clan know it. Buchanan boys know it... The MacKowski Gang—well, theyre a different animal themselves.'

'Theyre another clan?'

'North,' Jacoby said. 'From up in the mountains where theres abandoned mine claims. Mean sumbitches.' He spat. 'Whole mess of them too—dont know how many anymore. They just move around, take what they want. Clan like ours could live off of what they leave in their wake.'

'I take it we're not on friendly terms with them.'

Norman expected Jacoby to laugh at the foolhardy question as he usually did. But Jacoby said, no, no they werent friendly at all. 'Rather run into the Buchanans,' he said. 'Things can get pretty scrappy with the MacKowskis. Done took out a man of mine some time back.'

'Sorry to hear that,' Norman said. 'Who, I mean what kin was it to you?'

'The name was Lucas Brown,' Jacoby said. He let the name hang in the air for a minute. 'Shot my friend—another old timer like me—Lucas Brown, they shot him through the belly an he died by chokin on his blood.'

'I'm confused,' Norman said.

'Of course you are,' Jacoby replied. 'I havent told you about the miracle of life.' By the light of the stars, Jacoby's visage hung like a wisp of smoke, the white of his beard catching the few faint glimmers of the night. 'We'd been in a shootout with the MacKowskis over a job. Had each other pinned up pretty good. One of his sharpshooters had a good perch right outside a mineshaft. Great cover, except for the rocks above the frame. I took a charge an blasted the rocks above where this fella laid an the rocks came down, a whole avalanche. Thats when we rushed them. Chased them to the mouth of the mines.

'I went to dig the sharpshooter out of the dirt, figurin I might could use his body in the future. Oz an me start shovelin rocks out of the way an we hear this gasp. The man had lived. We pulled him from the rubble an he told us his name an I told him that he was dead. I looked at him an said he was Lucas Brown now—born an brought back to life. He accepted the new life. Been with us ever since.'

Norman listened to the snoring of the man and his child.

'Dont think of Lucas as any different,' Jacoby said. 'He's come into the clan an had two children. He's one of us. If I never told you otherwise, you wouldve sworn him to be one of my kin. Some day you'll be like that too.'

Though Jacoby couldnt see him, Norman nodded.

'Alright,' Jacoby said. He yawned. 'Careful with the merchandise. Dont let anything get to him in the middle of the night.'

Again Norman nodded dutifully.

They each lay down on the salted flats. Norman tipped his pack with the body onto its side. He stretched his arm out and pulled the corpse close to his, close enough he could smell the dusty fumes of rot wafting from the ragged scalp. He shut his eyes tight and pressed his cheek against the skull bone.

In his mind Martha looked younger. She spoke like a university woman and invited him up to her office. Such is the logic in dreams. Sometimes the imagined world is better understood than the one built around us. But in all the strangeness of imagery and composite characters we recognize ourselves, our stories. Even as Norman imagined himself following Martha up a mountain staircase to her office—the same office he occupied in the waking world—the deeper darker regions of his mind recognized another form hiding in the shape of Martha.

Doctor Blanche had been crying—that much came through when her voice cracked on the word doctor. Her blouse hung untucked from her skirt, a run in her stocking on her right leg.

'You alright?' Norman asked.

Doctor Blanche reached for the bottle of bourbon on her desk, but as her hand neared it, her fingers curled up in resistance.

'Fine,' she said softly. Then she repeated it as if trying to convince herself. 'I'm fine.'

'Something happen?' Norman asked.

Her curled hand went to her mouth and she squeaked and nodded. 'I was attacked,' she said.

Panic shot through Norman's system. 'I'm gonna call someone.'

'No,' Doctor Blanche said. She suppressed a sob. 'It was my husband.'

'Your ex-husband.'

'Nothings official,' she said. 'He's still entitled—thats what he said.'

'You mean—'

'He was in my garage,' she said. 'He shut the door and ran the air compressor so the neighbors couldnt see or hear…' As her voice trailed off, she reached for the bottle and drank from it directly. 'When he was done he said it was the best fuck he'd ever gotten out of me.'

'We could call and file a complaint,' Norman said.

'Girls might be burning their bras out on the quad, but the police department is a mans mans mans world and you know it.' She smirked ruefully and said she couldnt imagine the humiliation of telling some sweaty palmed cop about how her husband recited their wedding vows through gritted teeth while he ripped the pantyhose from under her skirt. 'The cop'll probably gather all the boys at the station to have a listen.'

'Submit a written complaint?' Norman said.

She set the bottle back down. 'No,' she said. 'Lets just talk about work.'

Norman pulled a chair up to the side of the desk and Doctor Blanche slumped back in her seat. Her blouse fell open enough to expose the bra underneath, rankled hickey atop her breast. Without thought she refastened her blouse and regained her professional demeanor. 'So tell me about this grant you wrote. Ghost towns is it?'

The harshness of the afternoon light screwed Martha's brow and she shaded her eyes with her hand. The extra wrinkles this caused made her look older. Norman approached, the merchandise on his back. As he neared the woman, he reminded himself of the dreams of last night. Any sensuality he had conjured up in the dream world showed no evidence here now. Her hair draped haggard and limp, her skin coarse and prickled with darker hairs.

'Brought a friend back, did you?'

'Yes mam. Jacoby says it's his merchandise.'

Raybur walked from the door of the couple's abode and exchanged glances with his wife. 'He just say he hauled the merchandise his own self?'

Norman answered for her. 'Yup.'

Together they cast their gazes up the slopeside, up toward Jacoby's house. The old man made his way up the graveled tailings, his arms outstretched like a whirling dervish.

'Well,' Raybur said. 'You better take the merchandise up to his place.'

In the months he'd been living in Jacobyville, Norman not only became acclimated to the heat, but also to the constant ascending and descending of the slopes. Zigzagging as he climbed helped ease the burden on the knees. Leaning into the slope maintained a center of gravity. He learned to spread his arms out wide and lock his legs every few steps. Doing so gave him several half-second breaks as he trod uphill. In much the same way, he carried the merchandise to Jacoby's house.

Given his head start, Jacoby was already on his front porch when Norman reached the bulldozed space the house sat on. The great square void of the vertical mine with the crane wreckage lay just beyond the porch. Norman walked wide around it as if the darkness could suck him in.

'They tell you to bring that up here?' Jacoby asked.

Norman stooped over to catch his breath—the climb with his cargo being more taxing than he expected. He shook his head, said he thought they wanted it up here.

'Always thinkin,' Jacoby said. 'Cant get one of my boys to think at all—other one thinks he thinks. Now Ive got you an you never stop thinkin.'

Norman began to slide the knapsack and corpse off his back when Jacoby told him to come inside. He repeated the offer right away and waved a hand over his shoulder, beckoning Norman to follow.

The interior of Jacoby's house looked no different than most of the ghost town abodes. Jacoby's might have more of a roof than most of the buildings, simply by virtue of being nestled against the wall of rock, though everything else was the same. He owned a proper table and chairs—objects Norman had not seen since before coming out this way, objects men had purchased and moved out here to the desert and abandoned altogether, objects no one had thought of since they were left behind in haste of another fortune. Heaps of rubbish and scrapped lumber littered the floor and gathered in the corners. In the wall facing the cliffside there was a stout square door Norman assumed to be a root cellar or a jam cupboard.

'You can drop him right here,' Jacoby said and Norman let the body fall from his back.

'Cooler in here,' Norman observed.

'Dont get much sun,' Jacoby said. He circled around the table, sat and motioned for Norman to do the same. 'Prime real estate once upon a time—that's why the manager picked this spot.'

'That and he could oversee all of the mining operations.'

'True,' Jacoby said.

Norman's eyes continued to adjust to the dimly lit room. He kicked at a piece of debris on the floor, then realized it to be a human thumb.

'Got parts all over the place in here,' Jacoby said. It was half an apology. 'Sit down please.'

Norman did as he was asked. He studied one of the piles of rubbish in the far corner of the room and realized it to be several crumpled bodies, the skin peeling away like paper, the mange of hair streaming about the floor.

'What do you do with them—the bodies?'

Jacoby reached into a footlocker and extracted a mason jar. He unscrewed the lid and gulped at the liquid inside, passed it to Norman who also drank. The burning of the fluid scorched the inside of his nose and cauterized his mind. He placed the jar back in the center of the table and settled back into his chair.

'There are men who want these bodies,' Jacoby said. 'Theyd pay good money to have that dead fella you carried out of Waterson.'

'What do you need money for?'

'I dont,' Jacoby said. 'Before money, men traded things. You want this body, I need water, food, tools, medicine. It's a good system.'

'Someone actually wants these bodies.' Norman said it as a statement.

'Oh yes.' Jacoby picked up the jar and made a toasting gesture and drank deeply enough to dribble some of the fluid from the corner of his mouth. 'Our great benefactor is interested in all things dead and gone and non-existent.'

The stupor that quickly overcame Jacoby uneased Norman. The old man sat slightly askew and suppressed a hiccup. His eyes glassed over as if he verged on crying, but he blinked and the tears were gone. 'You still have moments when you think I'm a madman.'

Unsure of how to answer him, Norman remained silent.

'It's alright,' Jacoby said. 'Thats your mind bein tired. Easier for you to think of me as a lunatic. Those are the same moments when you look back on your life in Indiana an contemplate whether what you did was criminal or not.'

Norman swallowed and suddenly the room felt hotter.

'Yes,' Jacoby said. 'Yes. You are a criminal. No doubt in my mind. The world out there'—he waved his hand like he would swat flies—'it doesnt matter. It's a dream. When you think of your crimes in that world, youre daydreaming. When you wake up, I'm a goddamned sage and Jacobyville is a paradise.'

'Tell me about this benefactor,' Norman said. He shifted in his chair and reached for the mason jar. It was nearly empty and a string of backwash floated in it. He did not drink it.

'You dont see any evidence of a benefactor?' Jacoby asked. He feigned surprise. 'You look around my village an you dont see any sign of a benevolent force behind all of this?' He leaned forward in his chair and spoke as if what he said commanded secrecy. 'Just bein alive in this place is evidence enough for me.'

'The real miracle is survival,' Norman said. He had been droning on about ghost towns in a pseudo-lecture for nearly a half-hour. Doctor Blanche's eyes opened and closed, her pupils dilated into pinpoints. She nodded lazily. 'Some of the towns had to get their water shipped in. When the water stopped, the town literally dried up.'

She reached for the bottle again and nearly knocked it over. In a voice not her own, Doctor Blanche swore. A tear rolled down her cheek.

'I can drive you back home,' Norman said.

Doctor Blanche's chin toughened and pocked. She sniffed and struggled to stand.

'Youre dreaming again,' Jacoby said.

The memory of Doctor Blanche vacated Norman's brain.

'Got to be careful with memories,' Jacoby said. 'They'll make places that never were. And soon you wont recognize where you are.'

'That doesnt make any sense,' Norman said. He used the back of his hand to scoot the mason jar toward Jacoby—but the old man ignored the gesture.

'Why havent you fucked Martha?' He asked the question as if it just occurred to him in that moment.

'She's a hag,' Norman said.

'I seen the way you lust at her,' Jacoby said. 'She'd have you—she's had all of us at one point or another.'

'Thats another reason.'

'Dont be coy,' Jacoby said. 'Thats not it; thats not it at all.' He tilted his head back and duffed the last of the jar's contents. 'Marthas a memory for you—she's the woman you done had your way with, aint that right?'

As Norman pulled into the driveway, the headlights caught the fissure of the front door ajar.

'I'd better check the house out,' he said. Doctor Blanche acknowledged his suggestion with incoherent mumblings, her eyes closed and her forehead pressed against the glass of the passenger window. Norman reached over and unbuckled her seatbelt, his hand brushing over the top of her legs. For the moment he leaned over her, he could smell her perfume, the oil of her hair. Again she murmured like a child who cannot escape a dream. Norman shook his head and climbed out of the station wagon. Outside the car he stood for a while, looking through the windshield at Doctor Blanche resting motionless. He recalled her words from earlier—about being attacked, still married, about how she didnt want to go to the police. He walked around to her side of the car, opened the door and, with considerable difficulty, lifted her to her feet.

'It's a struggle in your mind, aint it?' Jacoby asked. 'How do you reconcile your actions when you recount them?'

Norman sat long and brooding, trying to sort one event from another.

'I was helping her into her house,' he said.

'Because she was in need.'

'Yeah. She was in need. I put her on the couch in the living room and checked the rest of the house.'

'Check it for what?'

'Her husband,' Norman said. 'He attacked her. I was helping her out.'

'I'm sure you were checkin for her husband,' Jacoby said. 'I just dont think your motives were pure because once you looked everywhere, you locked the door.'

The deadbolt latched. How many seconds had Norman stood listening to the tick of the grandfather clock in the living room, he could not tell. After some time he had walked to the threshold of the living room and flipped on the nearest light switch. A lamp at the opposite end of the room lit up.

Doctor Blanche had managed to take her shoes off and reposition herself on the sofa. She lay facedown, her hair sprawled out around her, her bare legs sticking out toward Norman, the space between them shadowed and naked.

'I went to the living room where I had put her,' Norman explained. 'And she was already asleep—passed out really.'

'From drinkin,' Jacoby said.

'Yeah,' Norman said. 'I wanted to make sure she wouldnt throw up, choke on her vomit.'

'But you got close…'

Norman grabbed one of her ankles and shifted her leg to the side. The gap between her thighs widened and her skirt pulled up higher around her waist. With his free hand he rubbed the crotch of his pants. As he stroked the denim of the jeans, his fingers caught the zipper pull. Tooth by tooth he opened his pants and pulled out his penis. He let go of her ankle and slid his hand up the back of her leg, shoving the skirt aside. In the glass face of the clock Norman could see his reflection. He pressed himself into her.

'How fresh was she?' Jacoby asked.

'She wasn't; I told you already.'

'But you liked it,' Jacoby said. 'This was familiar territory.'

It happened quickly. Her body remained limp and Norman grabbed her legs, thrust himself in and out a number of times and came. The hand of the clock had barely moved. With his erection already waning, he looked around the room. He found her purse and sorted through the contents. A pair of pantyhose was wadded into the bag and he used it to wipe the jizzum from her vagina. Then he wiped himself down and stuffed the soiled hose into his pants pocket. Doctor Blanche lay so still Norman feared she might have died and he leaned in close to study her face. She breathed. Then he kissed her cheek.

'I dont think she ever knew,' Norman said. 'I mean it only happened once and it was quick and I cleaned up.'

'You really think she didnt know?' Jacoby asked.

'I spoke to her on the phone—by accident—right before I came out here.'

'Aye,' Jacoby said.

'She said she wanted to talk to me about my research on ghost towns.'

'The same conversation you had before you abducted her and raped her.' Any trace of amusement had left Jacoby's face.

Shamed by the words, Norman sat with his hands folded in penance. 'There were rumors going around the department.'

'Rumors?' Jacoby said. 'Stories, faint memories, accusations.'

'We wouldve made love if she'd been awake…'

'Dont lie to me,' Jacoby said. 'Dont lie to yourself. Consider this: A strong woman in a state of peril needs your help. You come to her aid, then take advantage of her. The only question here is whether or not she is consciously aware of your… indiscretion.'

Something in Jacoby's choice of words comforted Norman and he eagerly agreed, saying yes repeatedly and nodding his head.

'So perhaps this woman—'

'Doctor Blanche.'

'Aye. Doctor Blanche. Perhaps she doesnt know. You took her home an comforted her and what she feels for you is love. All the rape she experienced, she attributes to her husband—the one person who is protected under the law for forcin himself on her.'

Norman dwelled on the idea of Doctor Blanche feeling love for him. He imagined kissing her on the lips—her wanting him to kiss her on the lips. The notion passed and it seemed unlikely, a fantasy.

'No?' Jacoby asked as if he had been privy to Norman's thoughts. 'Maybe this will comfort you: Maybe she knows what you are an what you are capable of doin. She heard the rumors of the woman you lived with an she put herself in a vulnerable state after her trauma an you raped her an somewhere deep, deep in her mind, she knows.' Jacoby leaned back in his chair and whispered in a small voice. 'She knows, but doesnt know how to feel about it.'

The new notion took hold of Norman's imagination. Since the rape, he'd recapitulated the events in daydreams, replaying them over and over. He slowed down his every move when he imagined the scenario. It seemed as if he could watch it again as a third party.

The sternness of Jacoby's countenance broke into a smile. 'There you go again. Always thinkin.' He wagged a finger in a mock chide.

'Cant help it,' Norman said.

'I know,' Jacoby said. 'Thats why youre still alive out here.'

His smile was grandfatherly and his eyes twinkled with merriment. Without a gesture or hint, Norman knew the audience with Jacoby had ended. He stood and headed toward the door, turning around to thank the old man, but Jacoby spoke first.

'The one from before,' Jacoby said. 'The one you lived with—I know about her too. I know you killed her.'

The words cut through Norman like a razor and he acknowledged them with a single nod.

'And you loved her.'

'Yeah.'

Jacoby waved his hand to expel his guest and Norman pushed through the door. The harsh light of the desert—and the heat of the desert—blasted onto his face like it poured through some furnace porthole. He squinted, shading his eyes with his hand to no avail, struggling to discern what lay beyond the threshold.

A hand patted Norman on the chest, another on his back.

'Whoa, there,' Oz said.

Norman still squinted against the light, his eyes aching from adjustment.

'Watch where youre goin,' Oz said. 'Fall to your damn death that way.'

Another few seconds and Norman's eyes had adjusted. The square void with the collapsed rigging lay no more than a few steps in front of him.

'My eyes,' Norman said. He blinked a few times. 'Theyre havin a hard time—'

'Pa keeps it dark in there,' Oz said. He began to walk back down the slope toward the other residences. Norman followed. From this elevation Norman could see Raybur's place tucked into the crook of the small valley and the shed the brothers called their home on the other side of a crest. Farther out, when the slopes of the mountains met the flatland of the desert, scrub scorched into nothingness.

'You an him have yourselves a good talk?' Oz asked.

Norman said, yeah, sure, he guessed they did.

'That seems to be all he wants to do anymore,' Oz said. 'Talk with the professor boy, sit in the dark an talk talk talk.'

Norman made something in the way of an apology.

'No matter. Thats just his way. Half of what he says he dont mean. Half of what he says aint even true.'

They walked a while in tandem, around the skirt of a slope until their shadows had spun out in front of them. Oz stopped and rested his hands on his hips, scanning the horizon as if there might be something out there. There was nothing and Norman knew it.

'Gonna have to do some doin,' Oz said.

'Do what?'

'Less talk, more doin,' Oz said. 'We're gonna need you to come along an help out with this Wyrick.'

'With the Wyrick?'

Oz looked at Norman and repeated the word again—Wyrick. 'Whatve you two been talkin about if you aint been talkin bout the Wyricks?'

'They another clan, like the Buchanan brothers or the MacKowskis?'

Oz spat and swore. 'Foller me. You, me an Gay Jim got our work cut out for us.'

They shuffled down a slope. Off in a gulley somewhere Norman heard Lucas Brown's children singing and playing saying that London Bridge was falling falling falling down.

2.

The brothers sat on stumps of wood outside their shack. They leaned forward, using pebbles to represent people and splinters of wood to signify mountains or shacks or mineshafts. Raybur stood over them, thumbs hooked into his belt loops.

'An is that one there a mineshaft or a mountain?' he asked.

'Neither,' Oz said. 'It's the goddamned embankment on the reservoir.'

'Why you use such a short stick?' Raybur asked. 'The water tower is twice the size of the reservoir. Here, use this one.' He picked up a stick from the makeshift map.

'You just moved an entire mountain range.'

Gay Jim giggled and picked up one of the pebbles and tossed it through the door of the shack.

'Good job, shithead. You just threw yourself clear into Nevada.'

Raybur chuckled.

'Aint funny,' Oz said. 'Yall always want to horse round, but we aint gonna be ready for this next Wyrick.'

Raybur said to calm down. 'It's just the deal. Action dont come until later.'

'Never know,' Oz said. 'Gotta be ready for action even on the deal. Norm here dont even know what a Wyrick is.'

'Goddamn,' Raybur said. 'What the hell you an Jacoby been talkin bout if you aint been talkin Wyricks?'

Oz didnt wait for Norman to answer. 'Here,' he said. He used a piece of broom straw as a pointer. 'We got a buyer we use for our merchandise. We call him Wyrick. Dont go by any other name, just Wyrick. We'll meet with him somewhere hereabouts.' He pointed to a couple of rocks with the straw. 'We try to only meet with him on the outskirts of town. Dont need Wyrick seein too much of where we live.'

'Damn straight,' Raybur agreed.

'We might exchange merchandise with him at the deal or we might have to wait for the action.'

'The action?' Norman asked.

Raybur sighed, muttered to himself, then said, 'First time we meet with Wyrick, we set up a deal to be made. When the deal goes down—could be the next day, could be in three months—thats called the action.'

'Important thing is to never trust the Wyrick,' Oz said. 'Never.'

'Thats why Jacoby does all the negotiatin,' Raybur said. 'He can smell a Wyricks bullshit from a mile away.'

'Me an Gay Jim'll make sure we're in rifle range, well hid and such. Raybur here'll be our signal man, let us know from what direction Wyricks approachin.'

'Jims gonna have a gun?' Norman asked.

Oz snapped the straw in half, stood up, pulled the pistol from his pants and handed it to Gay Jim. In his hands the gun seemed like a toy; he cocked it and laughed while Oz scrounged for a chunk of wood. Then, in a single motion, Oz tossed a piece of wood high into the air, toward the sun. Gay Jim's gaze followed the trajectory of the wood. He stopped laughing and his eyes narrowed. He raised the gun and fired. The silhouetted wood broke apart, its debris littering the slopes. The short hard pop of the pistol seemed to never sound.

'Gay Jim can have a gun,' Oz said. 'Sure a shot as any you'll ever meet. Dont need brains to put one through your eye, college boy.'

Norman nodded, said he could see that. Raybur smirked and changed the subject back to the matter at hand. 'Should I be up on the ridge or farther out in the flatlands?'

'Flatlands,' Oz said. 'Pa thinks Wyrick is gonna come round the long way. Wants you in the shack that sits out there a ways.'

'Sounds fine.'

'How we know when Wyrick is gonna show up?' Norman asked.

Oz looked up from his model town and stared at Norman. 'Jacoby tells us.'

'An hows he know?'

Gay Jim farted and waved his hands above his head.

'You just cant get your mind around it, can you?' Raybur said. 'There are just some things Jacoby knows. Sure as the sun'll set, Wyrick will show the day after morrow.'

That night no one lit a fire—not a lantern, nor a candle, not a bonfire or even a match. Above the village, the moon glided over, full and round like a paper disc, casting its own reflected light out across the desert space. Unlike the direct light of the sun, the moon gave dimension to Norman's surroundings. Shades and gradients marked the space between things in a way the daylight obliterated them. The flat washed world of the desert expanded into region and country where time rolled out long before him. Distances could more easily be gauged, details on far away objects more easily discerned. If Norman looked to the line of telephone poles in the daytime, their spacing was a trick of the brain—the farther poles simply drawn smaller than those in the foreground. But now, in the moonlight, Norman not only saw their spacing and their scale, but he also took in, quite possibly for the first time, the enormity of the universe. For all that surrounded him was swallowed in the mammoth of the desert—an entire life, a village, even generations of a family whose moniker had become lost to time. And still this place, no bigger than a blemish on the crust of the Earth, the Earth itself no bigger or more permanent than a bubble breathed by a minnow in an ocean.

Above Norman the skies teemed with stars, some steady and bright, some blipping in and out of space and time. Voices carried down the slope to where Norman sat contemplating his place in this universe and he turned. Martha stepped out of the doorway of Lucas Brown's house. She smoothed out her ragged dress and ran her fingers through her hair. She stopped, her fingers curled around her ear, her head canted to the side as if listening for something on the wind. But no sounds came from the night and there was no breeze. Then she turned to stare at Norman. From the distance of a few hundred yards, her figure looked slim and young. She began walking to him and he rose to his feet. When he spoke, it was barely a whisper.

'Late evening for you.'

Her reply came as little more than a whisper too. 'Is for you too.'

'Full moon keeps me wake.'

As she approached her facial features developed a definition.

'Keeps most everyone awake,' she said. 'Full moons end up bein my busiest nights.'

94

In the moonlight, Martha looked younger—perhaps a vision of what had been years ago. As she drew near enough to touch, Norman felt a compulsion writhe inside of him. He stuffed his hands into his pockets.

'Raybur know youre out?'

'Does he know I'm whorin?'

'Thats not what I meant.'

'Yes,' she said. 'He knows. Stayin alive out here means givin up your body.'

The words sounded strange to Norman and he felt queasy. A pool of saliva formed under his tongue. 'Youre okay with that?'

She smiled, tight-lipped. She blinked twice. 'Boys round here been talkin bout how much time you an Jacoby been spendin together—how much you two talk.'

'Yeah,' Norman said, he supposed they did.

'He let you live cause he loved your mind.' She said it tenderly, as a mother would to a child. Then she reached out and stroked her fingers through Norman's shaggy hair. 'Jacoby treats the mind different than he treats the body.'

For a long while Norman studied the woman, her eyes like antique glass, her skin hued blue in the nighttime light. 'I saw the bodies he keeps inside the house,' Norman said. 'A pile of arms stacked like firewood. There was a thumb just lyin on the floor.'

'And the Madonna?' Martha asked.

Though referenced, Norman never understood who or what the Madonna was, and he asked in shadowy reply, 'What about the Madonna?'

Martha smiled as if privy to a joke. 'If you dont know,' she said, 'then maybe Jacoby aint as keen on you as Oz an Lucas Brown think.'

'What is it?' Norman asked. 'Can you tell me about the Madonna?'

'It's hard to put into words.'

'I need to know.'

Same as before, Martha smiled. She pulled Norman's hands from his pockets and cradled them in hers. 'The Madonna,' she said. 'She is love.'

The police officers who had responded to the call had treated Norman with indifference. At first only three arrived, but when they saw the scene, they called more officers. Only two officers seemed to be interested in Norman's role.

'You found her in the shower?'

'Yeah,' Norman nodded. 'She had been at the rally at the university.' The officers exchanged glances. 'She came home, got in the shower. After a while I checked in on her.'

'About how long?'

'I dont know, twenty minutes.'

'She didnt normally take long showers?'

'Yeah, well, I mean, she didnt say anything when she got home from the rally and I just wanted to see if there was anything wrong.'

'Thats when you found her.'

Norman looked at the notepad the officer used to write down his answers.

'She was laying facedown in the water,' Norman said. 'I pulled her out of the water and tried to pump it from her stomach.'

'Why dont you sit down?' the other officer said. He guided Norman to the barstools by the counter.

'Are those the clothes you were wearing when you found her?'

'Yeah.'

'Youre awfully wet.'

Both of the officers studied Norman, gauging his reaction. Down the hall he saw another flash from the camera in the bathroom and a disembodied voice give the okay to move the deceased.

'I ended up getting in the shower to move her,' Norman said. 'I'm not a strong guy; I'm just not capable of moving a body around.'

The lead officer shifted his weight from one foot to the other, then looked at his partner again.

'Obviously this is hard. We just want to get a full picture of what happened, thats all.'

The other officer cleared his throat and said they had two more questions and they needed them answered honestly and to the best of Norman's recollection.

'Did your girlfriend—girlfriend, right?' Norman nodded. 'Did she use any drugs—marijuana, narcotics?'

After Norman sat quietly for a few minutes, the other officer said, 'We want to know about her. We're not asking anything about you. Did she use?'

'I was trying to get her to quit,' Norman said finally.

'Our other question is about your sex life.'

Norman felt the back of his neck go afire, same as when he had called the police two hours before. He responded as he had many times in the last couple hours, by nodding.

'When was the last time you and Miss McGuffin had sexual intercourse?'

Norman had the answer rehearsed. 'This morning, right before the rally.'

The officer didnt write anything down.

'This morning?'

'Yeah.'

'Not after she arrived home?'

'No. She got in the shower when she came home like I said.'

'Thing is,' the other officer said, 'it looks like she maybe had intercourse more recently than that.'

For a second, Norman stood still, considering the words. Then, as he had practiced in the bathroom mirror, his face grew dark and he drew a few deep breaths. He stepped backward, his mouth open. One of the officers reached out to steady him, but Norman swatted his hand away. Then he collapsed onto the couch and asked what else he didnt know.

3.

Up on the ridge Jacoby lay out beneath the oak scrub, hands cupped over his eyes. Norman lay next to him, squinting in the same direction as the old man.

'There it was,' Jacoby said. He tugged at Norman's sleeve and pointed. A light flickered from the end of the ridge. Rifle in hand, Jacoby began to scuttle down the side of the slope on the seat of his jeans. Without question, Norman followed him. At the bottom of the slope, Jacoby stood and trotted toward a toppled water tower.

'Wyrick'll be pullin round this tailing in about three minutes.'

'Pulling around?' Norman repeated. 'Like in a car?'

Jacoby stopped in his tracks and looked Norman over. 'This fella wont see us, understand. He dont exist an neither do we.'

The top of the water tower tank had popped off leaving it lying like a giant littered tin can. The top lay like a Chinaman's hat on the ground next to it. Inside the empty vessel Norman and Jacoby squatted side by side. The metal walls were hot to the touch and the men crouched to avoid touching their skin to them. While they waited, Jacoby pulled the pistol from his waistband and checked the chambers.

'So light out there, a man cant see into a hole like this,' Jacoby said. His voice reverberated in the container and it enveloped Norman. 'Like one of those cosmic black holes— nothing escapes.' He chuckled. 'Shot a man in here once. Saw him dive in after Oz took a bad shot at him. Took my thirty-aught—guns got an arc like a rainbow—an bucketed a shot into here. Figured it to be like two objects in a void—the bullet an the man would meet an become one.'

Outside the gravel crunched under the tires of an approaching car. In the desert place the form of the car looked strange. As it rolled to a stop, Norman recognized it as a Lincoln Towncar. The tinted windows trimmed in chrome, the bumper and spoked hubcaps and the reflection they cast of the landscape was warped and negative. An antenna stuck straight up until the engine cut off, then it retracted into the hood. The driver door opened and a man stepped out. He was dressed to match the car—black suit with a white nearly reflective dress shirt.

Norman felt Jacoby's hand pat his leg. The old man raised the pistol and pointed it at the stranger. Unaware of the immediate threat, the stranger craned his neck around the landscape, the flat lenses of his sunglasses reflecting whatever he saw. He took several strides so he stood in front of the grill of the car and called Jacoby by name.

'Mister Jacoby,' he called again. 'Wyrick here—down from the main office.' He waited and when there came no reply he said the supplies were in the car.

Jacoby's arm extended until the pistol suspended in front of Norman's face, the sight set on their visitor.

The man raised his arms over his head and the shoulders of the suit bunched up around his ears. 'I'm not armed.'

Jacoby sighed. 'Alright,' he called and grabbed Norman by the sleeve. He tucked the pistol back in his pants and they emerged from their hiding spot.

'I'll be damned,' Wyrick said. 'I didnt see you in there.'

The old man didnt respond; he just smiled enough to expose the browned roots of his teeth. Wyrick studied Norman, but not to the degree Norman studied the man in return. He looked unreal in his unpractical garb, his clean look.

'Our stuff,' Jacoby prompted.

'In the car.'

Jacoby walked around the man, leaving Wyrick and Norman to look at one another. As Jacoby rummaged through the contents in the trunk of the car, he hummed and muttered to himself. Wyrick cleared his throat and widened his stance. His forehead shined in the sun.

The old familiar idea of escape surfaced in Norman's mind. In the past Norman had taken comfort in the idea of getting away. But now a surge of panic shot through his body. When the thoughts of escape were more frequent as they had been in the past, the thoughts were just that—they had been departures in themselves. He would imagine himself returning to Indiana, telling his stories to an awestruck Doctor Blanche. Then he'd stop the fantasy and set back to the work at hand in Jacobyville. But now, in front of Norman, an automobile proved that a return to life as he had known it was possible. Thirty, forty miles is enough to isolate a man—some generations of settlers never moved beyond that.

'The instrument?' Jacoby asked. He crawled from the back seat of the car with a long soft leather case in hand.

'Yes sir,' Wyrick said. 'Yours to do with as you please once the job is complete.'

'That right?' Jacoby said. 'Little gift from the big man, huh?'

'Guess so.' The Wyrick managed a smile.

'I'm takin care of the bodies too?'

'Body,' Wyrick corrected. 'Single target.'

'Of course,' Jacoby said. He unzipped the leather case and withdrew the rifle. The polished beauty of the gun struck Norman in much the same way the automobile and Wyrick did—an otherworldly artifact. The wooden butt of the rifle shone like a mirror, the sunlight gleaming off the barrel and the mounted telescope sight. 'Real beaut here, chief,' Jacoby said. He turned to display the gun to Norman, who nodded in approval.

'I was told not to write out directions,' Wyrick said. 'Just to tell you the logistics of the situation.'

'Aye,' Jacoby said. 'Sounds right.' He slid the bolt of the rifle and looked down the length of the barrel. 'Tell the details to my assistant here while I unload the car.' He gestured to Norman and sauntered away, still familiarizing himself with the new firearm.

Wyrick turned to Norman and spoke in a flat monotone as if reciting a recipe from memory. 'The target is a Japanese man—five foot tall, black hair, clean shaven. I will be with him, wearing the same outfit you see today. Time of day for termination is twelve o'clock noon, forty days from now. Point of contact is Dalton Wells.'

Jacoby stopped unloading the car. 'Why there?' he asked.

Wyrick responded with a question of his own, asking if the locale presented a problem.

'Nope,' Jacoby said. 'A long walk for sure—just an odd location for business.'

Wyrick sighed and hesitated before speaking again. 'Target is a Japanese businessman who wants a good reason to make a deal with the organization.'

The evidence must have been in the last statement as Jacoby began to laugh. 'Yes,' he said. 'Yes, alright. Good.' He hefted the last of the crates from the trunk. 'Other half of the goods upon completion?'

'Thats what I was told,' Wyrick said.

'We'll need lye powder too.'

In the evening all the residents of the village gathered in Jacoby's house to sort through the goods. Gay Jim opened each box, giggling the entire time. Sticks of beef jerky, powdered soup mixes, iodine tablets—each package contained a hodgepodge of desert necessities. Bullets and shells and gunpowder, socks and a pair of scissors. Jacoby sat in his rocking chair, holding his gun like a newborn. Like the other villagers, Norman sat amidst the mess of food, ammunition and bric-a-brac. Because

Jacoby's house remained forever dimmed in the shadow of the mountain, several kerosene lamps sat with fat wicked flames about the room.

'Is it the government?' Norman asked.

Jacoby stopped rocking and leveled his gaze at Norman. 'Whats that?'

'Who you work for,' Norman said. 'Is it the government? I mean we're mercenaries, right?'

The conversation attracted the interest of Gay Jim and he plopped himself on the floor next to Norman. The usual flood of body odor cascaded over the immediate vicinity.

'Mercenary,' Jacoby said. 'Now thats a loaded word.' Most all the fellow residents fell silent and refocused their attention on the exchange. Lucas Brown's children played at the far end of the room, taking bullets and setting them up like pins and rolling a marble at them. 'Aint never been a war fought in this land without the aid of men who kill for money—thats what a mercenary is, you know—a soldier for hire. Had Germans during the revolution—only folks called them Hessians. Scalpers in the Spanish-American War. Even the Civil War had their share—only they gave them name, rank an their own unit.'

'I get it,' Norman said. 'I get it. Whats going on here isnt new. I just want us to call it like it is.'

'What we do dont got a name,' Raybur said. 'Aint nothing to call it.'

'You aint never been in a war, son,' Jacoby said.

'Neither've you from what I can tell.'

Gay Jim opened a packet of green powder and dipped his finger into it. He licked it clean and repeated the process.

Somewhere in the shadows, one of the children knocked the bullets and they clapped in delight.

'Thats where youve been wrong,' Jacoby said. He began rocking again as if suddenly relaxed by reminiscing of a world since past. Lucas Brown, Oz, and Raybur and Martha sat like children and listened to the word of Jacoby. 'Some folks will have you believe the very first beings on this planet begat some boys who initiated the first act of homicide in this world. And whether this is myth or fact, it is truth.'

'Yessir,' Raybur said. His wife nodded in agreement.

'The murder,' Jacoby said, 'is in all of us. No treaty or word of law, no armistice or declaration can change our basic nature. Since the beginning of time, our species, our curious species, has thrived on violence. Weve created industry around the termination of life. Some are slow an some are, well, what we do.' He smiled. 'If you need me to summarize the entirety of human depravity, consider two men workin in a field.'

As he launched into his extended analogy, Norman looked around the room, first at the children as they emerged from the shadows to listen—wide-eyed and filled with wonderment—then at the villagers frozen in their byzantine devotion. Finally Norman looked at Martha. In the lantern light she looked her age. Upon feeling Norman's gaze, she turned her head, smiled and returned her focus to the patriarch's fable.

'The field is a barren place. Not a tree or flower or blade of grass in sight. Neither man has tools and it is a struggle to survive. And survivin is the only thing that seems natural. They could separate from one another, true. They could wander the whole of the Earth—the many fallow fields that cover the surface of the planet—in search of food. But they both know this is not an option. And the one says to the other, If we work together perhaps we can survive this place.

'But the other knew better—call it a primal instinct, call it being human—an he attacked his brother, rippin the throat from his neck. He ate the flesh of his brother an wore his hide. He drank his blood. Then he planted the dead mans teeth as the first seeds of the world to come. He wrung the contents from his bladder an liver to water the crop.

'In time the first harvest of society came. Babies hung like blossoms from the boughs of trees. And the man plucked them from the vine, peeled back the fine soft skin an ate them as fruits. Others he let shrivel an still more he plucked squirmin with life an planted them.'

Jacoby paused for a breath.

'Is this a story you dreamt up on your own?' Norman asked.

'Why dont you just let Pa finish?' Oz asked from the corner of the room.

'Always with the questions,' Raybur said.

Gay Jim began to clap and Lucas Brown swore at the sudden disarray in the conversation. Jacoby held up his hand to silence them all.

'This is the same story youve heard a thousand thousand times,' he said. 'Part of what makes us different from every other animal on this planet is our constant search for our beginning—our origin. What I just told you was the first epoch of mankind. Our gardener, the living brother, became fat an lazy an old. He let some of the fruit mature and turn into young men themselves. At first he considered killin them, but found that to be too much work. He shirked the one responsibility he had as steward over all creation an let others come into existence. They will kill one another, the gardener said to himself. And he was right. The blossomed young men did murder one another an in doing so, the ones who survived became beings hardened by carnage and made all the more lethal because they lived. This is the second epoch of man.'

Jacoby looked about the room before he continued as if reading from some holy script.

'But in every group there are some men who have apportioned to them some part of the divine benevolence that spawned them into being. And these men, each on his own, creates a place without feature, without tree or flower or blade of glass. And with two babies transplanted from the world beyond, they stand in the barren field an the one says to the other, If we work together, we can survive. And his brother—a descendant of violence itself—slays him without thinkin, breaks his skull into a spade an aerates the soil with his rack of ribs, plants the teeth.'

'This,' Jacoby said, 'is the progress of our world. We have moved past any epochs and entered an age of ultimate cruelty and bloodlust, where killin is the only way and something as great as the apocalypse—the very end of time—can slip by unnoticed. There are no mercenaries in this garden—just us who harvest life so life can continue such as it is.'

Around the room murmurs of agreement met with shaking heads. In his mind, Norman envisioned the place Jacoby described.

'Thats terrible,' he finally managed to say.

'Whats that?' Jacoby asked. The others stopped their side conversations and once again focused on the two men.

'If you believe that, whats the point of living?'

As he prepared to answer the question, Jacoby stopped

rocking. 'If all we did was live, nothing else could exist. Preservin humanity means continuing the long an sacred traditions of violence an murder an cruelty.'

Outside the night had fallen completely. The light from Jacoby's house could be seen from the nether slopes of the mountains. Rare clouds shaped like mares' tails blotted the luminary orchestra of the stars and everything beyond the confines of Jacoby's quarters was cloaked in darkness.

'Go,' Jacoby told them. He waved his hand. 'We got to open our gifts an have us a story. Now it's bedtime. Go.'

Oz took a lantern from the table, led Gay Jim by the arm and they left. Raybur and Martha did likewise.

'Mind if me an my kin take your last lamp here?' Lucas Brown asked.

'Thats fine,' Jacoby said. 'Just hand me that taper there, would you?'

Lucas Brown took a half-burnt candle from the windowsill and handed it to the old man. When he and his children left, darkness engulfed the room until Jacoby struck a match and touched it to the wick of the candle. At first the flame danced wildly, then it tamed and burned steadily.

'You stayed,' Jacoby said.

'Yeah,' Norman said.

'Youre disenchanted.'

'I wouldnt say that.'

'But you feel differently about me, about Jacobyville—the whole enterprise.'

Norman pointed a finger at the old man. 'It's that, right there, I cant tell what is actually you, whats just some story, whats part of whatever this is.'

'I shouldnt use words like enterprise you mean. I should say, The whole shebang, right?' Jacoby exaggerated his accent and laughed. 'Youve made me into something I'm not; youre havin a hard time seein me as something besides the desert hermit who took you in.'

Norman had nothing to say in return.

'Youve heard us talk of the Madonna, yes?'

'Yeah,' Norman said. 'I have.'

Jacoby stood and beckoned Norman to follow. He went to the stout squared door in the rear of the house, where the house met the mountain. 'I call her Ma,' Jacoby said and he swung the door outward. Light flooded the small chamber and Jacoby stepped aside to reveal the haggard form of a seated woman. A rancid odor emanated from the body. Around her a multitude of jars hung from hooks in the ceiling, small rubber tubes running from each of them and connecting with her in various spots. Her naked body was spotted and gray and flabby. The nest of pubic hair gaped where the blackened yawp of her vagina fell open. Her legs had been amputated, as had the majority of the fingers on her left hand. For what Norman saw before him, he could only take this woman—the Madonna—for dead. But one eye opened and the pupil shrank and danced about in her skull.

'It's me, Ma,' Jacoby said and the eye looked at him and blinked. A raspy breath escaped her lips and she sucked in another lungful of air as if she were a creature of the deep, requiring oxygen every so often.

When he left, Norman was not given a light. He stumbled off the porch and let his eyes adjust to the darkness. He remained mindful of the open shaft directly in front of the house and he took a circuitous route to avoid any pratfall. As he walked slowly, feeling his way through the night, he spoke to himself, muttering in a hushed whisper.

'Out talkin to yourself?' a voice asked.

Norman stopped and turned. The glow of a lamp with a wick trimmed low illuminated the source of the voice; it was Oz.

'Trying to feel my way back home,' Norman said. The light continued to approach.

In a minute's time Oz sidled up to Norman and turned the knob at the base of the lantern. The flame grew, throwing out a luminescence that flooded their surroundings and sent their shadows spilling down the slope as jangly forms.

'Pa, he'll send a man off on a cloudless night without so much as a match to light his way.'

'I noticed.'

'I'm sure he's got his reasons,' Oz said. 'Mans got a pattern to him, certain way he does things. Comes as part of livin out here.'

Norman did not answer; he simply walked in step with Oz, the light leading them on as a carrot put on a stick to fool an ass.

'Like tonight,' Oz said. 'I knowed he was gonna show you our Ma—the Madonna—when he done started in on the creation story. An I certainly knowed it had happened when you came out of the house without a light and youre talkin to yourself.' Oz stopped walking and, because he held the light, Norman stopped walking too. The desert dweller raised the lamp so they could see each other's faces and they studied one another in the yellow light. 'I know the pattern of men who see Ma an what they do next, what they begin to think about us.'

'I think this place is a nightmare,' Norman said. The words choked on their way out and they had the air of a confession.

Oz remained unmoved. 'The whole world is a nightmare, brother. Most people just dont know it.'

He lowered the lamp and they walked in silence to the door of their abode. Oz held the lantern above his head again. 'Go on in,' he said. 'Tonight I'm gonna stay with Lucas Brown.'

Though Norman did not move, Oz turned his body, eclipsing the lamplight, and began to saunter away. Norman put his hands out in front of him and felt the wooden frame of the doorway. He walked into the house, kicked off his boots and stepped gingerly toward where his bedroll lay. In the darkness he detected another being.

'Oz asked me to be here,' Martha said.

Norman stumbled forward, unable to see the source of the voice. He only found her once he felt the tepid warmth of her bare skin. His breathing quickened as did his pulse. 'He said you would be ready for me,' she said. Her hands pulled at the waistband of his pants and Norman assured her that yes, he was ready.

Afterward Martha lay so still it seemed as if she had vanished into the night like smoke or dreams or memories. Norman had asked her to be still during sex—limp. When she moaned, he shushed her. Though there was nothing to see, he closed his eyes and imagined his encounter just minutes before. He recounted how Jacoby backed out of the jam closet where the Madonna sat and told Norman that all of civilization had been born of this woman's loins. His gaze drifted down between the cauterized scarred stumps of leg. The crone's eye circled in its socket and she blinked.

'If you planted your seed in her, you would be the latest in a long line of men to do such a thing.' Jacoby had grinned. 'An thats your pleasure, aint it?'

As hard as Norman tried, he could not look away from the Madonna. The words Jacoby spoke sounded distant and Norman took his time responding to them. 'It's not that,' he said, wanting to explain himself more thoroughly.

'She cant fight back,' Jacoby said. 'An yet she has the power.'

In her rocking chair, the pan of refuse beneath her and the kerosene radiance cast about her, the Madonna appeared as a gargoyle or a deity of the grotesque proclaiming damnation over all the world.

'Yeah,' Norman finally said and he stooped inside the closet and embraced the Madonna. Her baggy skin gathered between his fingers like leavened dough and her shallow breathing barely moved her ancient worn breasts. He lowered the waist of his pants and pressed into her and began thrusting. Together they rocked back and forth—just the creaking of the chair, his breathing, and the refrain of Jacoby saying yes yes yes. The lamp began to swing and all that Norman could see—Doctor Blanche, the one glassed eye, Grace, the sloshing jars of medicine, the soiled pantyhose, a broken beer bottle—all blended together. Only when Norman climaxed did the images fall away from his mind. Jacoby's hand rested firmly on his shoulder as if laying a blessing on his follower. Norman backed up. The old woman blinked once, the hollow space of her mouth quivering.

'You aint so different from other men,' Martha said. Her voice cut through the abyss and startled Norman.

'I'm not like you,' he said. 'I'm not like Oz or your husband or Lucas Brown.'

She placed her hand on his chest and rested her head on his shoulder. 'All men, everywhere, are the same.' Before he could retort, Martha posed a question: 'Youre really the same as you ever were, aint you? You just dont hide it around us.'

'No,' he said. 'Out here Ive done much worse.'

'Worse aint the word for it. Youve just always held yourself back.'

'Not always,' Norman said.

He had grabbed Grace by the wrist and the water spilled out of the shower stall, pooling on the floor and soaking into the bathmat.

'I was raped,' Grace said again. Her lip pulled in and she started to whimper.

'Shut up,' Norman said. The words surprised him as they came out of his mouth. 'Shut up. You are a whore.' He began to step into the shower, twisting her wrist so she turned into the stream of water.

'What are you doing?' she cried. Then she spat out a mouth full of water. Norman grabbed a clump of her hair and jerked her head back.

'Let every guy fuck you except me,' he said. Water soaked through his pants and filled his shoes. As he undid his belt, Grace struggled against his grip, slapping backward. He heard her feet slide across the bottom of the tub. She made a futile effort to grab the shower curtain for balance, but it tore free of its hooks and when she fell the rest of the way down, she hit her head on the edge of the sink. On the floor she rolled back and forth, atop the plastic sheet. A knot formed on her head and the skin pulled tight. Her eyes were closed.

Norman did not shut off the water when he stepped from the shower. He looked down on her, this helpless naked form, murmuring to herself. Then he wrapped the plastic over her face, held her arms to her sides and raped her.

'You done knowed what you was doin,' Martha said. 'You done knowed it while you was doin it.'

'Yeah,' Norman said.

4.

For a few years in the early nineteen forties, Topaz thrived as one of the largest towns in all of Utah. The settlement spawned into existence after the bombing of Pearl Harbor when the government relocated Japanese citizens to various camps, many of them in unsustainable areas. The buildings—the schools, barracks, and stores—were constructed from cheap material and quickly deteriorated in the desert environment. Most of what remained of Topaz thirty years later consisted of piles of debris and some concrete pads. Such was Norman's knowledge of the ghost town.

'Of course you know about Topaz,' Jacoby said. 'But do you know about Dalton Wells?'

'Cant say I do,' Norman said.

All the men had walked a considerable distance. Jacobyville, with its women and children, had long sunk below the horizon, setting just before the sun. Jacoby asked Norman what he knew of Topaz, but decided to answer his own inquiry.

'When the prisoners in Topaz acted up, they were relocated to Dalton Wells—an isolation center.'

'I dont think they were referred to as prisoners,' Norman said.

The other men trailed behind at a distance, preferring to keep a conversation of their own.

Jacoby admitted he misused the word. 'Youre right. They werent called prisoners. But if you saw one of those camps when it was operational, you'd say otherwise. Barbwire fences, assigned living quarters, curfews, a sentry on duty...' For a moment Jacoby's thoughts seemed to drift elsewhere. 'Then theres Dalton Wells. Thats where the internment camps sent their troublemakers. Call a guard a name, play a prank, violate curfew, murder an rape an they send you off to Dalton Wells.

'First group of men—sixteen of them—came into Dalton Wells from a camp in California. They didnt get a trial. They didnt get a lawyer or a counsel of any sort. Just'—he made a grandiose sweep of the hand—'taken in the night and placed at a camp originally built by the Civilian Conservation Corps.'

They walked in silence for a ways before Norman asked whereabouts this Dalton Wells place existed.

'Out Moab way,' Jacoby said. A few seconds later he clarified, saying just north of Moab, not far from the highway. 'Be a good place to make a run for it,' he said. 'Few miles along the highway with your thumb out an someone'd pick you up.'

'What happened to the men they took to Dalton Wells?' Norman asked.

'The prisoners.'

'Yeah, the prisoners.'

Jacoby chuckled. 'Well, those sixteen, they was just the original lot. More came in an they was made to work. Guards killed a couple of them. Beat nearly all of them at one point or another.' He shook his head as if he could not understand the brutality of what he told Norman. 'Then they shut the camp down—moved the men to an Indian reservation out in Arizona... People've always been in the business of movin bodies around.'

The band of men fanned out across the arid plain, each of them trudging his own path toward a common destination—a place consisting of little more than myth and name.

They camped on the first day in the same manner as they would camp in the week to come. Once the orb of the sun glowered just above the crest of the earth behind them, they ceased walking and tended to their specific duties. Gay Jim and Oz continued on, scouting out what lay ahead. From time to time, they stopped and listened, guns drawn. Raybur helped Jacoby secure the rations, checking each man's pack for whatever supplies were needed. Together they concocted a meal—Jello powder and tuna, bullion and jerky, rice and Kool-Aid.

The pairings of men left Lucas Brown and Norman in each other's company. They were delegated the task of setting up camp—laying out the tarp, building a fire if needed.

'Easy job now,' Lucas Brown said. 'Wait til we get into them mountains. Aint gonna be sleepin on a tarp no more.'

'Grounds no good?' Norman asked.

'Jesus,' Lucas Brown said. 'You is dumb. Colder up in the mountains. We actually got to pitch a shelter, something we can get inside of.' He held up the wadded tarp and handed Norman one of the corners and pointed, said to go thataway. As they walked apart, Lucas Brown kept talking over his shoulder. 'Up there we gotta watch out for the MacKowskis.'

The tarp pulled taut and the men lowered it to the ground, letting the cushion of air escape from under it.

Norman chose his next words carefully. 'The MacKowskis. Are they as big a threat as everyone makes them out to be?'

Thinking of how to respond brought a smile to Lucas Brown's lips—a sight never seen by Norman either before or after this moment.

'Smitty MacKowski can track a man by his smell,' Lucas Brown said. 'Mean cuss—Jacobys fond of sayin Smitty dont got a tooth in his head or a heart in his chest.' He lowered his voice. 'Prolly true. But if you asked me I'd give the edge to old Smitty. Jacoby talks like he's smarter; Smitty acts smarter.'

They each staked the tarp through the grommets in their respective corners.

'What you mean by that?' Norman asked. 'Bout Jacoby only talkin like he's smart.'

'Look,' Lucas Brown said. 'We know youre fond of hearin the old mans philosophy of life an the universe an all, but the truth is there aint any magic to what we do. There aint any sort of mystery. Bodies get traded. Men get killed. The smartest men in the desert know this. An it's the only thing they need to keep in mind.'

'Smitty knows this?'

'He does.' After a measured pause, Lucas Brown said he should know. 'Runnin into Smitty MacKowski is like runnin into the devil hisself.'

They finished securing the tarp and Norman asked if they should scrounge for firewood. Lucas Brown hooked his thumbs through his belt loops and gauged the sun—now just a vestige of coal—and said he figured so. 'Might be one of the last times for a while yet. Cant have no light in the mountains.'

Dinner consisted of egg noodles, mustard, and freeze dried peas. In gathering what few pieces of driftwood and scrub they could, Norman found a tire tread and they burned that too. Stinking of oil and resin, the burning tire sent a stream of inky smoke roiling into the dusky sky. Gay Jim and Oz returned from their scouting expedition.

'Nothin out there,' Oz said. Gay Jim hooted in agreement, pulled the gun from his pants and licked the barrel.

'Fine job, boys,' Jacoby said. 'Sit down, have some dinner.'

Raybur used a ladle to serve slop from the bucket.

'More than likely this will be the last job for the year,' Jacoby said. 'The supplies we get from this one have got to last us through the winter months, so lets be extra fuckin vigilant and extra fuckin thorough.'

A chorus of agreement came from the men.

'Got mountains comin up too,' Jacoby said. 'And you know what that means... Norman?'

'I done tol him bout Smitty,' Lucas Brown said.

'Good,' Jacoby said. 'Extra fuckin vigilant.' He used his boot knife both as a utensil and as a device for gesticulation.

He pointed at Norman. 'The mountains is serious business, son. We got us a stopover in a swell at the edge of the desert. Probably come up on it the day after morrow. Then we gotta make passage through the mountains. More desert on the other side once we get through. Always more desert.'

The swell gurgled out of the horizon while they walked across the flats. It rose like the plume of a smoldering volcano in the way ash holds stagnant in the air. Only this vision was indeed stone. At first its contours showed a different shade of blue against the blue sky, but as they drew closer and the stature of the landmass increased, the colors became more distinct.

Out to the left—to the north—the mountains cropped the sky with jagged peaks and rounded valleys. Snow capped the most distant mountaintops. Of the many tricks the desert plays on the mind, this one wrought the most deceit. With each step the men took toward this mammoth form it grew in size, but seemed no closer. They camped one night in the shadow of the monolith and finally on the afternoon of the next day ventured to outmost rocky inclines, entering via a slot canyon.

Instead of spreading out wide, they proceeded forward in single file, a ribbon of sky cut into the stone above them. Norman saw a bird flit across the ridge crests and realized how long it had been since he had seen anything other than human, insect and snake. If any one of them coughed or spoke or kicked a stone, the sound echoed through the narrow corridor.

They walked uphill through the passages with the ridges overhead occasionally collapsing together slicing the sky into a mere sliver. As they walked, Norman stared at the back of

Raybur's head. He wondered about Martha, if Raybur thought about her, worried about leaving her alone in the village with the Madonna and children to care for. He took a sip from his canteen. He wondered if Raybur ever became jealous over the other men fucking his wife—or if, on some level, it titillated the old codger. With little more than these few stray thoughts, Norman became a fount of hatred for Raybur. Then he stumbled over a loose rock and his carefully built hatred faltered with his step.

'Come to the clear spot here,' Raybur said over his shoulder. 'Be able to see all the way into Colorado.'

Up ahead, the skinny passage broke into a wide berth and as the men stepped from the slot canyon out onto the plateau, they stood shoulder to shoulder. In the panorama Norman could look out on the yellow and white blotches of the desert land—and, in a single turn of his body, he could gaze upon a mountainscape that looked to ramble on forever—the peaks green and brown and white.

They descended from the swell along faults—flat graveled stretches held together by debris or conifer roots. Twice Jacoby stopped and foraged some pine nuts, hulling them from the cone and then dispensing them amongst his clan, each man nodding his head in gratitude.

They came to a ghost town of sorts—a stopover as Jacoby called it—a couple of slatwood buildings nestled into a crook of the swell at the edge of a larger canyon. A dilapidated shed sat near the bottom of the valley. Evidence of another shed and a gravemarker lay even farther out, a few upright chunks of driftwood might have formed a fence years ago.

'Make camp,' Jacoby said. He set his pack down and told Lucas Brown to check the shed at the foot of the slope. 'Make sure we aint got any surprises in there. Be a good place for Oz an Gay Jim to keep a lookout.'

As Lucas trod off toward the building, gun in hand, Jacoby took Norman by the elbow. 'Foller me,' he said and they began walking up the gravelly slope toward the house.

As they drew close, Norman realized the house sat on a footing of shale. Over time—between winters and rains and minor seismic tremors—the house must have shifted to its current catawampus state. A hulking massive boulder dwarfed it. They approached the rectangular opening where the door used to be and Norman looked back over his shoulder. The shed sat at the bottom of the slope, the only thing visible between the barriers of rock.

'Dont forget to wipe your feet before steppin in,' Jacoby said.

A hot pungent stink of rot flooded Norman's nose. He could taste the smell on the back of his tongue and he gagged. As Norman's eyes adjusted to his dim surroundings, the source of the smell manifested. He stepped backward, nearly falling out of the doorway. A body, hanged with a noose, creaked ever so slightly in the center of the one room house.

'Goddamn,' Norman said. His eyes stung with raw, hot pain.

Jacoby gathered up the neck of his shirt and pulled it over his nose and mouth. As he approached the hanging figure, he withdrew his boot knife. He lay a single hand on the body to quiet the creaking and he examined the corpse—first opening the jacket, then patting down the torso, and finally taking one of the dead man's hands in his. He let the hand go and the body began swaying again, the short length of rope creaking as it pulled on the rafters. Jacoby looked around the room and said there it was. He kicked a crate toward the hanging man. He stepped onto the crate and called for Norman to help.

From where he stood outside the door, Norman watched Gay Jim and Oz take turns jumping from a standstill. After each jump they marked their distance with a rock. Raybur officiated over the childish proceedings.

'Get in here an make sure the body dont hit the floor too hard,' Jacoby said.

When Norman turned his head to address the old man the smell magnified again. The body hung stiff—the skin curdling off the flesh, yellow and black and brown. The eyes stared out as two empty sockets, the crust of blood dried black. 'I dont think I can,' Norman said.

'Fresh dead is hard to take,' Jacoby said. 'I know. Still gotta plug my nose too. But we gotta cut this thing down so we can have a place to sleep tonight.'

Norman inhaled deeply—only through his mouth—and stepped forward to help Jacoby.

They placed the body farther out on the slope, behind the giant boulder. Norman carried it by the ankles while Jacoby walked backward, holding the corpse beneath the arms. Lucas Brown noticed them carrying it and began climbing up the slope. He arrived, panting, once they set the body down.

'Look him over yet?' he asked.

'Just a quick look,' Jacoby said and he knelt next to it. He used his boot knife to probe the mouth. 'Got all his teeth.'

Lucas Brown nodded, said this was a stroke of good fortune.

'Were we expecting this?' Norman asked.

Without looking up from his work, Jacoby instructed Lucas Brown to tell Norman the truth.

'When we got us a stopover like this place here, sometimes Wyrick'll string up a body that needs taken care of. Usually a body from another job.'

'But all we're doing is settin it a hundred yards from the house where we found him.'

Lucas Brown's brow folded and he looked from Norman to the old man. 'He dont rightly know what any of this is, does he?'

'What?' Norman asked. 'Whats that mean?' But the two men—long desert companions—stared down one another as if Norman was not present.

'It's something that needs experience,' Jacoby said. Then he looked to Norman. 'Wyrick hangs a body from another site at the stopover as a security precaution for us. If another clan or gang—or by some ungodly chance, the law—has been out his way, there'll either be no body or the body will be missing some key parts.'

'The teeth,' Lucas Brown said.

'Aye,' Jacoby said. 'The teeth. Sometimes theres other bones, maybe an organ—a mans heart, brain or eyes—but the teeth are like rare gems to us.'

'Teeth,' Norman said as if learning the word for the first time.

Lucas Brown sighed and turned, walking back down the slope. At the bottom Raybur still officiated over the jumping contest.

'Dont pay his sour mood no mind,' Jacoby said. 'Man cant think outside of himself—cant figure out why people dont know what he knows and then cant figure out how to tell them everything we know.' Then he squeezed the dead man's cheeks until the mouth opened and began prying out the teeth with the knife.

—

A detective had called wanting to meet with Norman. The investigation into Grace's death felt low on the police's priority and Norman reasoned that a call from the detective meant only good news. If he were to be arrested, no one would call first. Norman set the meeting up for his office at the university.

The detective wore an orange-brown suit, patterns running in little squares in the fabric. He was balding, wore thick framed glasses and his skin was shiny. When he sat down in the office, he leaned back so the lights reflected in his glasses and Norman could scarcely see his eyes.

'Want me to shut the door?' the detective asked.

Norman shook his head, then asked if there was any reason to.

The detective smirked and said probably not. 'Had to tell the office secretary—or receptionist, assistant—whatever we're calling the office broads these days—had to tell her who I was.'

'Everyone around here knows whats going on,' Norman said. 'Grace worked here too.'

'I know.'

The detective leaned forward and the lights cleared from his glasses and Norman could see his eyes. 'Youre all clear,' the detective said. 'Your story checks out, though I cant quite get a bead on who Miss McGuffin was.' He waited, stared at Norman.

'Yeah,' Norman finally agreed. 'Difficult to say, I guess.'

'You think you know someone—know them intimately, know all the details about their life...' The detective's voice drifted off. 'Well, you know.'

Norman nodded.

'More to a woman than her body,' the detective said. 'Suppose I dont need to tell you that.'

He pulled at his pant legs and stood to leave. 'Lets hope our paths dont cross again.'

As forecast, the night dispelled any heat from the daytime. With the plunging temperatures the stink of rot diminished inside the house. The six men lay on the floor under the tarp. Accustomed to the desert life with its erratic climate, the Jacoby clan fell to sleep quickly, leaving Norman awake. As he often did, Norman lay on his back, staring at the ceiling.

By now the fall semester at the university must have started. By now they would have filled his slot with an adjunct instructor. His parents would have been contacted, someone from the university informing them that they lost their second son—he went out into the desert and never returned. He wondered if anyone had searched for him. Maybe the local sheriff drove out to New Daisy and found his station wagon—what the clan left of the wagon—in a mineshaft. Maybe they were piecing together the clues and tracking him to Jacobyville. Maybe when they all returned from this excursion, the police would be waiting and Norman could tell them how this family of hermits, and several others like them, rob graves and trade bodies. When he returned to the university, everyone would want to hear about his time with the desert people and he could write a book about it. Doctor Blanche would fawn over his book and ask him to talk about Martha.

'What was she like, Martha?' Doctor Blanche would ask.

Norman imagined himself paying Martha a few compliments, then looking at Doctor Blanche and saying, 'When I was with her I thought about you.'

Doctor Blanche's lips parted and she smiled, her teeth framed by red lips. And then Norman imagined pulling the teeth one by one until her mouth gaped hollow and bloody. He shut his eyes as if to expel the image—but the idea had not come from without.

5.

When they came upon the road, it stretched serpentine north and south, taking on the gentle contours of the land. Since leaving the stopover, the band of men bivouacked through the mountains and took a pass back out into the desert country where they walked two days without respite.

From farther away, the pavement of the road looked like water—as if this were some arbitrary creek sliced through a scab of wasteland. But as they drew closer, Norman watched an otiose vessel blink onto the horizon and inch along. When the truck passed in front of them, it zoomed by and grew distant on the southern horizon.

'Route 191,' Jacoby said. He took a map from his pack and studied it for a moment, gauged the sun. 'Dalton Wells is up across the way a piece.'

They crossed the road.

On the other side, they continued walking at an angle to the road so it never left their sight. Another truck passed some time later. Jacoby fell back, letting Raybur take the lead.

'This is your big chance, son,' Jacoby said.

'Hows that?'

'When we crossed that road back there, tell me the feelin of civilization under your feet didnt stir somethin inside of you.'

Norman smirked and asked if the old man had forgotten about the apocalypse—the end of the world no one knew about.

Jacoby rested a hand on Norman's shoulder and they slowed their pace, allowing a gap to widen between them and the other men. 'I wish you'd go,' he said. 'Run away an see what a ruin the world has become since youve been gone.'

'Why'd I do that?'

Jacoby pulled on Norman's shoulder until they stopped and looked into each other's eyes. The old man looked past whatever defenses Norman built to safeguard against Jacoby's omnipotence. 'Because now you can truly see the world.'

Dalton Wells lay in a shallow spot off the highway. A couple of concrete obelisks—squat and rounded, whitened by the sun—marked the entrance where a gravel road had since been scattered into nothing. About a dozen cottonwood trees dotted the ground. The place proved smaller than how Norman imagined it. Gay Jim slumped against one of the trees, sighed and peered upward into the canopy of leaves.

'Got a box over here!' Oz called and Jacoby and Raybur went to inspect the finding—a small black box. As he wandered the grounds, Norman heard Oz cursing, saying the Wyrick couldve found a plastic box or something that wouldnt get so damned hot.

If ever there had been a prison here, the evidence had vanished. A few barren spots, a concrete patch, few piles of rubble and nothing else remained. The rumble of an approaching semi sounded long and low, grumbling down the road. It passed and whined off into the distance.

'Alright!' Oz yelled. He waved his arm for everyone to gather around.

When they assembled around the black box, Jacoby spoke. 'Tomorrows our work day,' he said. 'We're gonna set up tonight, make a dry run, make sure we get this right and get out.'

Oz took over speaking. 'Box here had some ammo for the instrument Wyrick gave us an a map of how it's going down.' He unfolded a sheet of notebook paper with a hand-drawn schematic on it. An X on a rectangle marked where the action was to take place. Norman took the rectangle to signify one of the concrete pads. Another X with a circle around it was drawn along a line representing the slight elevation facing the road. Oz pointed to this symbol. 'Wyrick wants our man with the instrument here.'

'I dont got a problem with that,' Lucas Brown said. 'Be able to see these sumbitches come up the road. Wont never have our backs to the action.'

'Aye,' Jacoby said. 'Round noontime—sun wont make no difference.'

Oz folded the map, placing it into his shirt pocket. He told everyone to find their places. As the men each began to move, Jacoby took Norman by the arm. 'Youre with me, son.'

Twice Jacoby used the rifle they called the instrument to shoot the black box they called the target. Gay Jim climbed a tree on the opposite side of the gravel drive and obscured himself amongst the leaves. Norman and Oz lay with Jacoby up on the ridge.

'It's not a tough shot,' Jacoby said.

Oz held up the binoculars, adjusted the focus and lowered them. 'I put a glass bottle down the slope at one hundred feet,' he said. 'Give me somethin to gauge the distance when the suns right above us. Figure the center of that patch of concrete to be bout a hundred fifty yards as the bullet goes.'

As he rose to his feet, Jacoby groaned. 'Keep the lenses of those binoculars shaded tomorrow. Dont need no glint comin off of them an givin the Jap a tip off.'

Oz nodded. 'We ready for clean up?'

'Aye.'

Placing his pinky and index fingers in his mouth, Oz let out a shrill whistle and Raybur and Lucas Brown ran up out of the arroyo near the back of the encampment. They stopped at the pad, picked up the box and ran to the road, where Gay Jim already stood after jumping out of the cottonwood.

When they finally all met under the shade of the tree, panting and tired, Jacoby said they were done for tonight, and tomorrow they would change the future of this world again.

They awoke early, every one of them, and no one spoke. Each man seemed beckoned from his slumber by a specter sent by the dawn sun. Their breakfast consisted of dried grains and water, some raisins—few enough to count. Down in the arroyo, Jacoby dumped his canteen into the dirt and used his fingers to knead the mixture into a stiff mud. Silently, the men painted their faces and necks, their arms and the backs of their hands with the mud. Then, with no more than a nod to acknowledge each other's presence, they went to their stations.

On the ridge, Norman, Jacoby and Oz lay side by side. The sun as it neared its zenith beat down on their backs, the threadbare shirts providing no impediment for the rays. Jacoby had rubbed down the stock and barrel of the rifle with a handful of grit and the luster the gun once held now became chalked and dull. Norman's eyes ached in their sockets from squinting; his neck shook from the tension of scanning the empty space.

The same shrill whistle Oz unleashed the day before resounded again. Then all lapsed back into silence. From out westward way, obscured by the right arm of the ridge, a car approached, the only portent of its coming marked by dual fins of dust rising up in the air. As the plumes dissipated into a stagnant haze, another set came immediately thereafter, marking a second car.

The dust clouds drew closer and Oz lifted the binoculars to his eyes, his hand cupped over the top. A few seconds later the cars ambled up the gravel road, past the stone obelisks. The first car Norman recognized as Wyrick's. The automobile behind it—a red Oldsmobile with a tan cloth top—looked even more out of place. They idled to a stop beneath the cottonwood where Gay Jim perched amongst the leaves.

First the door of Wyrick's car opened and he stepped out, wearing the same outfit as he had more than a month ago. He held a suitcase over his head and walked out from the shade of the trees to the concrete patch.

Then the driver of the Oldsmobile stepped forth from his car. Like Wyrick, he dressed all in black—his hair and glasses also black. Only a patch of parchment yellow marked his countenance.

'Target,' Oz whispered and Jacoby eased the butt of the rifle into his shoulder, closed one eye and peered through the telescope sight.

The Jap strode across the open space toward the concrete patch and Jacoby thumbed back the hammer of the gun. It clicked. To Norman's ears it sounded like thunder. His eyes darted to the Jap. The man kept walking, his hands swinging freely by his sides.

'Twenty-five yards,' Oz whispered.

Below, Wyrick and the Jap exchanged some words of greeting. The Jap glanced back over his shoulder at the cars parked under the cottonwoods. He pointed to the suitcase and said a few more words. Wyrick nodded and squatted, opening the case on the concrete.

When Jacoby said 'Good,' it came out as a long breath, which he held at the end.

'Five yards,' Oz said. Then, 'Mark.'

The shot rang out and vanished, the rifle bucking against Jacoby's shoulder. He drew in a sharp breath and Norman watched as a fleck of what must have been part of the Jap's scalp flapped off the back of his head. A vapor cloud of blood pillowed around his head before he fell sideways, his knees buckling beneath him.

Wyrick took two steps forward, leaning over the body. He turned, looking up toward the ridge. He used his hand to shield his eyes as if saluting the executioners. Perhaps the ringing of the first shot muted the report of the second—Norman only saw Wyrick step backward and a red circle appear on his white shirt. His hands went up to his chest and he staggered for a moment before collapsing next to the Jap.

Oz let out another whistle. Like they rehearsed, Raybur and Lucas Brown ran up from the arroyo, pistols drawn.

'C'mon,' Oz said and he dragged Norman to his feet.

Jacoby had already jumped up, holding the rifle like an Indian Wildman of western lore, and ran down the slope in elongated strides.

Gay Jim jumped from the tree onto the roof of Wyrick's car. He opened up the back door of the car for Lucas as he threw the bodies inside. Raybur's path diverged and he ran to the Oldsmobile, using a knife to slash open the cloth top. He took out a rag, set it aflame and tossed it into the car. Jacoby paused at the concrete pad where the attaché case still lay open, stacks of banded hundred dollar bills spilling onto the ground. Two bloodstains marred the ground where the bodies had fallen. Jacoby reached into his pocket and pulled out a plastic bag. As he caught up with the old man, Norman saw the bag contained teeth and Jacoby placed them in the case, snapping it shut and leaving it set on the pad.

'Get in, damn it,' Lucas Brown said.

Norman hesitated. The back seat was already occupied by the corpses of the Jap and Wyrick—and Lucas already smeared with blood and dirt. Raybur shoved past him and sat on the bodies, saying they better get moving before the fireworks started. The engine of the car roared to life and the discordant sound of music pumped out of the car's speakers. Jacoby rode shotgun and Oz yelled for his brother to hurry the hell up. The red Oldsmobile erupted in flames and Gay Jim climbed into the center of the front seat. Oz followed him, slamming the door, and together the eight of them—six still breathing, two corpses—circled around Dalton Wells and followed the gravel road out.

'Give me some damned room,' Lucas Brown said. He kicked one of the corpses.

'Cant scoot up,' Oz said. 'My legs are longer than yours.'

'Boys,' Jacoby said. 'Keep it down. We dont have all that far to go.'

The rankness of sweat and mud and blood filled the small cabin of the car. Norman could see out the windshield and Route 191 came into view. The taste of metal filled his mouth.

'Car comin,' Raybur said.

'I see it,' Oz said. He let off the gas where the gravel road met the highway.

'Sheriff?'

'Nope, just some regular folk slowin down to see where that smoke is comin from.'

They pulled out onto the road and Norman felt the car's suspension sag beneath their collective weight. They drove perhaps two miles before Jacoby farted and cracked his window.

'Lectric windows,' he said. 'Livin a life of luxury, this Wyrick was.'

A couple miles later, Oz decelerated and they rumbled off the pavement and onto the desert flat. Raybur looked out the back window and gave the all clear. The car accelerated until the ground streaked by in a menagerie of salt and dirt and lichen. Inside the bodies jostled together, every once in a while upset by an unexpected bump and followed up by a half-hearted apology from Oz.

They drove a while, until the radio had turned to static and then some. Oz rolled the car to a stop. The swell had come into view and each man used the break to urinate. Oz went around to the trunk and took out a ten gallon gasoline can.

'Hope this'll last us,' he said.

It did. They drove up into the swell, the undercarriage of the car scraping over rocks, the bodies inside tossing about. By now Norman surrendered himself to the blood and his clothes were soaked through and stank of metal, his tongue tasting like copper. At dusk Oz turned on the headlights and they cut a path through the darkness until the small pool of light caught sight of a shack.

'Home again, home again,' Jacoby said and Norman recognized the shack as the one sitting at the base of the slope where the brothers competed in their jumping contest.

With some grousing, the men lumbered from the car, the headlights still illuminating the shack. Oz popped the trunk open again and took out a toolbox. The men spent the better part of an hour pulling the boards off the side of the shack. They knocked out the studs until they had completely opened up the end of the shack. Oz then put the car in neutral and they pushed it into the shed.

'Perfect fit,' Jacoby said and they began fastening the boards back onto the frame, driving the same nails through the same holes. By sunup the work had been completed and they retired to the house at the top of the slope and slept the better part of the day.

6.

The exhaustion and the cold of the night stirred outrageous dreams in Norman's mind. Whatever dreams he initially had became lost to the darkness.

As the night grew colder, Norman turned and the tumblers of the brain also turned, unlocking different compartments of his being. He began to dream he had returned home to his apartment and Dusty stood in his kitchen proffering a beer to the prodigal wanderer.

'You must be thirsty,' Dusty said. But the voice that came from him was not his.

'I am.' Norman took the beer and they stood a long time before Dusty suggested they take a seat. The geography of the apartment did not resemble what it had been in the waking world, but Norman sat down as if this was a familiar place.

'Comfortable couch.' He said it had been a long time since he had a good comfortable sit-down.

'Secrets in the padding,' Dusty said, gesturing with the butt end of the beer bottle.

Norman took the cue to stand up and pull the cushion off the couch. He flipped it up on its side and found the zipper. As he pulled the small metal tab of the zipper along, the teeth popped apart one by one until he could see the dismembered body of Doctor Blanche folded and stuffed into the upholstery.

'Aw shit,' he said and stepped back.

In the strange ways dreams rewrite logic, Dusty now stood behind Norman and wrapped a length of nylon around his neck, pulling until his airflow diminished into nothing. The smell of rot and semen filled his nose just before he could breathe no more. And by then it was too late to cry out.

—

Whatever dreams circulated in Norman's brain were interrupted by the report of a gunshot. Gay Jim whooped and Jacoby cursed. Norman sat upright, his skin peeling from the dried blood. Lucas Brown also sat bewildered, clutching his shirt to his chest as a blanket. A second shot ran out, the ricochet off a rock evident from the elongated metallic note.

Norman crabwalked on his hands and feet, keeping low to avoid the windows. Another whoop rose up and echoed down the rocky chamber. Norman looked out the door. Down the slope Gay Jim and Jacoby crouched behind a boulder, their firearms in hand. Gay Jim popped up from behind the boulder, hollering some nonsense, and fired his pistol at the shack sitting at the bottom of the slope. Wisps of dust where the bullets hit flitted up into the air. He slouched back down behind the rock. Holding out his hand like a beggar, Gay Jim accepted the bullets Jacoby doled out.

'Whats going on out there?' Lucas Brown asked.

'Dont know,' Norman said. 'Some mischief probably. I'll check.'

He pulled his boots on and ran from the door of the house to the rock where the men hunkered down.

'Mornin,' Jacoby said. He could barely keep from smiling.

Gay Jim turned back around and steadied the rifle across the top of the boulder. He bit his lip and his breathing slowed and then came to a stop. His hand tensed, tightened, squeezed. The gun lurched, throwing his shoulder back, shaking his mop of greasy hair. The salvo carried off the rocks and rolled out into the flat below.

'What you aiming at?' Norman asked. 'The window?'

'Naw,' Jacoby said. 'Wont do no good to hit the window.'

'Be a shame to bust out one of those windows,' Norman said. 'Pane of glass, that old, intact like that…'

Jacoby pressed one bullet after another into the gun. 'That dumb sumbitch aint gonna look out the window if he values his brains.'

Norman looked down at the shack where they had stored the car. 'Someones in there?'

'Two someones. Started comin up toward the house.'

'Jesus. Did you shoot them?'

'Dont reckon I did,' Jacoby said. 'Fella had a satchel with him. Might have a gun. I just took a pot shot at them an they ran for cover.'

Gay Jim stood and shot at the shack again. This time Norman jumped at the noise.

'They those other family—the MacKowskis?'

'No.' Jacoby shook his head. 'If theys the MacKowskis, you an me an Jim here—the whole lot of us—would be dead. No. These are just some poor backpackin folks who stumbled across a ghosted house out here in the swell.'

'Theyre just some hikers?'

'Far as I can tell.'

In Jacoby's hands the gun looked like a primitive tool—something dredged from the depths of a cave.

'Let them go,' Norman said.

'Cant,' Jacoby said. 'They done seen us an seen the car in that shack too.' He stood, squinting down the barrel of the rifle, and fired. He waited a second, then sighed. 'Well, Jim, we're outta range up this far. Bullets knockin into hundred year old hardwood. The two of them probably layin under that car in there. Aint no one dyin.'

Gay Jim shook his head excitedly and bit his tongue. He craned his neck backward, until he stared up into the sky and he cawed like a bird of prey. Norman winced at the sound.

'Nothing can be done about it now,' Jacoby said and he grabbed Norman by the sleeve and made him watch.

Oz crept out from behind some rocks piled near the shack. He crouched and approached the broadside slowly, close to the ground, the double-barrel shotgun in his hands. Norman turned and looked back up at the house, where Lucas Brown and Raybur watched from the doorway. Gay Jim peered over the edge of the boulder, nearly hyperventilating.

'Watch,' Jacoby said. Oz blew a hole in the corner of the building. The echo of the gunshot crashed up the chasm of rock to where Norman witnessed the scene. Screams followed, muted by sheer distance, yet channeled upward by the passage in the rock. One of the figures inside the shack, half-flung through the wall by the blast, tried to limp away. His right boot left dark footprints with each stride.

Gay Jim laughed and clapped gleefully.

'Go on, son.' Jacoby gave his son a handful of bullets for his pistol before Gay Jim went bounding down the slope, arms flapping wildly. Once he came close enough, he stopped, leveled the pistol at the injured man and fired. The man doubled over.

Jacoby cackled. 'Right in the gut.'

Norman's eyes burned from watching, from not blinking.

'Hey hey,' Oz called. Another figure tried to slide out under a broken slat board, but Oz intervened. He grabbed the figure by the hair and pulled her to her feet. She protested, clawing and grunting.

Jacoby crossed his wrists on the boulder and rested his chin to watch. 'Oh boy,' he said. 'Look what we got here.' He turned to Norman. 'Now thats a good lookin woman.'

Mid-stride Gay Jim changed his course from the man he'd shot to this captive woman. As he trotted, his hand pulled at his belt and his trousers fell to his ankles. He stumbled as he stepped out of the pant legs. His erection waved out in front of him. Oz clubbed the woman with the stock of the shotgun and tore at her clothes. She shrieked, trying to free herself from his grip. When she kicked at Gay Jim, he grabbed her leg and yanked the denim shorts from her body. Then he ripped the underwear from around her thighs, leaving her exposed. Oz yoked the woman by the shoulder and Gay Jim forced himself into her. Together they dropped her to the ground. With one arm, Oz held the woman by the neck and used his free hand to pull his jeans down.

'Oh boys,' Jacoby said quietly. 'Guess it has been a while since theyve had a piece of cunt other than Martha or the Madonna.'

Norman rested his head against the rock. Sweat beaded across his forehead. He vomited.

'Dont look away now, son.' Jacoby grabbed Norman by the scruff of the neck, directing his gaze back down at the scene unfolding below.

The woman screamed and swore when Oz waved his member in front of her face. She gritted her teeth, letting out a primal sound. Oz took the pistol from Gay Jim's hand. He held it by the barrel and swung the butt at the woman's mouth. Broken teeth falling into the back of her throat stifled the screams and cries for help; the pleadings for mercy stopped altogether once he forced himself into her mouth.

'Make them stop,' Norman said.

'Cant,' Jacoby said. He sighed.

The two brothers continued thrusting themselves into the woman until she relented and went completely limp. Her protests stopped and they moved her as they wished. Jacoby stood, taking his rifle with him, and began to descend the slope.

From his vantage point, Norman saw the first victim, the man, move. No one else saw it, but his hand moved toward the satchel. Without a second thought, Norman called out after Jacoby in an indistinguishable cry. The man pulled out a small handgun and squeezed off a shot. Gay Jim howled, grabbing at his buttocks, letting the woman fall from his grip. She lay like a rag doll. Jacoby whirled the rifle to his shoulder, fired, and the injured man writhed on the ground.

Raybur and Lucas Brown cursed and ran barefooted from the house, past where Norman propped himself against the rock and down to where Jacoby and his sons stood over the bodies. The surface of the stone felt cool on Norman's face. Gay Jim limped around, naked from the waist down, howling in agony. Ignoring his son's injury for the moment, Jacoby walked over to the man. He knelt next to him and searched for signs of life. Upon finding a pulse, he turned the man upright and held his head up by the hair, forcing the man to watch Oz rape the woman—her head and arms dangling as Oz only gripped her by the thighs. He threw his head back when he came and dropped her to the ground. Then he walked over to the man and stomped on his head.

—

They loaded the man and woman into the car with the bloated corpses of the Jap and Wyrick. Oz and Raybur wore rubber gloves as they opened up plastic bags of greenish white powder and began sprinkling it over the bodies.

'Lye,' Jacoby explained to Norman. 'Helps the bodies decompose—burns the flesh right off the bones.'

'Jesus Christ,' Oz said.

'Whats it now?' Raybur asked.

'This ones still breathin.'

They gathered around the open door. He obviously wasnt talking about the man whose neck could no longer hold up his head. Rather, it was the woman lying motionless on her back.

'Felt her breath on my cheek,' Oz said. He placed a gloved hand over her bare chest and said he could feel a heartbeat too.

'I'll take care of that,' Raybur said and he funneled the bag of lye into her mouth. She coughed and moaned and he closed her mouth and pinched her nose. The woman's throat lurched with stifled coughs. Then she lay silent and Raybur said that was that.

Gay Jim lay on his stomach in the house, his naked ass with a swath of cloth tied around it. The bullet had passed clean through the left cheek of his buttocks, leaving two small round holes. Amongst the supplies from Wyrick, they were given a first aid kit. Jacoby put it to use right away, cleaning out the wound with iodine and rubbing ointment at the entry and exit sites.

Lucas Brown inventoried the rest of the supplies: ammunition, dry goods, some cash, medicines of all types—including

IV jars with hoses and syringes, more bags of lye, some cotton shirts and socks, a jug of kerosene, matches, two pocketknives, a few jugs of water, a solar oven, jerky, coffee, three boxes of tea bags, and a compass.

'This is what you get paid for killing a man?' Norman asked.

Other than Jacoby and Gay Jim, the others paid Norman no mind. Gay Jim, of course, giggled so his nearly bare ass shook in the air.

The old man held up two fingers—a gesture Norman first associated with the protestors at the university, but he then realized simply meant quantity out here. 'Two,' Jacoby said. 'We were paid to kill two men.'

'And this is what you get in return.'

Raybur and Oz sorted through the goods, Lucas Brown checking them off a list. It was an orderly operation. Finally, Jacoby replied that yes, that was the nature of the trade.

'And since you just did in our friend, Wyrick, do you just move on to dealing with someone else?'

Like a seasoned poker player who studies his opponent more than he plays the odds, Jacoby waited to respond. 'Theres always another Wyrick,' he said. Norman tried to interject, but Jacoby continued talking. 'Literally, boy. In a few months time—maybe even a number of weeks—a new Wyrick will meet with us an set up a similar occasion, telling us of his quarry an how to kill him. In the end, because he goes by the name of Wyrick, he too will die.'

Jacoby's explanation compelled Norman to ask the next question—who sends these Wyricks to unwittingly set up their own deaths? The inquiry made Jacoby smile and he wagged his finger at his pupil. 'Sent on by a higher power,' he said. 'As long as they keep visiting us, life in the desert is possible.' He stopped abruptly as if he revealed too much.

'What about the hikers?' Norman asked. 'Killing that guy and his girl, that wasnt about life in the desert. That was you all acting like a bunch of fuckin animals.'

'Watch your tongue,' Lucas Brown said. 'Seen what we can do an talk to us like that.' He sniffed.

'Join your friends in the back seat of that car in the shack,' Raybur said.

'Nothing like thats gonna happen,' Jacoby said. 'Norman is one of us. He's not used to seein first hand the price we pay for livin like we do. This is his first time.'

The answer quieted the men, but did not appease them. Oz and Raybur began comparing their pocketknives, casting sidelong glances at Jacoby and Norman.

'Those people'—and Jacoby made a vague gesture to the shack that lay beyond—'they saw too much of our operation here. It's trite to say, but they had to die.'

'It's the way you did it.'

'What do you mean?'

In his throat the words felt huge, like he couldnt bring himself to say them. Jacoby said the words for him. 'Did we have to rape the girl?' He smiled. 'You want to know if we had to do it.'

Norman nodded.

'You should know better than the rest of us, Norman. You should be able to tell us there is no choice.'

'Thats not true.'

'Youre lying,' Jacoby said. 'Youre not lyin to me, though; youre lyin to yourself. You want to believe you are not one of us.' Jacoby leaned back and smiled the satisfied smile of an armchair philosopher. 'Before men came together and formed what we call civilization, the world was little more than a tumult of rock an steam an bone.'

'Is this another one of your visions?' Norman interrupted. 'I'm tired of you explaining how fuckin crazy you all are with some nonsense metaphors.'

All the men stared at Norman before turning their focus to Jacoby, waiting for his response.

'No,' Jacoby answered evenly. 'This is not a metaphor. What I am tellin you is the history of our species, our planet, the fate of our universe.' His eyes locked with Norman's. And like a frightened child, Norman refused to blink. His eyes began to water.

'I asked about the couple yall killed and you pretend to know the fate of the universe.'

'The couple existed in the universe, did they not?'

Norman imagined walking out of the house, going down to the shack where they stashed the car and climbing into the back seat. He would curl up and die in the back of the car, lying amongst the other dead. But he couldnt move. His legs would not allow him to stand.

'When you woke up this morning you didnt even know those people existed,' Jacoby said. 'You heard a gunshot an came runnin. Remember?'

For a moment Norman recalled his waking.

'What do you suppose we—Gay Jim and me—were doin?'

'I thought... I thought you were just shooting at the shed—playing really.'

'Thats right,' Jacoby said. 'You didnt even realize that some living human beings were in that shack—not until I told you. And chances are those people were not real until Oz here blasted open the side of the shack and you saw their bodies.'

In his mind, Norman replayed the moment he saw the injured form of the man emerge from the building.

'You knew they existed,' Jacoby said. 'You trusted my word. But like a crime youve committed or a thought buried down in your subconscious, only an act of violence could dredge it out.'

Norman stared at the floor without blinking, studying something not there.

'The world has always been a violent place,' Jacoby said. He patted Norman's knee. 'Civilization came about when man harnessed the power of fire. And fire with its burning an charring, its melting an cremation, means destruction. We've used fire as a tool to forge the gears in the machinery of civilization an progress—the turnin of those gears—is only made through the continuation of violence. That couple today—those strangers you care so much about—they stepped into the gears, got burned by the flames. Theres your metaphor. What you witnessed, Norman, is what folks at your school call progress.'

In a voice weakened by his thoughts, Norman said he didnt understand.

'Youve had dreams,' Jacoby said. 'Youve tried to envision the dawn of time an know what I say is true. Stay or go, there wont be much difference. This life an the next are just points on a timeline—past an future.'

THREE

Gratis

I.

At first winter came on only as a figment in the nighttime. In the darkness, a blistering cold settled on the houses of Jacobyville and Norman imagined the wooden slats freezing and splintering along the warp of the grains. The nails frozen into shards of glass. The jags of windowpane like blades of ice. Norman lay on his back in his house, watching his breath manifest into fog. Outside the stars shone down cold and sterile.

Morning came and the brutality of the cold vanished. Any suffering intoned in the absence of the sun absolved with the dawn. As the sun peaked in the sky and reflected off the rock and the hardpacked earth, all became warm again. Norman did not speak of the cold to anyone. Since returning from their mission out to Dalton Wells, Norman limited his interaction with the men. If ever he confided in someone, it was Martha.

'At first I felt like I belonged here,' Norman said. He pressed his body against hers, trying to siphon what warmth he could from her. 'But I keep thinkin—I mean, I cant sleep cause of the cold—and I think that maybe I'm not supposed to be here.'

Martha placed the palm of her hand against Norman's cheek and shushed him. 'Nothins out there,' she said. 'Jacoby told you as much. You cant go back. It's a different place now. It's all gone.'

'I'm goin to escape,' he said, giving voice to the idea that had been in his head for so long. He said it again. 'Dont tell them, but I'm plannin to escape.'

In the dim light of the moon, their visages glowed bone white and their eyes looked like deep transoms revealing all they had seen—time past and time now.

'Oh Norman,' Martha sighed. 'You can try to run away, but you aint never gonna escape us.'

'Youre talkin like Jacoby,' Norman said.

'You want to be free,' she said. Pity resounded in her voice when she said that freedom wasnt real.

'You could come with me,' Norman said.

Martha pressed her index finger against Norman's temple. 'It's in here,' she said. 'Run away. But in here'—and she applied pressure to the soft spot of his skull—'in here, youre a prisoner.'

The pupils of Martha's eyes darted back and forth and Norman knew she couldnt come with him. He rolled over and felt the cold flood his body. He began plotting his escape. First he thought of the supplies he needed. In his time living with the Jacoby clan he remained in constant amazement at how little sustenance people need to survive. As far as supplies went, he'd take only what he deemed absolutely necessary.

From the time he first came to Jacobyville, he knew the one true path out of Jacobyville to be the electric lines. Eventually the lines would have to intersect with some form of civilization. It was a law of man. Years ago it was water—follow any trickle of water and eventually it would lead to a town. Then, when water became transportable, it became rail. Follow a rail line and you would end up in a settlement of some type somewhere. But rail died and so many of the train lines now ran out into the desert without terminus. Electric dominated these days—the great ropes of wire bounding coast to coast, connecting cities with sparks and buzzing.

He'd have to head out at night, walk fast to stay warm and sleep during the daylight hours. He calculated how fast he would have to walk to outrun the Jacoby clan. He imagined what he'd tell people, what his colleagues at the university would say. His parents would embrace him like their long lost son.

But Dusty. After their fight it was possible Dusty had gone to the police saying he had suspicions. They would have gone to his landlord and prowled around the apartment. Or now that his lease had expired, they would have tried to sell his furniture in an attempt to recuperate some of their unrealized profits. Someone might buy his couch and when they sat on it, they'd adjust and readjust, finally deciding to open the cushion and inspect the padding. Inside they would find the soiled pantyhose. The thought caused Norman to shudder, and Martha, half in sleep, put her hand on his chest, murmuring how cold it was.

The next day, Oz sauntered over to the door of Norman's abode. He leaned against the doorframe with his forearm and watched as Norman used a nail to punch new holes in his belt.

'Trim down with the life we lead,' Oz said.

Feigning too much investment in his work, Norman didnt look up from his work. Oz continued on. 'Jacobys called a meetin, wants everyone there.'

Norman nodded.

'If you got a problem, you could always bring it up,' Oz said.

For a moment Norman sat still. 'Nothing I could say would change anything.'

Oz stood up straight and looked out across the ghost town, said he supposed Norman was correct. 'Only one person round heres got that kind of sway with words. Maybe you should talk with Pa. Tell him what you think. Talk with him fore you do somethin rash.'

Norman stood and laced the belt through the remaining loops on his jeans. The waist rode low and bunched in parts as the belt now acted more like a cinch cord. Together they walked from the house, down the slope and around the tailing to the meetinghouse. Everyone else had already arrived.

Jacoby spread his arms wide and invited everyone to sit. Over in the corner, the children continued to play. The old man cleared his throat and said the first order of business concerned the weather. 'Gettin cold out an we dont need anyone freezin to death.'

'Amen to that,' Raybur said.

Jacoby nodded in acknowledgment. 'Means that the time of years come for us all to move into my house. I want everyone to bring their blankets, clothes an small belongings to my house right after this meeting.' He looked directly at Norman. 'If you need it to stay warm an survive, it should come to my house.'

'We really got space for one more?' Lucas Brown used his thumb to point at Norman.

'Need someone to keep your Pa company,' Raybur said.

Jacoby chewed the side of his cheek and before he could speak, Oz said that was the Madonna's job.

'Mans gotta talk, though,' Lucas Brown said. 'An she aint much for talkin.'

With a clap of the hands, Jacoby said the next order of business concerned a new Wyrick deal.

'We just got done with one a month ago,' Raybur said.

'I know it's a little soon for another Wyrick,' Jacoby said. 'But the payoff is sweet an Ive been told we'll have lots of time between the deal an action.'

'When're we talkin bout this Wyrick showin up?' Oz asked.

'Three days time.'

'Contact point?'

'Use the mineshaft on the south side of the mountain,' Jacoby said. 'Have him meet us inside. Give Raybur a chance to check out the car an supplies.'

'Supplies we gettin up front gonna make life easier?' Raybur asked.

'Aye. Winter'll be easier for all of us. Action wont be til springtime—I already know that. I'll get the rest of the details when I meet with the Wyrick.'

Oz and Norman climbed up the mountain, higher up than Norman ever cared to explore. When they reached the spine, the ragged edge, they traversed it. At the onset of their excursion, Gay Jim followed them, but had since turned back. The wind whipping off the desert pan jetted up the slope of the mount and flapped in the wayward's clothing.

'Scared of the mine,' Oz said after his brother turned around. He raised his voice, competing against the bluster of the wind. 'Cant blame him much, bein like he is.'

Norman asked what happened—said he knew Gay Jim hadnt always been this way.

'True,' Oz said. 'As a boy he was always lively—gettin into trouble, runnin around like the fool he is now.' Oz slowed his pace to walk next to Norman. With the constant uphill climb, his speech became labored with pauses. 'We played round Jacobyville, same as Lucas Browns children do now. We came up here into the mountains where people used to dig dig dig.' He panted. 'Gay Jim, he went down into a mineshaft, opening not much wider than his shoulders. I waited for him to come out, seein what he might find; he was always findin things.'

The peak of the mount came into view and they turned off the ridge and started down the slope. Being on the leeward side of the mountain, the wind nearly ceased altogether. Farther down the slope, Norman spied a tailing.

'We takin the long way around?' he asked. 'Couldve just walked around the base.'

'Thats where the Wyrick'll go in,' Oz said. 'Our job is to always make sure Wyrick is never in control of the situation, but let him think he is.'

Norman said he understood, then asked what happened after Gay Jim went into the mine.

'Nothin,' Oz said. 'I waited an he didnt come out. I didnt pay it no mind cause he knowed the caves an shafts an such better than me. He liked goin in and sneakin around, tryin to scare me.' Oz stopped and picked up a slender piece of driftwood to use as a staff. He continued down the slope, using the stick to stabilize his descent. 'I got tired an went back home, told Pa what happened when I realized Gay Jim was still missin.

'He grabbed me by the neck, took the rope an we ran up the slope with Raybur. The opening was too narrow for either of them, so they tied the rope round my waist, told me to scramble in there, feel round. I cant forget it—Pa held my head in both his hands and told me to hold my breath as long as I could, then to breathe real shallow like.' He demonstrated and as he did so, he stopped walking. 'He told me I would get confused, feel sick. Just yell when you get a handle on him, Pa said. Said he'd pull us both back with the cord, said not to fight it. The air in mines is bad—stale, no good for breathin.'

'You found him obviously,' Norman said.

'Third time in, yes.' Oz started walking again. 'I begged the old man, Please dont put me back in there. It was dark an I was just a boy. Scared, really. Later, Pa'd tell me it was the lack of fresh air that made me act like a fool. Said Gay Jim bein in there that long, thats what made him go fool for the rest of his life.'

They came to a circle of white rocks with a wooden pallet sitting in the center. Using the toe of his boot, Oz lifted the pallet, revealing a hole like a well. Norman peered down the hole. Like the shaft outside Jacoby's house, this one sunk down into eternity. Oz knelt by the hole. A rope secured to a stake dangled down into the narrow shaft and Oz hauled up a few feet of rope until a canvas bag appeared. After he untied the bag, he let the rope fall back into the shaft.

'We'll have our gear on the ready up here,' Oz said. He unzipped the bag and sifted through the contents. 'When we get a signal from yonder'—he pointed out past the mouth of the mine below—'then we spelunk on down through this air shaft.'

'This is the air shaft?' Norman asked.

'Yeah,' Oz said. 'Life'd be a whole lot different for me an Gay Jim if we'd known about air shafts an mines. Dont matter that we know how to check for movin air an such—Jims afraid all the same. Cant blame him.'

Oz handed Norman a smooth piece of metal shaped like the number eight, said when the time came, he'd lace that through his belt and wind the rope through it. 'Whole thing works by friction, you let the rope through nice an easy an you'll slide down without a hitch.'

He said theyd be watching for a signal from Gay Jim letting them know the Wyrick was coming. 'Pa an Lucas Brown will be down in the mine already, Raybur'll hide by the entrance. I'll stay up here while you go down, let them know the signals been given. Whole thing shouldnt take but a couple minutes.'

They camped out on the mountain, keeping a small fire and huddling together for warmth. When he woke, Norman could not recall his dreams. Oz crouched over the few embered remains of their fire and stoked them into a single tongue of flame. 'Enough to brew up some coffee,' he said and crushed a few beans in a pan of shallow water.

They hardly spoke as they kept vigil over the desert vista. The sun climbed higher, behind the thin haze of clouds, forcing them to squint. Once the sun rose to its apex, Norman saw a glint, then another.

'That the signal?' he asked.

Oz nodded, tossed the long-cold dregs of coffee out and laced the rope through the figure eight. He kicked the wooden pallet aside and told Norman to step into the hole backward.

'You have to trust me on this,' Oz said. 'Just step backward.'

Norman hesitated. On the horizon, dust kicked up behind an approaching object.

'Runnin out of time here, Norman.'

Norman couldnt see the bottom; he couldnt hear anything either. 'Why cant you go?' Norman asked.

'First good question you done ask,' Oz said. 'But I aint got an answer for you—Pa said it's gotta be you.' With that he pushed Norman backward so he fell into the hole. He plummeted some distance, scraping his arms and legs and face against the narrow passageway before the rope pulled tight and he jerked to a stop. He hung, suspended in the shaft for a couple moments, and then started letting the rope out little by little. 'Hurry the hell up!' Oz called from above and Norman let out even more rope. Cooler air rushed up past his feet and rocks around him felt slick with dew. Darkness engulfed him and he felt stone under his feet.

'Jacoby!' he called. 'Lucas! Wyricks on his way.'

A faint light shone from around a corridor. After releasing the rope, Norman started for the light.

'Just hold it,' a voice hissed. It was Lucas Brown. 'We want the Wyrick down here near us.'

Somewhere in the shadows, Norman heard Jacoby hum a reply of agreement.

The sound of a car's engine grumbled down the long corridor and suddenly stopped. A car door slammed and another voice called out Jacoby's name. The voice called out for Jacoby over and over again, drawing closer all the while. Something about the voice seemed familiar to Norman.

When a dark form came around the bend, Lucas Brown took aim at him with a pistol. Jacoby said, 'Mister Wyrick, yes?'

The man said that he was. 'Having some trouble seeing you in the dark here.'

'There a reason you need to see me?' Jacoby asked.

'I guess not.'

A long silence followed with neither man knowing exactly how to proceed. As his eyes adjusted, Norman could see the Wyrick more completely—a taller man with hair so blond it glowed white. Norman supposed it to be a trick of the brain—perhaps a touch of oxygen deprivation, but he knew this man, this Wyrick.

When the Wyrick spoke again, outlining his instructions, Norman recognized the man as his brother. A gasp escaped his lips, audible to everyone. For the first time, the Wyrick realized more figures other than he and Jacoby inhabited this space.

'You were sayin about the north country,' Jacoby said.

'You'll be in MacKowski territory, we realize—'

This time Lucas Brown interrupted. 'Why not use them then?'

An uneasy silence prefaced the answer. 'Theyve been compromised,' the Wyrick said. 'We're afraid the target wont be dealt with properly—theyre no less reliable, just cant be trusted on this job.'

'Got an envelope with the information in it?'

There was the rustling of papers and the Wyrick asked if they should get the goods out of the car.

'Already got my man unloadin your car,' Jacoby said.

Wyrick and Jacoby began walking back toward the mouth of the mine. Norman took a step before Lucas Brown grabbed his arm. 'We're waitin here,' he said. 'Best not to let him see your face.'

2.

Snow fell on the ghost town and it did not melt. The skies remained overcast and brooding, a slated expanse of gray without break, without horizon, without division between this world and heaven. At first Norman felt like the snow would pile deep and drifting as it did in the Indiana winters. But the flakes merely blew about, sifting in the wind like ashes. The powdered snow tumbled in the breezes, the pellets of ice knocking against the houses with their boarded sides and tin roofs. This alone was the sound of winter in the desert.

He pulled the collar of his shirt up around his mouth and staggered down the slope. A gust of wind cascaded up the channel between the mountains and he shuddered when it whipped through the rags of his clothes. He tottered on, trying not to bend his legs, as if the cold had paralyzed him. He'd seen the wooden slats of the houses grown brittle and broken with the cold and he felt as if the same could happen to him. The fury of the winter desert proved every bit as vicious as the summer. A drift of snow—a blanket of snow as they called it in Indiana—Norman realized would be some comfort. Aside from providing insulation as the inches accumulated, the snowfall would remind Norman of a place he once called home.

The channel in the mountain opened up as the slopes curved to either side and the wind cut sheer and unforgiving into the exposed parts of Norman's body. He pulled up the collar to cover his neck some more, but found his hands and wrists receiving the brunt of the cold's brutality. He craned his head sideways, hoping to deflect some of the wind.

In his pocket he cradled his pilfered goods—a box of matches and a length of twine, a stub of candle and the discarded jokers from a deck of playing cards. The hardpacked desert earth froze so hard his footfalls tapped like rocks across concrete. Twice he looked over his shoulder, back up toward Jacoby's house where they all spent their nights. But he saw no signs of life, of movement. Norman rounded the skirt of the slope and the house slid out of view. He counted his paces, taking care to return his gait to its normal measure. At twelve paces, he stopped. A rock shaped curiously like a human head sat on the side of the slope. Norman clambered up the incline of loose rocks and reached behind the stone. The touch of stone against his fingertips felt white hot, but he knew this to be another of the brain's tricks. The rocks themselves might have actually been colder than ice. Carefully, he lifted a few smaller stones until he found the rusted can beneath. With a single yank, he pulled the can free from its cache.

Inside the can, Norman had already stashed four one-hundred dollar bills, a green Coca-Cola bottle, a longer candle and several tissue thin leaves of paper. For a moment, the cold seemed not to exist. This can, he knew, contained all he would need to survive outside of Jacobyville—though when he would eventually leave, none of these objects served him any good. Desert living requires more of the mind than of the body.

After depositing his goods and hiding the can once again, he stood to leave. His legs somehow felt more limber—until the wind met him with full force. The air rushed around him, scorching blistering lines across his face through the thinner spots of his beard. He squinted, the wetting of his eyes stinging with the same ferocity as everything else in this forsaken environment. Putting one foot in front of the other, he bowed his head and began contemplating the task of walking out across the frozen desert pan. He wondered if Jacoby or his sons—if Jacoby and his sons—would come after him, what they would do if they caught him. He imagined what he would say to the first civilized people he met, how he would plead with them to call the police, how he could reassure them that he was not a desert lunatic. He thought of returning home and talking to Dusty, to Doctor Blanche, to the police. All he needed to do was walk out of here following the telephone poles. And when he looked up to study the telephone poles, Jacoby stood before him.

Norman followed as Jacoby had bade him to do. They walked with only the cry of the wind and their metronome footsteps, trudging up the slope of pilings toward the Jacoby homestead. The wind came at their backsides, pushing them along. Several times the wind blasted Norman so hard, the air escaped his lungs. As they walked, Norman wondered if Jacoby had seen the stash of supplies, if Jacoby knew he planned on escaping. But Jacoby said nothing and now they walked in silence.

The smoky gray clouds of dusk welled up above the mountains like the smolder of a slowly erupting volcano and a darkness unlike any Norman had ever witnessed began to fall on the world.

'Felt the clouds comin on,' Jacoby said. 'Get to be my age you feel things like that. Knew it'd be gettin dark an figured I better fetch you.'

Norman nodded. The haziness of the late afternoon evaporated into night as if Norman had been struck by a sudden blindness. They stumbled the final leg of the trail to the house.

'Watch that shaft now,' Jacoby said.

Norman's eyes scanned through the growing darkness and found the patch of deeper black carpeting the nighttime black. He took Jacoby by the elbow and they led each other to the porch.

Inside the house, almost everyone slept. The creak of the door roused the brothers, but no one stirred otherwise. A single candle set on the corner table flickered as they shut the door. Martha and Lucas Brown lay together; the stench of the Madonna wafted across the room.

'Startin to get cold,' Jacoby said.

Unsure if this was a joke being made out of the obvious, Norman sniffed.

Jacoby rubbed his palms together, blew into them and cleared his throat. His sons sat up on the floor, rubbing sleep from their eyes. Oz blinked a few times before asking if he should build up a fire.

'No,' Jacoby said and he sat down cross-legged and withdrew a pack of matches from his coat pocket. In the gloom of the candlelight they looked curiously like the ones Norman stowed in his can at the rock. His mind began to race. Jacoby never stepped anywhere near the rock; he couldnt have taken them. But then Norman's thoughts turned in his head and he supposed he might have remembered incorrectly or not at all.

Jacoby struck a match, sending it alight with a pop and a hiss. Sulphur floated in the air like incense. He pulled a kerosene lantern toward him across the floor.

'Norman,' Jacoby said. 'Tell us about the cold.'

Still entranced with the pack of matches, Norman sat down on the floor dumbly. He leaned back and bumped into Gay Jim.

'The cold,' Jacoby prompted again. He opened a hatch in the side of the lantern and trimmed the wick.

'The cold,' Norman said.

'It's the thing thats been on everyones mind—the cold, the winter.' He shrugged.

'You know more bout the cold than I do,' Norman said. 'Looks like you got winter here same as where I'm from.'

'Aye,' Jacoby said. 'But your winters are not the same as ours.'

'Colds the same anywhere you go.'

Oz guffawed and Gay Jim followed suit. The children began to climb out from a pile of bedding in the corner, asking if it was morning yet. Jacoby raised a hand to silence them all. 'It snowed where you lived.' It was not a question, nor was it a statement. Something in the strange intonation of Jacoby's voice compelled Norman to answer.

'Yes, it snowed.'

'Not like this, though.'

'No, not like this at all.'

'You didnt let it bury you.'

'Bury me?'

'Aye.' Jacoby leaned in close to the lantern so light cascaded over the ruts of his face from underneath and his eyes appeared as deep welled sockets without color or hint of life. The fine white hairs of his beard set aglow and what wasnt shadowed looked to be composed of flame.

'No,' Norman said. 'People still need to get out and do stuff.' A feeble explanation and he knew it.

Jacoby clucked his tongue—a sound that sent Gay Jim into a wild series of yawpings and guffaws. In the corner, the children now sat up, fully awake and watching the men. Lucas Brown grumbled about the fool and his goddamned giggling. Oz tugged at his brother's sleeve to silence him, but even then Gay Jim could only stifle his laughter.

'Never know whatll send that idiot off.' The voice belonged to Raybur. No one noticed him sitting outside their circle, outside the skirt of light cast by the lantern. 'As you were sayin, boy.'

Norman blinked and swallowed. 'People got jobs to get to, I guess. We get snowed on and we clear it away.'

Now Jacoby shook his head. 'All these folks all rushin round—all these folks an their jobs. Busy busy people out there in the world.' He brought his hand up to his mouth and chewed at the skin around his middle fingernail. He spat quietly. 'How they keep the roads clear?'

Norman's brow twitched. 'We plow the roads,' he said. He was quiet for a moment, then continued, saying they had big trucks that drove around, scooping the snow off the roads.

'They do more than plow, though.'

Norman agreed. 'They salt too.'

'Hows that?' Raybur asked.

'Salt,' Norman repeated. 'The plow trucks throw down salt behind themselves as they go.'

'To melt the snow,' Jacoby said and Norman nodded. 'To keep the roads clear,' Jacoby added. 'So busy people can go to their jobs.'

As if on cue, Gay Jim guffawed. But Oz's question cut his brother's laughter short. 'Howd they do it?'

Norman studied Jacoby and his face of fire, his bottomless eyes. The old man's eyebrows raised and the dark lines of his forehead cut deep and black and cruel.

'What do you mean?' Norman asked.

Jacoby took over: 'He wants to know how the salt was dispensed. Did they throw it out with shovels or pour it out a little at a time like a dump truck?'

Though he knew the answer—for he'd seen the snowplows troll the winter roads of Indiana since he was a boy—Norman struggled with explanation. 'They got these pinwheels,' he said. 'Spreaders, they call them. They throw the granules in different directions.'

'Like to scatter it?' Oz asked.

'Yeah, it throws it out evenly.'

Now came Jacoby's turn to laugh, the phlegm catching in his throat and adding a moist crackle to his voice when he finally spoke. 'If I were to go out an measure all those grains of salt, the distances between each one, are you tellin me theyd all be even?'

'Thats not what I meant.'

'What'd you mean by even then?'

Norman sighed. 'Well, it's approximately the same.'

'So the spreader throws out salt approximately the same as... what?'

'Approximately evenly.'

The absurdity of the conversation or perhaps the ineptness of Norman's answer caused Jacoby to laugh more heartily. Gay Jim joined in with his whoops and hollers. Even Oz sniffed.

'So what youre sayin,' Jacoby said, 'is it is even—but not even at all.'

'I'm not sayin that at all,' Norman protested. 'It's close to bein even.'

'Like two is about equal to three.'

Fatigued with these petty arguments, Norman relented, saying sure, he guessed so.

'But what if you were a fraction, a really small number?' Jacoby asked. 'If you were one one-hundredth of one, then two becomes a very long way from three.'

'Youre not lettin me finish my story.'

'I think you finished it already.'

'You missed the point then.'

Jacoby rocked back from the lantern light. Suddenly his face tamped into a much darker hue, like the coals of a fire still angry from conflagration. 'No, son.' His voice was a measured tone. 'You missed the point of your own damned story.' He shook his head in mock pity. Then he pointed his crooked finger, the jag of fingernail, at Norman. 'When the universe exploded into existence it was pure happenstance— a ball of dense matter spreadin itself out evenly, or about evenly. Those small variations, those fluctuations in the matter speedin out across the nothingness that wasnt even yet outer space, created gravity, orbits, the illusions of time an place. Particles slammed together an stuck, snowballin into planets. Our own sweet Earth was a perfect recipe of hydrogen, calcium, oxygen an every other elixir to make the cocktail of life.' A crooked smile spread across Jacoby's thin chapped lips. 'Proximity to the sun superheated the fens an bogs an swamps, cookin up a primordial soup, until finally after simmerin so long, basted with the ashes an lava flows, the accident of you slithered out.'

Norman met Jacoby's words with sarcasm and he thanked the old man for the compliment.

'It's a hard recipe to perfect,' Jacoby said. 'Harder recipe to maintain. Soon you got life squirmin all over the damn place, clingin to every rock, festerin in the cool damp places, infectin crack an nook an cranny, thrivin in hard to find places, unreachable spots. But the sun keeps bakin away and we're liable to boil over with life. Run here. Run there. Make babies. Dig a ditch, tell a story, buy a whore, sell a whore, fuck, shit, sleep, dream, wake, think think think. But you, boy, youre just one one-hundredth of one in an infinitely big universe that only gets bigger an more crowded. You were your biggest an most important when your mother expelled you like slop from her womb an you wailed an coughed blood. Thats when your words mattered most. You end up spendin the rest of your life tryin to fight the nature of the universe.' He shook his head again, but now he did so without mock pity, without irony. Pity could not be feigned and the old man looked truly saddened by what he had to say. 'And you will lose.'

Norman sighed, trying not to let Jacoby's words affect him. In the silence, where even the fool Gay Jim sat contemplative, staving off the thoughts given to him proved difficult. He shifted on the floor and looked out the window. A break in the gauze of clouds revealed a waning sliver of moon. Below, the shadowed crags of mountaintops cropped up like paper silhouettes against the night.

Jacoby followed Norman's gaze. 'Aye,' he said knowingly. 'The stars. Lookin to the stars for an answer. It was written in the cosmos some have said. Wishin on stars—the first star you see, the fallin stars. Something happens an we say the stars are all aligned.'

This time Norman let out an exaggerated sigh.

'Sorry to have offended our resident scholar,' Jacoby said, placing a hand over his heart. 'You dont believe in coincidence? Of course not; youre a man of science. But what Ive just told you is that all of life—life itself—is coincidence. Stars have to line up because that is what they have been assigned to do in this giant natural order. If you look at the stars like you are now, youre lookin at the things sprayed out by the pinwheel of the big bang—and they lay approximately evenly.'

'I know,' Norman interrupted. 'I know what youre goin to say: They look evenly spaced but theres actually lightyears of variation between them.'

The pity writ in the ruts of Jacoby's face deepened. 'Oh, my sweet boy,' he said. 'You didnt understand your own story despite writin an editin an revisin it. You painted the perfect image—the stars like flecks of salt spread out on the roadway. Little stones of salt on the great black expanse…' For a moment Jacoby seemed to consider his own thoughts, the universe of his mind. Silence resonated like a singular empty note in the night until Jacoby spoke again.

'You own a car?'

A flash of anger pulsed through Norman's body. 'I did until you all took it and took me.'

Unflinching, Jacoby clarified. Said he meant to ask if Norman had a car back in Indiana.

'Got my brothers car when he left for the army,' Norman said. 'Same car you all took.'

'You ever take it on the highway in the winter?'

'Yeah.'

'How fast you go?'

'Speed limit.'

'An whats the speed limit?'

'Sixty, I guess.'

'Sixty or about sixty?'

'Sixty.'

'So in three seconds you go two hundred and sixty-four feet.'

Norman blinked, staring at the old man, trying to discern if the calculation was correct, if it was a smoke screen, a test, or something Jacoby had committed to memory. 'Sure,' Norman agreed.

'Lets say your granules are spread out in the fashion of the universe, according to the grand design of the almighty pinwheel—the salt trucks speed, the depth of the snow, the surface of the road an such. Your wheels spinnin over the grains of salt, poppin them into dust. I'll admit, theyre spaced evenly from our perspective as we're glidin over them in a car at sixty miles per hour. But then, just a few grains fall askew an you hit a patch of ice. And you lose control of your car for three seconds—two hundred and sixty-four feet—an you slide off the road into a ditch. The violence of the impact slams your head against the dashboard. When they find you the next morn, your body is cold an your blood an brains are frozen in a trail across the dashboard, the glass of the windshield cracked like a spiders web. That is the design of the universe.'

It was a trick, Norman knew, but for a long moment the world—his current predicament included—seemed to make sense. Sudden euphoria is a fleeting thing, usually reserved for those who seek respite in death. But Norman was nowhere close to dying; his life would go on for a long time—outliving his counterparts by many years. And unlike the dying man who accepts the gift of bliss as a last rite, Norman asked what it all meant.

For his part, Jacoby, the reluctant shriver, said it was writ in the cosmos. 'What happens from here on out is the plan of forces larger than you, larger than me even. Try as we might, we cant stop what happens from here on out. It's been set in motion since the dawn of time.'

3.

Jacoby's words circulated in Norman's head, causing him to lie awake, staring headlong into the darkness of the tin roofed ceiling. He shivered. But he did not feel cold. Under his blanket he managed to stay warm enough. The thoughts Jacoby had put into his head—the dreams he had implanted—thats what produced this insomnia. Jacoby and Oz snored loudly. Raybur cleared his throat and rolled over. Every once in a great while the chair of the Madonna creaked and her stench floated from her cubby into the main room where they all slept. Norman blinked, trying to see a difference between this world and the one composed of dreams, the one holding him at bay.

He thought of going home, returning to his parents' house as his brother never had. The police might charge him with something—they might reopen the case with Grace, examine it in light of whatever Doctor Blanche said—but he doubted it since no one stopped him from pursuing his grant research.

Silently, he promised himself, promised God—and he promised Jacoby and the Madonna—that he wouldnt touch Doctor Blanche again. He imagined living as a hermit, only emerging from his apartment to teach. A life of celibacy, he decided. For a long while he considered this and why it bothered him so much—a life of no sex. Then he whispered it out loud, 'I am a rapist.'

A second truth hit him. He could stay here forever. No one would ever find him. Like the rest of the Jacoby clan, he could give in to the wildness of the desert and let the land and Jacoby and the whole Wyrick system shape him. He didnt have to be celibate; Martha loved him just as she loved her husband. And unlike the taboos of the outside world, Norman felt no pang of guilt when she came to his abode still smelling of Lucas Brown. He felt no embarrassment when he crawled atop of her and she called out other men's names. He relished the animalistic moments when his body surged with adrenaline and all the important things turned to a liquid mixture of tears blood bile jizzum and sweat. In the dark, Norman felt a stiffness in his cheeks from the smile spread across his face.

He closed his eyes and resolved to sleep, perchance to dream. But then a third notion infiltrated the security he had built in his mind. His brother. Their current Wyrick. In the dark Norman reconstructed their interaction in the mine. He listened to the voice so distinctly Midwestern in his memory. He traced the outline of the Wyrick's face, how the man walked. But the chances were simply too great—his brother, a missing soldier in Vietnam, appears in the same mineshaft as him posing as a Wyrick. Life itself is coincidence, a voice told him. He thought of the Jap and his Wyrick, their bodies disintegrating in the back of a luxury car in a shack out in the middle of nowhere. The entire set up could have been Jacoby's doing, a test of Norman's loyalty, see if he would kill his own brother. They would pull Abner's teeth and sprinkle them over the west, making him complicit in whatever crimes their higher power conceived. He thought of Lucas Brown's children, the brothers, Jacoby, and the Madonna. Together they delineated the life one comes to lead in the desert world. There was no promise of life here, no promise of death either—just a withering existence. And Norman knew that living meant leaving.

Snow crunched under his foot as he stepped off the porch and out into the brazen desert darkness. The shroud of clouds had lifted somewhat, revealing the intermittent flitting of stars, the hairline sliver of moon, the occasional glimpse of the hazy red spot called Mars. Norman had become acclimated to the cold for the most part. He exhaled and watched the fog of his breath crystallize and float away like dust. For a moment he stood, half expecting the sound of Jacoby's voice to call him back, tell him that the place he had once called home didnt exist anymore—that it perished with the rest of civilization. But no plea or argument to stay resounded and the night quaked with thunderous silence. Norman took another step. The temperature dipped well below freezing, yet he seemed not to notice. He hiked down the slope trail, around the skirt of the mountain where he hid his supply stash. As he rounded the bend in the trail the wind blew evenly and the breeze cut him to the bone. Here the wind blew occasionally—out in the desert pan Norman knew it would be relentless.

He looked out over the expanse of the empty place, the shifting drifts of snow. Air snorted from his nostrils. He found the rock shaped as a human head and rolled it aside. His bare fingers found the metal rim of the can and he pulled it out. He tucked it underneath the blanket he wore as a serape. He looked down on the path before him.

'Yeah,' he said out loud, and the sound of his own voice startled him as it clashed with the stillness of the night. It seemed small. He said yeah again and began to walk.

Almost right away Norman recognized his escape as a bad idea. He continued to talk out loud as if by doing so he could convince himself better than through thought alone.

'They'll track me,' he said. 'They'll find my footprints in the snow and they'll track me down and Jacoby wont want to talk to me anymore and he'll kill me.'

He kept walking.

'Thats not true,' he said. 'Jacoby loves me; he loves my mind. I'm not afraid of dying. I havent been afraid of dying for a long time now—I'm afraid of the things that just exist.'

As he cleared the last boulder of the mountain foothills and stepped out into the flats, the winds hit him full force. A new, brutal cold charged by a relentless and whipping wind stripped him of any warmth. He choked on the air. The soft flesh patch residing at the back of his throat behind the tongue scorched with cold, sending a metallic taste like blood through Norman's mouth. He gingerly clenched his teeth, afraid the cold made them brittle enough to shatter. At first he thought his lungs would go cold in the same way of everything else, but he was wrong. It was the tubes leading into the lungs—the bronchials—that contracted and hardened with the cold. He numbed.

Wanting to keep his mind agile, he began calculating the risks of his escape. He had done this many times before, but now the calculations became about survival on a visceral level. First he needed to discern what time it was. He cast his gaze up at the waned moon, the white of it matching the desert. He knew nothing of telling the time according to the path of the moon. He didnt even know what day it was, what month. He gave up on trying to figure the time and guessed it to be after midnight—probably close to two in the morning.

Jacoby would be the first to wake as he always was. Right away he'd notice Norman was missing. Thatd be about six in the morning or thereabouts. Theyd mobilize quickly. Norman figured he had about four and a half hours' head start. He resolved not to slow his pace or stop. If he followed these electric poles as he originally planned months ago, he would eventually come to some sort of town. The world is only so big after all. At first he lied to himself, saying it would be only a matter of hours. Then he sobered himself and knew it would be days. The task of living seemed too much and thoughts of Jacobyville seemed to swallow him as he walked, until he realized he came to nearly a standstill.

'Keep moving,' he said. His body listened and he redoubled his pace. He felt that Jacoby would be waiting for him up ahead. Without breaking stride he looked over his shoulder at the footprints he made in the snow. If the wind kept blowing, it might cover his tracks. That too was a lie. Norman knew full well each time he stepped down, the crunching sound was his foot compacting the flakes. The energy created by compaction produced just enough heat to make a paper thin layer of ice.

Snow might cover it, but the divots would still be there, enough for Jacoby to follow.

Morning came on like a destination. In the distance, in front of him, the sun broke over a faint and far-off mountain range. When he left Jacobyville he figured his bearing as eastward; this confirmed it. He speculated how far the mountain range would lie from here, knowing the desert distorts distances. He picked up one foot and put it in front of the other. He could feel nothing now, except hunger. And thirst.

In his hasty departure, Norman hadnt taken any food. As he trudged on he sank his raw stiff hands into his pockets feeling for a grain of meal, a seed or kernel. But there was nothing. He considered scooping up handfuls of snow and eating them, but he knew from folk wisdom and Boy Scouts, TV shows with contrived plots, that eating the snow would dehydrate him more, lower his body temperature. He kept his lips pressed tight together. He knew each exhalation, the fog and steam and smoke pouring out of his mouth, meant less water in his body. Even with his mouth sealed shut, the snorts of steam from his nostrils spread out as clouds, the tiny ice crystals dancing in the early morning sunlight. And the cold burned up into his nose, a searing pain infiltrating his brain. The shock of it caused his eyes to water and the moisture made his retinas sting like they were stabbed with razors of ice.

He looked backward, where his footprints led back into the darker skies. But he didnt slow down this time. He didnt stop.

—

About midday Norman's body began to thaw. The clouds pushing through in the night must have marked a warm front. The blanket of snow became a ragged patchwork with intact spots of snow heavy with melt water. Some divots collected pools of water. Norman looked over his shoulder and, seeing nothing there, knelt by one of the pools. He cupped his hands and drew up enough of the water to wet his mouth. His teeth clenched. As the water traveled down the length of his throat and made it into the pit of his stomach, he felt a surge of relief. And as his stomach filled with water, his hunger for sustenance amplified. He searched around for anything edible, first looking around his feet, then scanning the horizon. There was only snow, dirt, sky, and cold. He scraped at the wetted dirt by the edge of the patch of snow. He picked the pebbles from the mud, then rolled it into a ball. He closed his eyes and put it in his mouth. Slowly he forced his jaw up and down. Then he swallowed. The earthen mixture possessed none of the qualities of food; it was not nutritious, nor did it prove tasty by any means. Most of all, it did nothing to satiate the bellowing hunger twisting in his gut. There was nothing else he could do. He continued on.

Once the sun canted past the midday mark, the ache in Norman's leg grew into a steady shake. His knees trembled and his feet landed unsteadily on the wetted ground. He cursed to himself in whispers. His pace slowed and he thought about turning back. He imagined first what Jacoby might do—if he would be welcomed.

Norman thought then of his father and of his brother. It hadnt been that long ago that the officer in full army regalia showed up at their house in Indiana, asking if Norman was the man of the house.

'No,' Norman said. 'Just visiting for the summer.'

'Whos there?' his father called from the kitchen. He had been husking some corn and came around the corner picking at the silk strings between the kernels. When he looked up he muttered a damnation under his breath.

The officer began his statement about Abner, the words pouring out in army cadence, then halting before he said, *suspected to be dead.*

'What'd you just say?' his father asked.

The officer finished his statement without repeating the phrase and said that a representative from the United States Army would contact them with further details surrounding insurance and benefits.

'Suspected dead,' his father said. 'Hear him say suspected?'

Before he climbed into his sedan, the officer replaced the hat he had kept under his arm.

Norman's father pointed the ear of corn at him. 'Your brother, he'll make it back. Just wait. He's too smart for the gooks to kill.'

'Dad,' Norman said. 'When Ma gets home, are you gonna—'

'Damn you,' his father said. 'There aint any news to tell your mother. And dont you breathe a word of it or I'll skin you alive.'

And to Norman's knowledge his father never did say a word of Abner's disappearance. For four years they waited faithfully for some news of his whereabouts. At first they made conversation as if he'd come home at any minute. When Norman's mother purchased a new car, she asked if they thought Abner would be confused, walking up to a house with a different car and all.

If Abner were to walk onto the long narrow gravel road Norman's parents lived on, theyd run to the front porch and holler for him, waving their arms in the air. Whether Jacoby might take this tact with Norman remained unknown.

A clatter followed by a low rumbling pulled Norman's thoughts back. He froze, only letting his eyes move. Another clattering resounded out to the west, closer this time and the rumbling grew more intense. It took a moment for Norman to process what he saw, but once he identified the source of the noise as a bread truck—a flat-paneled box on wheels—he began to run, arms flailing, begging for it to stop.

4.

The truck driver was a big man, nearly hairless, except for his eyelashes and some irritated stubble on the back of his neck. He offered Norman a stick of peppermint gum, which Norman chewed three times before swallowing it.

'Hows a young fella like yourself end up in the desert in winter?' the driver asked. The way he posed the question Norman knew he was wondering aloud rather than searching for an answer.

Norman leaned against the window, his forehead pulling against the glass. He watched the foreground whip past in a blur of yucca and scrub, patched blobs of snow. The road—shaded the same color as the desert dirt—hummed under the steel-belted radials of the truck while the things farther off—the mountains and clouds and destiny itself—appeared stationary, barely moving except in a hulking brooding fashion. Norman pulled his leg up to his chest, resting his foot on the bench seat.

'Look here, kid,' the trucker said. 'I'd like to help you out, but I think you need some time to sober up, dry out, get clean. Do what you need to do. Get right with the Lord.' The driver kept one hand on the steering wheel and leaned over, unsnapped the glove compartment and took out a laminated card.

'Here,' he said and Norman took it. On one side it had the Lord's Prayer typed out and on the reverse side it had the first verse of God Bless America. 'Helped me through some tough times.' The grumble of the truck engine filled the cabin before he spoke again. 'Town up this way, about five miles. Place called Gratis.' He asked if Norman ever heard of it.

But Norman didnt respond; he wanted to stay here forever, head against the window, trucking down a state route, stick of peppermint gum in his stomach.

They pulled into a Shell station and the driver cut the engine. Norman looked through the window at his reflection in the rectangular side view mirror. He hardly recognized himself. His once pasty skin now looked tough and craggy and his hair had grown longer than it had ever been, held in place by sweat and grease.

The truck driver looked down at the floor, at nothing in particular. Finally he said this was the end of the line.

'You aint going any farther?' Norman asked.

'I am, but I cant take you along.'

'I'm no trouble,' Norman said. 'I'm not a druggie or anything.'

The trucker raised his hand to silence Norman. 'It's none of my business. I try to do right by the Lord and give folks a lift when they need it.' He sighed. 'It's hard being a trucker these days. Drugs an hookers at all the truck stops, extra money to be made on the routes if you make deals with some folks. Put the two of us together—a man tryin to do right an a man who needs to get right—an one of us'll end up back where he started.' He began to tell a story about a fellow trucker who, against his better judgment, agreed to take a truckload of Mexicans across the border—mostly women and their youngins trying to meet up with their pops who'd crossed on their own and sent money back home. 'Well, he no sooner started en route to Las Cruces when he lost control of the rig an ended with an e-lectric line layin across the trailer.'

'I'm a professor of Anthropology from Indiana,' Norman blurted out.

The driver looked sad; he frowned and blinked slowly. 'I knew you was in deep when I seen you traipsin all by your lonesome out there by mile marker forty-three.' He forced a smile at his passenger. 'Figure out whether you want to clean up an you can be whatever you want to be—professor, astronaut, congressman.'

Norman's gaze drifted back to the figure in the mirror—haggard, tired, and emaciated. He nodded, put the laminated card in his pocket, and climbed out of the truck. Twilight ushered the daylight away, the bitter desert cold returning with the shadows. From the looks of it Gratis was not very big; Norman could see from one side of the town to the other.

There might have been a neighborhood tucked away from the commerce district; still, this place was no more than a blip in the desert.

'Hey,' the driver said. Norman turned. The big, hairless man shuffled through his wallet. 'Here,' he said and took out two twenty dollar bills. 'Its gonna get cold tonight. Try to get a good nights rest an a hot meal.'

Norman reached for the money and the man held onto the bill even after Norman had it in his grasp.

'This moneys for food and lodging. Got me?'

Norman nodded.

'Promise me.'

'Promise,' Norman croaked.

The driver smiled. 'Alright. Sundown Motel is down this sideroad here, just a block or so. Nice diner across the street too. Might be open now—more of a morning place, but still.'

'Thanks.'

The driver bobbed his head once and said God bless.

Norman made it halfway down the block when he saw the sign for the Sundown Motel, the word vacancy lit up in hot pink underneath. One of the rooms had its light on. People moved inside.

He looked the street up and down. Not a soul in sight. He felt his mind slowing down. Diagonally across the way, a train caboose sat stationary in a park on a bed of gravel. A sign in front said Gratis Tourist Bureau. Most of the town had gone to sleep, only a few scattered lights left on—the vast swell of the desert darkness surrounding them.

He crossed the street and looked once more up and down the abandoned lane. Then he crawled under the caboose and lay down on the gravel and the ties between the rails. He pulled his arms from the sleeves of his shirt and pulled them up to his chest and fell promptly to sleep.

The laughter of children woke Norman. He lay on his back, staring up at the rusted chassis of the caboose. Daylight warmed the earth considerably and he stuffed his arms back into the sleeves of his shirt. He crawled to the edge of the rails and peeked out from behind the giant steel wheel. A playground stood nearby—a framework with chains and swings, a mock homestead erected from timbers. A woman with a nylon jacket and a fanny pack pushed her daughter on one of the swings. Norman crawled over the rails and out from under the caboose. He stood and dusted himself off.

The woman stopped pushing her child; both stared at the stranger. Norman managed a smile, but they returned his gaze blankly. He opened his mouth to say something—anything in the way of explanation—but suddenly the weight of any words seemed too much to articulate and he walked away.

Before he came through the door of Desi's Diner Norman could smell the food. The thick sweet batter of pancakes frying on a griddle all coated in hot lard, the crackling fat of bacon, the fruity and saccharine-laden syrups. He pushed his body against the glass door, catching a momentary and horrifying glimpse of himself.

The inside of the diner was gauche with yellow globe lights, orange vinyl cushioned booths, and faux wood veneer countertops. A waitress with her hair tied back walked the length of the counter, a carafe in hand. The cook, a lean tall mulatto, stood over a griddle, metal spatula in hand. Systematically he scraped and flipped, clanged and clattered, cursed and called out orders.

No one looked up at Norman. He showed himself to a stool at the end of the counter. A waitress with a handkerchief holding back her hair peered at the newcomer out of the corner of her eye. As she poured coffee, she turned and whispered something to the cook. The cook spun around, his thick framed glasses fogged with steam. He tucked one spatula into the front of his apron and put his hand on the counter in front of Norman.

'Hey, stranger, what'll you have.'

It wasnt phrased as a question and Norman knew what he meant. He reached into his pocket and took out one of the hundred dollar bills he took from Jacoby. He thumbed the bill, cleared his throat, asked if they had some sort of breakfast spread—a farmer's feast or a homerunner, something like that.

The cook leaned back from the counter, taking the spatula from his apron and called across the diner. 'Carla, tell this gentleman what we got in the way of breakfast deals.'

Norman didnt wait for the omelet to cool before he began shoveling it into his mouth. Chunks of ham and pepper scorched the raw spots in his throat. He chewed with his mouth open, bits of egg falling back onto the plate. He scooped up the hashbrowns soaked in ketchup and melted over with cheese and wadded them into his cheek as he took a swig of milk.

An old timer a couple seats down asked how long it had been since Norman had eaten.

'Couple days,' Norman said between bites.

'A couple days?' The cook turned from the griddle.

'Yeah.' Norman kept eating.

'Well hell,' the old timer said. 'You could stand to slow it down. You'll make yerself ill eatin like that.'

'A couple a days?' the cook asked again.

'Uh-huh.'

'You should be savorin that food,' the old timer said. 'Youre actin like this is your last meal and theys gonna send you to the e-lectric chair.' He said it with no guile, just two eyes peering out from behind a set of smoke-lens glasses.

'Took my chances not eating last night,' Norman said. He swallowed. 'Nothing round here was open. Woke up this morning and had to prioritize—eat first, then talk to the sheriff.' He slurped down the last of his milk and pointed to the cup. The waitress took it and began refilling it. 'Hopefully I didnt think it out wrong, otherwise this could be my last meal.'

A couple of folks in a nearby booth ceased their conversation and turned to listen to the vagrant traveler ramble at the counter.

The cook smirked. 'What do you mean?'

'I just escaped a kidnapping,' Norman said. He reached for the milk and looked up when he realized the waitress still held his cup. She stared at him blankly, a small gap between her lips. In his head, he said the words again, realizing the casualness with which he spoke. Now all the faces in the diner looked toward him.

A man dressed in camouflage with a hunting vest in the back corner booth of the restaurant responded first. 'Kidnapping here in Gratis?' he asked.

'No,' Norman said. His voice cracked. 'Out in the desert.'

'Your car break down or something?' the old timer asked. 'Some colored sorts give you trouble?' He shifted in his seat and nodded at the cook who waved him off.

'No, I went out on a grant—like a scholarship—to study ghost towns and these people, this family, they kidnapped me.'

'A family?'

'Yeah.'

'Like a mom and some kids, a husband and such.'

'They live in this ghost town—'

The cook made eye contact with Carla. She walked by swiftly and set the check on the counter before Norman.

'What was you doin in the desert?' the old timer asked. It was as if he missed the complete exchange. Still the question stirred something in Norman's mind and he thought of Doctor Blanche, of Dusty, broken beer bottles, soiled undergarments.

He took a shaky breath. He felt dizzy. His stomach churned. 'I came out here last June to study ghost towns.'

'June?' The old man threw his hands up and nearly fell out of his stool. 'June?'

Norman nodded. Then he asked what month it was now.

The man in the corner booth called out next. 'You sayin you dont know the month?'

Norman blinked. Suddenly the diner seemed much brighter. He looked down at his empty plate smeared with grease and ketchup and syrup, yolks of egg. 'Dont know,' he said. 'Guess it to be spring—March maybe.'

The old timer gave a single nod. 'March twentieth.'

Every remaining person in the diner was now watching Norman at this moment, enraptured by this stranger in rags, amused by his obtuse manner and voracious appetite.

'Was you a part of a commune out there, is that what youre sayin?' the old timer asked.

'No.'

'I read something in the gazette about these communes, how they get kids involved, get them hooked on the weed.'

'Mmm-hmm.' The waitress nodded her head.

All around the diner heads nodded in agreement.

'Sometimes kids dont know what theyre gettin into,' the old man said. 'They think they can live on peace an love an drugs.' A silence fell on the diner for some times, all the eyes of the diner-goers leering at Norman. Then the old timer spoke again. 'How you plannin to spend the rest of that century bill?'

'I'm not a druggie,' Norman muttered. He knew the response came off as less than convincing. 'I'm a professor at Indiana State University.'

The cook took a step forward, laughing. 'Alright man, thats enough. You know what—meals on the house.' He took the check from the counter and tore it in half. Norman began to protest.

'No, no,' the cook said. 'Take your smack money and get out of here.' He smiled and wished Norman luck.

People began conversing lowly. Norman spun his stool around and searched for some support. The rest of the diner patrons did their best to ignore the crazy man at the counter. He looked back at the old man, but he just shrugged and turned his eyes down at his mug.

As Norman snatched the hundred dollar bill off the counter and stuffed it into his shirt pocket, he caught the two men in the corner booth—the men in hunting garb—giving him a sidelong glance. Their eyes darted away and one man put his hand over his mouth, feigning a cough.

With a single yank, Norman pulled open the door and a sudden chill racked up his spine. He staggered around the side of the diner and emptied the contents of his stomach. The vomit came out in one continuous stream and splashed up on his pant legs. He stood upright again, wiped his mouth with the back of his hand. As he caught his breath, he looked at the town—the quiet shops, the now-abandoned playground, the peaks of roofs lined up in a housing plat out in the distance. At this moment, this place, more than any other, Norman felt, was a farce.

The Gratis police station wasnt hard to find. Like most every small town in America it sat next to a firehouse, a flagpole out in front. A six-pointed star painted on the window. Norman walked into the lobby, an area not much bigger than a bathroom stall. A woman sat behind a pane of glass with wires running crisscross through it. A hole cutout in the center for her voice to be heard.

She waited for him to speak.

'Want to report a crime,' Norman said.

The woman, as if activated by some magic phrase, snapped into action. 'What was the nature of the offense?'

Norman blinked, exhaled, pursed his lips. 'If it's alright,' he said. 'If it's alright I'd rather just tell the sheriff myself.'

'I need to know the nature of the offense so I can match you to the appropriate office.'

Norman looked behind the woman, at the three doors behind her, the names of men painted on the smoked glass. Two rooms were dark, their trashcans sitting out for the custodian.

'I was kidnapped,' he said.

The woman didnt look up from writing when he said it, so he repeated himself more loudly and directed his speech toward the hole in the glass.

'I heard you, sir.' She still didnt look up. 'When were you kidnapped?'

'What do you mean, *when?*'

'When did the crime occur?'

'Last June.'

The woman set her pen down. 'This happened over nine months ago?'

'Ive been kidnapped—gone—for nine months. I just got away.'

'Just got away?'

'Yesterday. I made it here and slept. When I woke up, I came here.' He felt dizzy.

The woman folded her hands. 'How'd you get away?'

Norman opened his mouth and the words came as a squeak. 'I walked out, away I mean, while they were sleeping.'

The woman wrote nothing down; she just stared, her eyelids half-closed, faint hint of amusement flicking at the corners of her mouth. The tick of the clock in the lobby became more audible. Her phone rang. She waited for the second ring to pick it up.

'Yessir,' she said. With her free hand she began scribbling

down some notes. She stopped and looked up at Norman before saying yessir again. 'One,' she said abruptly. 'Out here in the lobby.' She nodded to whatever the other end of the phone said. 'I'll do that, yessir.'

She hung up and smiled at Norman. 'That was Deputy Walsh. He'll see you in a couple of minutes. Go ahead and have a seat.'

'Deputy?' Norman asked. 'Is he a specialist in these sorts of crimes?'

'He's the deputy on duty. Have a seat please.'

'What about the sheriff, cant I talk to him?'

'He's on vacation in Austin with his wife. Deputy Walsh will be with you shortly. Go sit down.'

Deputy Walsh came off as the quintessential western constable. He had a thick mustache, light gray stubble on his cheeks, and clear blue eyes. He sat on the edge of the desk, a mug in hand. He offered it to Norman.

'It's tea,' he said. 'Go on. Good to calm the nerves.'

Norman took the mug, but did not drink of it. The deputy walked back around the desk and sat down, clasping his hands together and resting his chin on them. A medical bracelet peeked out of his sleeve.

'Kidnapped, huh?'

'Yes, sir. Out in the desert, last June.'

'Call them ab-ductions nowadays,' the deputy said. 'You is a little old to be kidnapped.'

'Abducted,' Norman said. 'Sure, I was abducted in the desert last June.'

The deputy repeated the words to himself, shaking his head. He stared Norman down. 'Level with me now: Was any drugs involved?'

Norman shook his head in return. 'No,' he said. Then more vehemently, 'No, no drugs.'

'Youre sure?'

'Jesus, yes.' He waited a moment. 'Just because I was out in the desert and I come into town dressed like a hobo you all think I'm a doper.'

'You all?'

'Yeah, everyone.'

'Everyone in this room?'

Norman glanced around the room—bookshelf, desk, grandfather clock. Otherwise empty.

'No...'

'Do you see other people in this room right now?'

'I meant the other people here in town, at the diner.'

'They thought you were on drugs?'

Norman looked into the mug. The liquid inside no longer steamed. 'Seems to be what everyone thinks.'

'You know I could do a drug test right now? Have you pee in a cup, see if youre lying.'

'Thats fine. Call the university; they'll tell you I worked there.'

'Might try that tomorrow. Chances are nobodys at your school on a Sunday.' The deputy took their conversation in his stride, as if he'd had this conversation a hundred times before. 'Had a lot of trouble with drugs round here. Not just Gratis either. Small towns are becoming outposts for these drug dealers—Mexicans, most of them. Got kids shoving balloons full of LSD up their asses.'

Norman gritted his teeth. 'Yeah, I was kidnapped—abducted. They werent into drugs and neither was I.'

Deputy Walsh sighed, reclined in his chair with his hands rested on the paunch of his stomach. 'Alright,' he said. 'Whereabouts were you ab-ducted?'

'Out near New Daisy, the ghost town.'

'And did you get an ID on your, your captors? A name, distinguishing features…'

'The main guy, his name was Jacoby. But they werent in New Daisy. We moved around a lot.'

'Right. Where'd you move around to?'

'All around. Cant remember it all.'

'You cant recall?'

'No, they kept me sedated at first. I just remember moving, but not in any certain direction.'

Walsh's eyes went alight. 'They kept you sedated.'

Norman's voice raised. 'Damn it. Drugs got nothing to do with it.'

The deputy kept his composure. 'I didnt bring it up this time. You did.'

Norman took a gulp of the tea. When the liquid hit the back of his throat, it scorched—not from heat, but from spices. Then he felt a surge of relief. He studied the deputy. Though he had a notepad on his desk, Walsh wrote nothing down. His eyes remained focused on Norman. Norman who hadnt bathed in nine months, who dressed in rags, who was without any ID.

'You dont believe me, do you?'

The deputy sighed and shook his head. 'Cant rightly say I do. Seen too many of you types go through here—everyone with a story.'

'You can call the university tomorrow.'

'I could and I will. Chances are they'll corroborate your story too.'

'Yeah.'

'You left last summer and havent been back since. It's the gap in between thats got me worried,' the deputy said. 'I'd bet my next paycheck you done screwed the pooch at this university and headed out here for a break of some sorts. Maybe even thought you wouldnt come back.'

'Youre speculating.'

'Speculating, telling you what I know from doing this a long time.' Walsh shrugged. 'Same difference, sonny boy. Maybe you thought about putting a bullet through your brain. Instead you took some drugs. Got caught up in something you dont rightly understand.'

Norman leaned forward, set the mug on the corner of the desk. 'I saw them murder people.'

'You witnessed a murder?'

'Yes. A young couple. They raped the woman, killed her boyfriend and her when they were all done raping. I saw an assassination too.'

'Excuse me?'

'Something government like. Agents are sent out with contracts, only then Jacoby kills the agent too. The agents dont know theyre targets. He kills them both and buries them in shafts and shacks with lye. And I think my brother might be their next target.'

'Your brother?'

'Abner. He went missing in Vietnam a few years back, listed as MIA.'

'So this is like a conspiracy?'

'Sort of. Yes.'

Deputy Walsh sucked in the side of his cheek. He glanced down at his blank legal pad. When he spoke again his voice sounded different; he used a tone better suited for conversing with a child.

'Son, I want you to wait right here an I'm gonna make some calls, see if I cant get to the bottom of this.'

The deputy closed the door behind himself, leaving Norman alone in the office. He could hear the deputy talking with the secretary. An eruption of laughter broke through the conversation. Norman stood, walked to the window behind the desk. It was already unlocked. He slid it open, popped the screen from the frame and stepped through.

As soon as Norman rounded the corner of the sheriff's station he felt watched. He looked over his shoulder to see if Walsh followed him. It wouldnt be more than a few minutes before he came back into the office and saw the open window and the missing screen.

But the police didnt bother Norman. They wore uniforms and drove cars painted black and white with lights on top. They had rules—laws—to follow. Someone else watched him now. He quickened his pace, glancing over his shoulder again. A truck rumbled through a four-way stop farther down the street. He walked faster. He began to swing his arms. Then his legs moved more quickly. He ran.

He ran three blocks, to where a Laundromat shared a building with a pizza parlor. A street lamp flicked on as dusk settled over the rooftops. Because the evening air was cool and damp, the windows of the Laundromat fogged over. The blurred outline of a Hispanic woman moved inside, switching her clothes from one machine to the next. Norman felt the gaze from an unknown source focused on him. He crossed the street and crouched behind a shrub and waited several minutes. Another truck and a police car drove by, headlights on. The woman exited the Laundromat and entered the pizza parlor next door.

The clothes stolen from the dryer were still damp when he put them on in the bathroom of the Laundromat. But they felt warm too. Norman cupped some of the granule soap in his hand, mixed it with water and scrubbed down his face and hair. He used the cloth towel dryer to mop out his hair. As he left the Laundromat the cold cut through the wetted cloth and the warmth evaporated. He passed the Hispanic woman on the sidewalk without looking at her.

All the way to the Sundown Motel he felt the eyes on him again. This time he didnt look over his shoulder. He walked at a measured pace. The pink neon letters of the motel blaring hot in the bitter darkness. At the edge of the motel parking lot, he stopped and examined the structure: a row of white doors with an office at the end. Dim lights backlit the closed miniblinds in the windows. Opposite from the office a few evergreens created a tree screen for the air conditioning units and a propane tank.

The desk clerk appeared to be hardly out of high school. A kid with dark skin and shy manners. The room at the end of the row cost twelve dollars and Norman paid with the twenty from the trucker. The boy began to thank Norman, but Norman held up the other twenty. 'If I dont get disturbed tonight this will be on the nightstand in my room come morning.'

The kid nodded.

'If God shows up, you dont know where I am.' The boy nodded, but Norman wasnt finished. 'I mean it—pretend like theres fucking lambs blood on that door.'

Again, the boy nodded. He handed Norman a key on a lanyard.

On his way to the room, Norman stopped at the vending machine and bought a Coke and several bags of chips.

He kept the lights off, letting his eyes adjust to the dark as they had become accustomed to doing. He peered out the peephole at the darkened parking lot, but there was nothing. He shook the pillows from their cases and rolled up the blanket from the bed. On the nightstand he found a pack of matches, a pad of paper, and a shortened pencil with no eraser. He took those also and went into the bathroom, shutting himself in complete darkness. He tore the pillow apart and stuffed the cotton batting under the crack of the bathroom door. Only when he had every fissure in the room sealed did he turn on the light.

It took another minute for his eyes to readjust. The bathroom buzzed white and tiled, sterile and fluorescent. He worked quickly, tearing three holes in the pillowcase. He slid the sack over his head and wore it like a tunic. Then he looked at his feet. The boots had worn through in places, exposing bare flesh. He had mended them over the last couple months with twine and duct tape. He sat on the edge of the tub and slid his feet free.

On the sink counter a plastic-wrapped disposable razor sat next to a cake of soap. He used the heel of the boot to crush the casing of the razor and freed the blade. Carefully holding the blade, he cut swathes from the shower curtain to line the boots. At least they would be waterproofed. For a moment he thought about throwing the razor away. Instead he cut another strip from the shower curtain, wrapped it in the plastic and put it in his pocket. Finally he took the bottle of Coke, and being without an opener, he placed the edge of the metal cap on the bathroom counter and smacked the top of it with the heel of his hand. The bottle opened and the saccharine scent of soda wafted up, bubbles of carbonation sounding like static. Norman resisted the urge to chug down the liquid, knowing the soda would only make him thirstier in the long run. He poured the contents down the drain and refilled the bottle with water from the tap, plugging the mouth with a wad of shower curtain.

He flicked out the bathroom light and all became cloaked in darkness. He opened the door and padded over to the window facing the evergreens. Underneath, the air conditioner units sat muted. Unlike the full-length windows facing the parking lot, this one was without a curtain and the iridescent glow of the town cut out in the darkness like a portrait. He unlatched it and slid the glass and listened. Outside it was quiet—not even the whir of a distant car or the din of some social club. Just silence. A hoot owl moaned and it fell silent all over again. Norman pulled the razor from his pocket and used it to slice the screen from the frame. He pulled the loosed mesh in and let it fall to the floor. Again he listened, but heard nothing. He pulled himself up to the opening and leaned out to see what he could spy. The parking lot lamps cast pools of light down the scant few cars. Across the street a cluster of buildings sat unlit and vacant. He looked the other direction, down the street.

He watched a traffic light turn from yellow to red. A junker car plowed through the perpendicular street, the sound of the engine chugging until it too, along with all else in this nighttime world, faded into nothing, nothing at all.

He tossed the pillowcase onto the ground, then the blankets from the bed. As soon as Norman hit the ground he felt the eyes again, the watching. He held his breath, thinking he could better hear without the whispers of his own breathing. But there was no sound. Whoever watched him—whoever had been following him—was looking at the door of the motel room and from where they sat his escape would be hidden by the evergreens. He lay down so he could look out under the branches. In the shadows, his body wedged between the air conditioners, he waited. He waited to see who was out there, who followed him through this world, and what they would do.

5.

He woke midmorning to the sound of the housekeeper. She swore in muffled tones, only made audible by the open window. Norman didnt remember falling asleep. Hurriedly he grabbed his belongings—the pillowcase, blanket, and the bags of chips. He took off at a trot toward the Shell station.

An elderly couple filled their car. Norman dropped his sack by the door of the station and walked in. Above the door a bell chimed and the attendant wearily lifted his eyes from his newspaper. Norman used the money he promised to leave on the nightstand to buy a dozen sticks of beef jerky and a bottle of apple juice. He also bought the Monday paper, the *Gratis Gazette*.

Once outside he stuffed his purchases into the pillowcase, looked around, and approached the old man who was now securing his gas cap.

'Sir,' Norman said.

The man shut the metal flap to the tank and straightened up.

'Sir.' Norman said it a little louder this time.

The man turned around, startled.

Norman did his best to smile and look the man in the eye. Still, he darted glances left and right, sure someone was watching him. 'Can I ask you a favor?'

'I aint giving you money.'

Norman stood dumbfounded by the reply.

'Got half a leftover sandwich in the car. I'll give you that, but no cash.'

'I was going to pay you for a ride.'

Now the man stood quietly. Unsure if the man heard him, Norman began to repeat himself, only to have the man cut him off.

'Ride to where?'

'Westward—if youre going that way.'

The man nodded. Inside the car, the man's wife craned her neck trying to see the stranger conversing with her husband.

'Need to go about fifteen miles. I could give you five dollars.'

The man spent a long time staring at Norman, like he expected a confession or a longer story. But his eyes were less accusing, less watchful, than the other hidden gaze. Norman glanced around.

'You in some type of trouble?' the man finally asked.

'No sir,' Norman said. 'Just trying to make it westward.'

'Why westward?'

'Trying to meet up with my brother. He's in some trouble.'

The old man's eyes narrowed and he rocked back and forth on his feet, hands in his pockets. 'Might be your brother can help you—nothing wrong with that.' Then he asked what was in the bag.

'Blanket, food, some toiletries. Take a look if you want.'

The station attendant stood up from his desk and peered out the glass doors.

'Got the missus in here,' the man said. 'She takes oxygen and reads the Bible, so there aint any smokin and there aint any swearin.'

'We always try an do for others like we'd have them do for us,' the woman said. Norman nodded out of politeness. She kept talking, one Bible-based cliché after another. 'Never miss a chance to be Jesus with skin on his face.'

Out the window, the desert passed by, neutral and ugly and forlorn. The telephone posts he had followed should be coming up soon, if memory served, but the ride into Gratis with the truck driver felt like a long time ago now.

'What about you?' the old man asked. The woman had stopped talking and she turned her attention to Norman. The old man's eyes peered back at Norman from the rearview mirror.

'I'm sorry,' Norman said. 'What?'

'You a believer?' the man asked a second time.

Norman's eyes connected with the woman and she nodded at him as if to goad him into the affirmative. All eyes on him.

'Raised Catholic,' Norman said as if that were answer enough.

'Whats that?' the man said.

'He was raised Catholic,' the woman repeated loudly.

'Doesnt tell us anything,' the man said. 'Knew a preachers son who went to prison for mo-lesting a little girl. Had a decent upbringing, that one. Then he promises to show her a puppy he's got in his bedroom. When she goes with him, theres no puppy and that boy, he mo-lests her.' He shook his head and said, 'Belief is somethin thats in you or it's not.'

The woman beamed at her husband, nodding as if she had never heard these words before. On the horizon, little posts like matchsticks sprouted from the earth, wire draping from one to the next. The one nearest the road canted slightly forward. Mile marker forty-two whipped by.

'Just let me off up here,' Norman said.

'Up where?' the woman asked. Her husband asked Norman to repeat himself.

'By those telephone posts up there.'

'Well, shoot, son. We didnt mean to offend you—' the old man started.

'It's fine,' Norman said.

The woman reached a hand back and patted Norman's knee. 'We just try to do for others like theyd do for us.'

The posts grew closer. Norman sighed. 'It's fine,' he said again. 'Just drop me off here.'

The man shook his head, but kept driving. The posts rushed by them. Norman turned and watched them start growing distant in a different direction now.

'Goddamnit,' he said.

The woman gasped.

'What?' the man asked. 'What'd he say?'

Norman leaned up close and spoke loud enough for the old man to hear, his wife staring on in disbelief. 'I said goddamnit, goddamnit. And if you dont stop this goddamn car the last thing you'll see in your life is me fucking your wife until her cunt looks like roast beef.'

Dusk fell with a dry cold. Most of the snow, save the occasional patch shaded by a yucca or boulder, had melted away. The wet from the snowmelt seeped into the ground and froze hard. To Norman it felt like walking on concrete. He cut a straight path, deviating now and again only to pick up scrap pieces of brush, some desiccated weeds, the spare twig—anything that might be of use.

The handprint the old man left on Norman's face felt fresh and raw in the cold, like it would never stop stinging. His cheek burned anew when he crouched in the last embers of daylight to start a fire. The flames seemed to lick at the spot, making it pulse.

The fire fueled by his findings and a roll of toilet paper glowed hot and yellow only for a minute, then lapsed into shades of red and black and in between. He added the last of the brush he collected and some strips of newspaper. He held his hands close to the flames and let the heat sear through his fingertips, until it felt like the flesh might melt and his fingernails would combust into flames. He ate three sticks of beef jerky and saved the wrappers. Then he unplugged the Coke bottle filled with water and drank down the contents. He crawled over to a nearby crescent of snow and packed the bottle full. The ice crystals scraped at his hands and he cursed himself for letting them grow so warm.

He sat by the fire—now just a single tongue of flame and some papery coals flaking in the wind. He pulled out the plastic jerky wrappers and twisted them together into a single braid of plastic. They were still slick with grease and he dipped the edge of the wick in the flame. It burned slow and steady. He set it on the ground a few feet away and placed the glass bottle next to it. He added more wrappers.

The toilet paper roll fumed dark and angry. Norman used the twig to poke at it, expose some of the unburnt tissue coiled inside. A couple yellow flames jumped to life, but only for a few brilliant seconds. Norman lifted his shirt, his tunic and coat, exposing his white underside to the flames. Then he billowed the shirts out in an attempt to capture the heat and hold it close to his body. He kicked the dying fire into ash and spread the warm soot out across the frozen earth. He stretched out on the ashes and shivered. Turning up on one side, he watched the flickering light of the other fire, how it glinted off the Coke bottle and how it melted the snow inside.

He woke. Eastward the sky washed gray and gloomy, a slight difference between the earth and heaven. But west—west broke flat and black, the stars blotted out by a matte of clouds. He sat up and ate a bag of chips, saving the wrapper in his pocket. The snowmelt in the bottle yielded little water but he drank it all down.

Before heading forth into the expanse, he stopped at a patch of snow and packed the bottle full again. He plugged the mouth of the bottle and slid it into his pants pocket, hoping the warmth of his body would melt the contents.

In the desert, there is little to do besides think. As he traipsed, putting one foot ahead of the other, Norman began to understand how a man like Jacoby came to exist. Out here there was nothing but time and space and a man could become big enough to consume everything around him. Start in a great emptiness and grow to fill it and a man could gain critical mass, swallow up the smaller men around him, the towns farther off, the countries, galaxies, life, the universe, God. With enough time a man could connect his every thought and create his own universe, larger and more webbed than the one men had collectively built with their small small minds.

Norman stopped, gauged the sun and sipped from the bottle. The day had warmed some and the sun appeared as a faint white apparition through the gauze of cloud. He thought of his time in Gratis, how the stories of his desert experience seemed too far-fetched for the people to understand—how when he recounted his past it sounded unreal to even his own self. He kept walking with the express purpose of putting distance between himself and that town. His step faltered and he felt watched again. He glanced back over his shoulder, out into the desert, and saw nothing. Each stride pushed him back toward Jacobyville, toward his brother, Martha, the things he'd lost in his last life. He redoubled his pace.

Evening came again and he made a fire much like he had the night previous. As he lay in the ashes he pondered for the first time since the graveyard in New Daisy if he might die, if Jacoby might kill him. Death felt like a power only Jacoby possessed—like the only thing keeping him alive right now was a presence in the old man's mind and if Jacoby were to stir from a dream about Norman, life itself would wash over in a field of white waking. Everyone else in the world seemed blind, alien, dumb.

Voices carried low across the night air. At first Norman tried to recognize the voices, thinking they were his thoughts. But they came from without. He sat up. Narrowing his eyes, he peered out into the darkness and slowly turned his head.

'Right there,' one of the voices said.

A white light blared directly at Norman and he put up his hand to shield his eyes.

'You weren't shittin,' the other man said.

The light flicked off and the two visitors drew closer. They wore hunting gear and carried rifles and canvas packs on their backs. Soon they came close enough for Norman to recognize their faces. These were the men from the corner booth of Desi's Diner. He still lay in the ashes of his fire when they crouched next to him and lit a small lantern.

'We follered you from Gratis,' the one finally said.

'Youve been tracking me.'

The man nodded. 'Got my curiosity goin with your tale at the diner. Figured you might be truthin instead of lyin.'

'Not me,' his companion said. 'I thinks youre wanted man— someone from the drug cartels. I been figurin that since I saw you leavin the sheriffs office through the window.'

'We been watchin you,' his companion said.

The one picked up the old Coke bottle, rubbed his fingers in the ashes. 'Cant believe them supplies is all you got.'

Norman's throat was dry and he swallowed hard. 'Whatre you going to do?'

'We're gonna help you kill these sumbitches, hear? You just got to lead the way.'

'Either that or youre done gonna lead us right into one of your communes or wherever it is youre growin pot.'

The lantern emitted a small amount of heat and Norman cupped his hands around it, casting huge shadows across his face. 'It aint drugs,' he said. 'You'll see that firsthand.' Then he chuckled and the companion asked what the hell was so funny.

Norman took a moment to appraise the men's gear—rifles with scopes, vests of many pockets, nearly all of them bulging with something, boots laced up to mid-shin. 'If you want to kill Jacoby, the leader of this village I was talkin about, youre gonna need more than what you got.'

The companions exchanged glances—one confused, one smirking.

'From what you said back at Desi's, this old man an his family, theyre just a bunch of hermits, right?'

Norman shrugged and nodded. His companion asked if they had any special guns, the automatic types. 'You know, the kind they issued in Viet-nam.'

'No,' Norman said. 'Rifles, shotguns, pistols.'

'Well, shit,' the man said. 'Aint nothing special then. Couple of old kooks with some muzzleloaders an hand cannons.'

'What were you plannin on killing this Jacoby fella with?' the companion asked.

Before Norman could answer, the man said, 'You did plan to kill him, right?'

'Yeah,' Norman said. 'I mean, hell yeah.'

'But you aint got no gun.'

Up to that moment, Norman hadnt considered the instrument he would use to kill Jacoby. He thought of something plausible to tell the companions.

'You come into Jacobyville, armed to the teeth like you are, Jacoby an his boys'll shoot you down,' he said. 'Come in there like me, an you'll at least get to see him, have a chance to crack a rock against his skull, put your hands around his neck.'

The man leaned into the lantern, warming the back of his knuckles. He stared into the light when he asked his next question. 'You think this is it for ya? Youre gonna die.'

Norman nodded his head. 'Yeah.'

'Shit,' the companion said. 'Aint no one dyin except the old kook. The two of us, we been huntin everwhere—big game huntin like bears an mountain lions, got some bounties on some wolves once.'

But the man paid his companion no mind. 'You think we're gonna die along with you?' he asked Norman.

The answer was simple. 'If you follow me, yes.'

'We done tracked an caught an escaped con out Nevada way,' the companion said. 'Sheriff had him listed as armed an dangerous. Came out without a scratch, didnt we?'

'Whats so special about this old man?'

Norman removed his hands from the lantern and the light illuminated his face. 'He knows what we're talking about right now,' he said. 'He knows what I'm doing before I do it.'

'What do you mean, he knows what we're doing right now?' the companion asked. 'Is he watchin us?'

Norman shook his head. 'Doesnt have to. Forget about sneaking up on Jacoby. Forget about playing tricks on him, being clever. He thought of everything already, seen it all already.

Right now, he's laying on the floor of his cabin, watching us in a dream, listening to this entire conversation.'

For a while, the men sat quietly as if there were prying ears out in the darkness. Finally one of the men spoke. 'Tell you what, sonny boy, me an my partner here will take turns keepin a watch tonight. Tomorrow we'll foller you at a distance. We wont develop no plan til we lay eyes on this ghost town of yours. Sound fair?'

'And you'll kill Jacoby?'

'If he's everything you say he is, yeah.'

Norman snorted. 'If he's what I say he is, that's why you wont be able to kill him.'

About midday Norman caught the first glimpse of the ghost town—one of the beehive kilns. The crown of the kiln was crushed in and it sat precariously on the hillside. The door gaped vacant. With the sun directly overhead and shaded, the structure cast no shadows on the ground around it. He pointed to it as he passed. The companions who trailed him took note.

While the companions walked with their rifles at ready, their heads constantly turning, Norman made no such efforts toward precaution. His feet dragged across the dirt, making rough scraping noises. The old man could be watching right now—watching from the interior of the kiln, from the bouldered slope of the mount. Watching him from atop a distant mount.

The day grew warmer. He paused and took off his tunic, tossing it to the ground. The men met up with him briefly. He looked around the abandoned landscape, waiting for the impact of the bullet. None came.

'I hope you aint crazy,' the companion said.

The man passed a canteen between the three of them. After Norman took a swig, he assured the companion he wasn't. 'Crazy is believing that gun and walking extra careful through the desert is gonna protect me from Jacoby,' he said.

They began walking again, toward the slopes of the mountain.

Cupping his hands to his mouth Norman called out. His hello echoed and died and there came no response. He stopped, squinted, shielding his eyes with his hand, looking for any movements in the folds of the slope. Further on, he knew, the homestead sat hidden from their view. He climbed. The first structures of Jacobyville came into view.

'You werent bullshittin,' the one said.

His companion let out a low whistle, said he'd heard there was a ghost town out thisaway. 'Heard stories bout it when I was a tyke.' He surveyed some of the structures, then said, 'But damn.'

'I'll flank out around the side here,' the companion said. 'You go straight up the middle an when they poke their heads out, I'll brain em. Got it?'

Norman tried to utter an agreement, but his mouth remained dry—his tongue stuck to his teeth, his lips gummed together.

'Here.' The man handed Norman the canteen.

'That sound like a good plan?' the man asked.

Both of the hunters fell silent, waiting for Norman's response. But Norman had none. He stood staring at them blankly, canteen in hand, the eyes of the men studying him—that familiar sense of being watched. He shook his head—not in disagreement, but in defeat.

'Oh, God,' the one groaned.

'I cant kill them,' Norman said and he knew this to be true.

'Fuck it,' the man said. He turned to the companion. 'Want to pack it in? Get out of here?'

The companion nodded once before a blast from behind Norman tore through the air. The hunter's face spewed a font of blood. He crumpled to the ground.

The man slid off the rifle safety and stepped backward three steps. Another report ripped open the fading strident note of the last blast. A scrap of the man's upper arm flew backward. Norman froze in place. The man cursed and attempted to lift his gun one-handed. A third shot rang out and pierced the man in the stomach. Thick oily blood gurgled out for a few seconds before he sat down on his butt. He coughed once, a mist of blood spraying from his mouth. And then he fell.

Norman stood, looking at his two fallen saviors, the stains of blood growing around their bodies on the rocky ground. Footsteps came up behind him. He felt a hand lay on his shoulder. Gay Jim crawled out of a crevasse no more than ten feet from where they stood and began hacking at the bodies with a hatchet. Norman doubled over, his stomach lurching. He coughed. Jacoby's breath tickled his ear when he welcomed Norman home and called him son.

FOUR

OED

I.

Martha kept her distance for the first couple days after Norman returned. Once, from across the slouch of the mountain, Norman felt her looking at him. He turned and saw her, dress hanging loose on her body, shuffling in the breeze. Light bleached out her features and she appeared no more than a specter.

When they supped in Jacoby's house Norman didnt make eye contact with her. Then, in the night, as they all lay sleeping—Gay Jim murmuring to himself, Oz and Raybur snoring—Norman thought of Martha and masturbated.

Finally, after three days, Martha found Norman outside, near the open pit of the vertical mineshaft.

'You came back,' she said.

Out of all the members of the Jacoby clan, Martha was the only one—save Jacoby himself—to acknowledge Norman's disappearance. As if under hypnosis, the men of the clan simply carried on as if he had never left. Norman used the toe of his boot to push a few pebbles into the mineshaft. A few rocks hit the lift, hanging twenty feet below; others continued on in silence.

'I knew you didnt come back for me,' she said. 'I know about you—who you are out there, on the outside. Jacoby told me, about your past I mean.'

Norman didnt look up from the pit. He stared down it. Wooden timbers cut like railroad ties reinforced the sides, hardened dirt spilling out like mortar.

'I told you, you cant get away,' she said. She stepped closer. 'Out here it's different.'

'How would you know?' Norman asked. He didnt look up, but knew how she stood, how her hair fell across her forehead and trailed down her cheek.

'We've all left at some point,' she said. 'We all came back too. Jacoby says the world here is somethin you take with you. Says once you see this place, you cant unsee it. Says you could go to the ends of the Earth an you'll still be lookin at Jacobyville.'

Norman nodded because he knew what she said to be true. Then he said the world out there—the town of Gratis, Deputy Walsh, Carla at the diner—it all seemed somehow false.

One corner of Martha's mouth turned up in a smile. 'The world out there is over,' she said. 'Ended a long time ago and we're all thats left.'

When Norman found Jacoby the old man squatted over the spent bullet shells. He looked long and hard at the casings, then looked down the slope, toward where the hunters had been shot, where now only a dusted-over patch of stain marred the ground. More than likely Jacoby heard Norman walk up, but the short shadow Norman cast in the midday sun caught the old man's attention.

'Can look at a bullet casing an tell what happened here,' Jacoby said. 'Tell where a man stood, how he held the gun. See where his feet were an if he ran afterward.'

He gathered up the casings in his hand and grunted as he stood. 'Told Oz an Raybur to clean it up—make it like it never happened—an this is what they leave.' He shook his head. 'Might as well reenact the whole thing right in front of a crowd.' For a time, both men stood staring at the stained earth, then further out, out into the desert pan and then out unto the horizon where the rest of the world existed. 'But you didnt come here to talk to me about my boys housekeepin.'

'No,' Norman said in agreement. He clenched and unclenched his jaw before saying what it was exactly that brought him here. He phrased it the only way he could: 'I need to know how you know so much.'

The old man's eyebrows raised, the bags under his eyes pulling tighter. He smiled. 'I know.' He motioned for Norman to follow.

They walked a circuitous path around the edges of Jacobyville. They passed out into the pan, farther out than where the itinerant camps of workers would have been set up a hundred years prior. The beehive kilns sat out to the east and grew distant as they walked.

Eventually they came to a collapsed structure, little more than a ragged hole in the ground with some stray lumber and a length of twine. Jacoby turned and crawled backward into the hole. As he disappeared into the shadows he bade Norman to follow.

Inside the air sat rank and stale, heavy with dust, the space so cramped neither man could stand. Jacoby lit a candle sitting on an overturned crate in the corner. In the yellow light, the old man looked jaundiced, sickly.

'Old storehouse,' Jacoby said. 'Keep some dry goods, salted beef an the like in here.'

In his head, Norman sifted through the research he did on ghost towns, thought of how storehouses were either kept in the center of town or on the outskirts depending on whether the rations were threatened by man or by animal. When this storehouse was built, the threat was from man.

'When I was a boy this was my hideout,' Jacoby said. 'There was a hatch back then. Less dirt down here too.'

He sat cross-legged and Norman did the same. With the candle flame at his back and his hat off, he appeared more a seasoned sailor or a spirit guide of ancient—or one channeling the other.

'I grew up here,' he said. 'It was after the boom years of whatever this town was called then. My father had moved my mother, pregnant with me, out this way after he heard someone say this place was gonna the be the next big thing. According to his source there was copper in this crag—the entire core of the mountain just solid copper through an through.' He sniffed and laughed. 'Most of us come into this world on the downside of things. The rail line had all been abandoned. Years later a locomotive would come through, pullin up the track behind it as it went. Probably sellin it for scrap.

'A few of us remained and we grew close—Raybur for one, others whove passed on. As children we played in the abandoned mines, the graveyards, the skeleton frames of the buildings we once called our homes. Our fathers toiled down in the mines until the inevitable happened an the main shaft collapsed. We never realized how alone we were, how far away everything was, until our fathers were all gone. My mother—the Madonna, our lady of the desert—she kept us safe, nursed us through our teen years.

'When a couple of other families tried to steal our rations, she helped me commit my first murder. I was fifteen.' He contemplated it, relived the whole episode in his mind, yet only said he used his father's carbine to do it. 'That was the way of it—life, I mean. And our life became the scavenging kind. She took in some other children after all the parents were gone. We learned to forage, collect; we learned how to survive on nothing.'

'This isnt what I was askin,' Norman said.

Jacoby nodded. 'You want to know how I know, but you dont want to hear the history behind it.' He grinned like an old devil. 'It clashes with the history in your mind, the history youve spelled out for your students. Thats fine.'

Norman began to stand up, but Jacoby placed a hand on his knee.

'Quite some time had passed and Ma had already given one of her legs to us so she couldnt get around. I wandered out far and away from Jacobyville lookin for anything to eat. Suppose it had to do with the world bein a different place back then. I came across a broke down car, a man sittin on the hood. Young fella, a lot like you used to be. Said he was doin some sightseein, headin cross the country—Los Angeles to Chicago. Car had overheated.

'To me he ranked no more than a stranger—same as me to him. I used a rock to beat in his face. Never had a man die so quietly as that one.' Jacoby made a sound effect and punched one hand into the palm of the other three times. 'I rummaged through his belongings, found some food—mostly cereal an cookies. But then I found this.' Jacoby shifted, reached behind the crate and pulled out a paper sack. From the bag he drew out a thick book with tabs and ribbon hanging loose from the spine. In a moment worthy of liturgical reverence he handed the book to Norman.

The golden lettering of the cloth cover shone in the candlelight: The Oxford English Dictionary. Norman stated the obvious. 'It's a dictionary.'

'Aye,' Jacoby agreed. 'And Ive read an memorized every word.'

The two sat quietly for a few minutes, Jacoby studying Norman's face, Norman contemplating the cover of the dictionary.

'What am I supposed to get from this book?'

The old man seemed surprised by the question. 'All the knowledge I have comes from that book. My ma only knew how to read a few words—enough to get by—an she taught them to me. I took those few words an broke them down into letters, studied the letters, made new words an strung them back together.

'Then I find this book with its words an definitions. All the elements of an entire universe as we understand it, broken down an printed onto pages, bound an numbered.' He exhaled loudly. 'There are no new thoughts. I'm sure youve heard that before. The advantage I have over everyone out there'—and he nodded in the direction of the storehouse entrance—'is that I live here.' He pressed his index finger into the powder dust of the dirt floor. 'Out here I live apart from everyone else; I dont have their laws—not in the combination of words they prescribe anyway, though Ive read them all already. My thoughts are not governed by teachers or politics, history, ideology. I dont have theories or religion. I do my own thinking. I can do whatever I want with those words an make whatever worlds I want. I can destroy. I can see all the way back to the beginning of time an I can see with crystal certainty what the future is like. Ive built an rebuilt our story so many many times.'

The resoluteness of his voice brought Norman into the fold, though the professor inside his head questioned why Jacoby would make this—this place, this time—his story. Again the old man looked astonished by the query.

'There is no other story,' he said. 'This is it. All the words contained in this book comprise all of the stories—an the words we will invent to make future stories. Every truth is contained in this book. Every lie, every human who ever lived—the entire universe as we know it can be constructed from these words. There is no more. Ive reordered them in a thousand thousand different ways. And all of the stories, like so many sentences, tell me one thing: The thing we call evil is the same thing as life an to lead the perfect life means to die.'

Norman's next question spilled out like he had waited for this exact moment to ask it. 'How does this story end?'

For a long time Jacoby sat motionless, only his eyes opening and closing, his breathing steady and shallow and rhythmic. 'Like every story ends—we die.'

'But how do we die?'

'Not together,' Jacoby said. 'You are not so fortunate.'

Life at the university felt like another lifetime entirely. His venture into Gratis, back into civilization, became a bad dream. Farther back his childhood ceased to be his, his brother no more than a memory, and all that came from that time, that past, faded into an ether of otherworldliness. He supped with Raybur and Lucas Brown, fucked Martha out in the open, shot bottles and cans with Oz and Gay Jim. He paid homage to the Madonna, sitting at the foot of her chair, his head resting in her lap.

As the days warmed up he went for walks, sometimes taking the children along, though he seldom spoke to them. They walked out into the desert flats, toward the storehouse, though never so close they could spy the hole in the ground.

At night Norman began the practice of recalling specific memories from his life previous to Jacobyville—a time he took to calling from before.

'I only ever taught what the university wanted me to teach,' he said.

Martha's head rested on his chest, a clump of greasy hair strewn across Norman's neck. His hand rubbed her back while he spoke. 'I had an office an a schedule. I had that apartment. I never realized how much fear I was livin in until I came out here.'

Martha had taken him into her mouth just a few minutes before, but he continued to grow harder and pushed on her back so she rocked rhythmically up and down. He raised his voice over the wet sucking sounds.

'I dont fear anything out here. Maybe goin back again—I think I'm afraid of that. I'm afraid the worlds ended without me.' Martha changed her angle, moved her tongue and moaned. A charge of energy shot down Norman's spine and he swelled. He struggled to maintain his thoughts. 'When I was out there, in Gratis, it all seemed so unreal—fake or scripted, like I was livin in someone elses head. But every day of my life from before was like that. Every day, until I acted on impulse. Then I developed new fears.'

Martha's head bobbed up and down and Norman thought of Doctor Blanche and how she had lain so perfect, so still, so lifeless. Suddenly his scrotum pulled tight and he ejaculated. Martha swallowed audibly. She slid his penis from her mouth and rested her head on his chest again. They lay in silence for a time, then Martha asked what had changed Norman's mind so much. He took a long while to respond—long enough for her to begin repeating the question.

'I know who I am now,' he said.

2.

Preparations for the excursion progressed quickly. They calibrated their long guns and rolled up their knapsacks with some rations. They wouldnt need much in the way of food since they were headed north into wooded country. Within a week of walking, Jacoby assured them, they would be able to start hunting—small game mostly.

'Wouldnt want to have to carry a deer carcass through the mountains,' he said. 'We'll kill up some rabbit an squirrel. That'll make for good eatin.'

The men all agreed, and for the first time in some months the thought of food made Norman salivate. None of the men were staying behind. Going north—going into MacKowski territory—meant taking an army.

'Now I know the Wyrick said the targets been compromised by the MacKowskis, but I dont see why that means we gotta do this,' Raybur said. 'We got to hike three weeks north into mountain country to do a job that shouldve been given to the sumbitches that would love to shoot them a Jacobyite?'

Everyone slowed their packing to listen as Jacoby answered. 'The body trade is complicated,' he said. 'Wyrick explained it. The target body needs to disappear.'

'You tellin me Smitty MacKowski cant find a mineshaft to drop him down?' Raybur asked.

'The target? Sure, he'll disappear easy enough. But what the Wyrick told me without knowing it is that after we put a bullet through his pretty blond head, we need to bring his body back out here to the desert.' The answer did nothing to ease the tension. 'Chances are that Wyricks body will feed us for a year.'

'You really think he's that valuable?' Lucas Brown asked.

'Yes,' Jacoby said definitively. 'I do.'

'What do you think makes him so valuable?' Norman asked.

'Might could be that he's your brother,' Oz said.

Norman stopped packing, the idea of his brother a sudden reality.

'Life by definition is coincidence,' Jacoby said. 'I said as much, you know.'

Norman did not move. 'And we've got to kill him—my brother, Abner?'

'Aint your brother no more,' Oz said. 'He's a Wyrick an that means one thing.'

'What about if he becomes one of us? Like what happened with Lucas Brown?'

Lucas Brown sniffed at the idea. 'Hate to tell you, dreamer boy, but I was always Lucas Brown an your brother was always a Wyrick, same as you walkin round here sayin youve always been part of the Jacoby clan.'

Norman started to say something when Jacoby interrupted. 'Lucas Browns got the right of this one. When we get north we'll see whose loyalty lies where.'

The trajectory out of Jacobyville took them along the same path Norman had used to escape. The six men fanned out walking at a steady pace. Every once in a while Norman would see a random boulder, a piece of driftwood, and convince himself he recognized it from his solo excursion. But these recollections were fantasy and he knew it. The path may have been the same, but this was strange country.

Like their previous ventures, they left Martha and the kids with the Madonna. Before setting out they each kissed the ancient woman on the head. She wheezed and her eye spun about wildly.

'Careful,' Martha said. She looked at Raybur when she said it, but Norman felt the words directed at him. She had never looked older, more ragged and beautiful than she did now. Norman lingered for a moment and kissed her. When he turned to leave, Lucas Brown watched him.

At dusk they bedded down, sleeping in a heap together. He thought of Martha and dreamt of Doctor Blanche. When he started awake again, he thought of Grace. Laying on his back in the desert, the smog of morning washing away the heavens, Norman came to the conclusion that each woman was the same as the next—just in different form.

Jacoby crawled out from under the tarp they used as a collective blanket and stood, surveying the desertscape. He arched his back in a stretch. Already, sensing movement, the others began stirring. Then a foreign sound caught their attention. Oz snapped awake, sitting upright.

'There,' Jacoby said and he pointed. A light flickered yellow and incandescent, distant on the horizon. The men abandoned camp and started toward it, taking only their guns. The bright spot drew closer and split into two—a set of headlamps. The state route, much like it had when Norman came out this way, lay closer than anyone realized. The old man broke into a trot and they ran to meet the vehicle. The headlamps grew more distinct and the vehicle took shape—a white bread truck. Norman's stomach knotted and he slowed his pace.

The driver, seeing the horde of vagabond people, downshifted and the engine grumbled. The brakes squeaked a little and he downshifted again. A hiss of air and the squeaking stopped. The driver rolled down his window.

'Morning,' he said. 'God bless.'

As he walked closer, Norman saw the driver—the same man who picked him up some weeks ago, a season ago. Coincidence is the cruel nature of our universe.

'You all in some sort of trouble?' the driver asked. He leaned his arm and shoulder out of the cab to study the six men gathered around the side of the road. Finally his gaze fell on Norman. His mouth tightened and his head shook almost imperceptibly. But Jacoby saw it. He looked from Norman back to the man leaning in the truck window. Quicker than he had ever moved, the old man pulled a revolver out of his rear pocket and, in one swift motion, shot the trucker in the side of the face.

The sound the driver made came out as a choked plea. He leaned back in his truck and the engine roared. The vehicle lurched once, then twice. It began to roll and Oz jumped onto the running board, grabbing hold of the rearview mirror. With his free hand he pointed the pistol through the window and squeezed off two quick shots. Then, with the truck gaining speed, he emptied the chamber and jumped clear of the vehicle. He hit the broken edge of the road and rolled. Farther on, the truck careened off the pavement and crashed into a telephone pole by the side of the road—the pole canted slightly forward.

The ragtag band of men ran to the truck, Gay Jim outpacing them all. He limbed up to the door and yanked it open, shooting twice more. The driver's body hung halfway out, only secured in place by his seatbelt. Jacoby slowed to a walk. Oz went around the back of the truck and pulled at the latch for the cargo. Raybur stood at the edge of the road, keeping watch for approaching vehicles.

'Lucas,' Jacoby said. 'Tear off a strip of cloth from something, would you?'

Lucas Brown went to the driver's corpse and ripped a sleeve from his shirt.

'Anything interesting back there?' Jacoby called.

Oz's voice echoed inside the metal bin. 'Dry goods—lots of bread.' A box slid aside and there was a thud. 'Here we go.'

Everyone gathered at the back of the truck and Oz handed them a crate. Inside the crate were a dozen blocks of white powder wrapped in plastic and held together with brown packing tape.

'He wasnt one of ours, was he?' Lucas Brown asked.

Jacoby shook his head once. 'No, couldnt be. Take the crate with us anyway.' He turned to walk away, but then thought better of it. 'Lucas, you got any teeth on you?'

'A few.'

'Leave a couple.'

As Lucas Brown tossed a couple teeth to the ground, Jacoby walked around the side of the truck where he studied the driver's face and shrugged. Then he opened the gas cap and stuffed the sleeve halfway in. Everyone backed up when he lit it afire.

They were fifty yards away when the truck exploded—an orange ball and a belch of black smoke.

The highway continued on running close to the foothills of the mountains. Disappearing into the foothills after the explosion proved only a matter of distance. The scrub flora of yuccas and sage and cheat grass became more verdant with scrag pines and stunted oak bushes. They followed the low passes between the mounds of rock and dirt. Small game—mice, ground squirrels, and the like—scurried through the undergrowth. Every once in a while, Jacoby withdrew a map from his pocket and pointed vaguely in a direction leading them ever north and slightly east. Oz and Gay Jim took these moments of pause to shoot at the varmints with buck spray.

In the evening they made camp again, this time stoking a big fire and roasting their game. They arranged their knapsacks around the fire while Raybur climbed up a nearby hill to survey their surroundings. As Oz pulled the first of the squirrels from the flames, Raybur trundled back into camp.

'Quiet up there,' he said. 'Couldnt see a damned thing for miles.'

Jacoby nodded, pleased with the report.

Then they ate, throwing the bones of the small beasts into the fire. In time, the fire quelled and only a few licks of flame and coal remained. Each man settled into his knapsack—Gay Jim, Raybur, and Lucas Brown already snoring. Only Jacoby and Norman sat up. Oz lay in his bag, propped up on one elbow, staring into the flames.

'You got questions about what you saw today.' Jacoby said it not as a question or prediction, but a simple statement of truth.

Norman took his time responding. 'Yeah.'

Oz tossed a few pine needles on the coals; they did not go aflame, but squirmed like dying snakes.

'I was a boy when I met my first Wyrick,' he said. 'We knew he was going to come, had it told to us. The deal was simple enough: A Wyrick, always dressed more for a job in some office somewhere, comes out to the desert with a target. He gives me a location, an instrument. Then, on an agreed date, I kill them both.

'Some time will pass an another Wyrick comes out with another target an it happens again. They give me envelopes written in code an I know what to do with the bodies, where to find bodies, how to switch them around.'

'Whats this got to do with the trucker you shot today?' Norman asked.

Oz threw another handful of needles on the fire.

'Everything,' Jacoby said. 'This is the way of it.' He sighed as if already weary of the world. 'You never let me finish my history of Jacobyville.' He searched his mental inventory. 'We lived on close to nothing throughout my childhood years. We learned to scavenge an gather. Like any other desert animal we adapted to our environment. And like some other animals, I grew to the size of my environment.

'Really, it was a good life—a peaceful life, though not an easy one. Then one day a stranger shows up.' Jacoby looked across the fire at Norman—his eyes like flecks of silver. He laughed to himself. 'You know this story already, dont you? A stranger shows up an the universe is disturbed—it's a common story we dont think about enough. What if the stranger shows up to restore order to the universe because your life—that peaceful happy nonsense—disrupts what has always been the natural state of the universe? What if the universe, always expanding, is naturally destructive, naturally inclined toward violence and isolation? What if peace is an anomaly?'

The story spread out across time—all of the night sky. And as Jacoby spoke, the stars above them rotated like a great glittering mobile. They moved through the mountains as he continued the story, each day merely a walk leading them into a darkness where their minds ran rampant through all space and all time.

'This stranger, he shows up dressed in jeans an flannel shirt—clothes with creases an no stains. He fanned himself with a straw hat. I didnt know any better at the time an I went out to meet with him, my twenty-two in hand. A friendly sort, he asked me my name. Never volunteered his. *You know you dont exist*, he said. I was a boy really an I just nodded. He looked around the ghost town an smiled. Then he said if he wanted, he could come back here with a dozen jeeps, some flamethrowers an a bulldozer an wipe this place off the map. He sounded so natural. He smiled. I just nodded.'

The crags of the mountains loomed darker and more shrouded in shadow than they had the previous night.

'*A man named Wyrick will be coming out here*, he told me.' Jacoby wagged his finger in the darkness and said to Norman, 'You know that game, the rules, the play—as long as men named Wyrick keep comin out here and plannin assassinations, you keep killin. It's simple enough.'

Tonight Oz drifted off to sleep and the fire burned down to little more than a few charcoaled remains, crusts of white ash forming at the edges.

'I dont get it,' Norman admitted. 'Did this stranger work for the government or something?'

'Norman,' he said, then repeated his name a few times until it became a whisper. 'You arent thinkin like youve been livin in the desert. I worry about you.' He paused. 'Consider your brother.'

'Abner.'

'Aye. Abner the Wyrick,' Jacoby said—and it only served to remind Norman what lay ahead. 'What are the odds of you runnin into your brother like you did? One in a million? One in ten million?

'I chalked it up to coincidence,' Norman said. 'How you said coincidence is the nature of life.'

The old man laughed out loud. 'Your problem is youre somebody elses kind of smart. You let other people still do your thinkin for you. Your brother, he did some very special things in that war over there.' Jacoby gestured into the night.

'Vietnam.'

'Yes, Viet-nam. He joined the special forces—ran missions no one knew about, wore a uniform with no name.

If he was caught, the government would have no idea who he was.'

Norman agreed, asking what this had to do with anything.

'What are the chances of two men runnin into each other in a war?'

'Not great, I guess.'

'What if they were sent to the same front?'

'Better, but still not great.'

'Now what if they were given the same assignment on the same front?'

'I guess they might meet up at some point.'

'Aye. Now lets say the men are both fightin on the same side.'

The scenario took a moment to draw itself out in Norman's mind. 'Are you sayin Abner an me are on the same side here?'

'What I am sayin is there is only one side, one thing that matters an that is war. Every war since the beginning of time—since even before we became the mistakes of life—is actually just a continuation of the previous skirmish. The world thrives on war. It's big business.'

'Youre telling me that we're fightin the Vietnam War right here, right now in the deserts of Utah?' Norman laughed in the old man's face and kicked what remained of the fire into nothing.

But Jacoby's voice cut through the darkness. 'Norman, there is no Viet-nam War, just war—pure and unbridled. The war just changes forms while the currency remains the same.'

'The currency?' Norman said. 'You mean this is about money?'

Now it was Jacoby's turn to laugh out loud. 'What desert have you been livin in for the last year? The currency of every war, of every economy is the same—bodies. People will predict that the wars of the future will be fought with radio, with television. Robot soldiers they say. I say bullshit. The ultimate cost of doin war is bodies, the only piece of property you ever own.'

The pines grew thicker, fuller, and their voices did not carry. The air became thinner.

'The stranger I met,' Jacoby said, 'there are very few like him—like me an you an your brother. The stranger lives outside reality, constructin his own story in the grander scheme of things.'

They ascended into the night sky, where the trees again scattered sparse and bare and nubbed, their trunks twisting like shillelaghs of old. Streaks of star flitted in and out of the sky, evaporating into the abyss without fanfare or note.

'The narrative is this: Most of the world does not want to think for themselves. They want their environment constructed, laid out, their days need to be planned an plotted, their problems are even given to them as simple formulas. They believe votin is freedom, choosin one brand over another is choice. Goin for a walk in the park is liberty. School is education. Church is faith.' Jacoby exhaled, nearly panting as if the list could go on, but his lungs just couldnt handle the strain. 'Your problems are limited to a few obvious plot devices—infidelity, career issues, property disputes. That is the existence of the world. That is what we few protect.'

They perched high up on a balding mountain peak, looking down over the whole of creation—the valleys cloaked in blackness with not a hint of lamplight between there and eternity. The sliver of moon above so thin it looked to be a single white hair curled and stuck on the lens of night.

'We protect whats not real then?'

'Aye,' Jacoby said. 'Whats not real an what is unreal. The reality of the drug cartels cannot meet the reality you saw in Gratis. We stand between them.'

It took Norman a long while to process what Jacoby said. 'What happens if these realities collide?' he asked.

'When they collide,' Jacoby corrected. 'When they collide, the world ends for those folks the same as it ended for you.'

The words Norman spoke next seemed to follow naturally. 'An if the war ends, the world ends.'

The conclusion made Jacoby proud. 'Aye. We keep the war goin, but never bring it home. The Wyricks can work for the government, sure. Their clients are informants—or the Wyricks are dirty agents. No matter. We turn them both into currency—into bodies. If a district attorney needs a body to make a case, he finds it in a shed out in a forgotten corner of the west, part of what is now drug territory. One cartel gains too much power. One of its captains is taken out, his body showin up as a hit by another too-powerful cartel. They fight each other out here in drug territory an peace in Gratis, Utah, is preserved. People go about frettin over promotions at their nine-to-five jobs and their sweetheart children.'

They sat in a valley carved out by a glacier an eon ago. The pines once again so thick starlight could not penetrate, nor could smoke from their fire escape.

'The problem,' Jacoby said, 'is that I am gettin old. So are the Buchanan boys and the MacKowskis. When you live on the outside people forget youre there, forget what you do. There arent many like you, Norman. And it's gettin harder to hold back reality.'

'You think the world will end soon?' Norman asked.

He could not hear the reply, but knew Jacoby nodded his head in the darkness.

'All those words,' Jacoby said. 'Take all those words from my book an add them up, turn them into the formula for readin the future an here is what it says: Forty years from now a van in Acapulco will pull up in front of a grade school an slide its door open. Two men will empty out a trash bag an a dozen heads freshly severed will roll out onto the school steps. Entire towns—little crossroads no bigger than a gas station an a few outbuildings—will become the capitals of the drug cartels. People who speak out against the cartels an their involvement with the government will be slashed to ribbons an hung from pedestrian bridges, warning signs draped around their necks.' Again, he shook his head, saying he read it in a book, that this was a portrait of our future. 'Bodies at shopping malls. Bodies dumped out on the highway during rush hour. Caves full of childrens bodies. Governments will take less covert actions to incite warfare. The only thing holdin back a tide of bloodletting an chaos an out an out violence in the streets of Juarez an El Paso, the only thing that keeps bodies off the highways an school steps, the only thing standin between the fragile thing we call now and a terrible future, is us.'

3.

The morning sun came and cast shadows of the mountain long and westward. The rolling verdant valleys bristled with life.

Creeks ran along rocky paths. Off—far off—in the distance, greater mountains capped with white stood soldier over this place. The men it seemed had come to the edge of the world, a place merely painted on the canvas propped up between this world and the space beyond.

Directly below them, down in the valley, a few patches where trees did not grow, tan patches of soil bleached by the sun. A few squat structures sitting in barren spots—their clapboard siding dry and gray-blue. The men stood looking down on the place when Jacoby sidled up next to them. 'That there,' he said, 'is Clawson.'

They began their descent.

Like most mountain mining towns, Clawson appeared on only a handful of maps for a couple of years between the end of the last century and the promise of a new one. It had been a silver claim, though not a productive one, so it never grew much larger than a smattering of mineshafts with a few permanent outbuildings. Men came, went bust, and left—many of them taking to the mountainside and working on their own claim, leaving smaller mineshafts tucked into the slopes.

Amongst the outbuildings was the bunkhouse—a modest two-story with a sagging roof and no façade; there was a chapel—not much more than a pile of stone and a crooked cross on top. Three outhouses still stood much as they had a hundred years ago—maybe the wood warped and whipped by the sun and wind. But most notable out of all the remaining structures was the cabin.

Nestled in the far end of the valley, perched slightly higher than all the other buildings, the cabin looked to be of another time. Instead of the vertical ill-fitted slats, the cabin's walls were constructed from milled lumber laid horizontally and overlapped to shed the rain. In place of the tarpaper, shingles made from slate covered the roof. Its glass windows after all these years were still intact. A wooden door creaked in the breeze.

'Spread out, boys.' And the men stretched out into a thin line, their guns drawn.

Raybur held his shotgun at waist level and inspected the mines while Oz and Gay Jim cleared the bunkhouse. Lucas Brown stood up on a boulder near the center of the encampment and scanned the slopes of the mountains surrounding them. He set the rifle across his shoulder like a yoke and gripped the ends.

'Come on,' Jacoby said. He motioned for Norman to follow. They stopped outside the cab. The old man whistled at Norman and held up his revolver. Norman nodded and pulled his gun from the sling under his arm. They thumbed back their hammers, one after the other, and Jacoby kicked the door open.

The interior of the cabin was barren. A single chair lay on its side, a small table pushed to the corner. In the hearth of the fireplace a few charred canes of another chair lay cold and black. Jacoby tucked the gun into his waistband and strode the rest of the way in. Norman followed. Their footsteps creaked across the loose floorboards. The top of Norman's head brushed against an oil lamp hanging from the rafter, its contents long evaporated. Jacoby stopped and inspected a canvas jacket hung from a peg on the wall, but it was dry rot and fell apart at the touch.

'Cleaner than a circumcised monk,' the old man said. He sounded disappointed. 'This is where it goes down.' He pointed to the doorway, then at the center of the room. 'Wyrickll bring the target through that door an I use this gun'—and in some sleight of hand he withdrew the semiautomatic pistol—'to put two bullets in him. Two bullets.' He snorted, said he'd never been given such an odd direction. 'Then one of you are gonna finish off the Wyrick—doesnt matter who or with what gun so long as it gets done.'

He shook his head and walked past Norman to the cabin door. He let out a short, shrill whistle and the rest of the clan crawled from their respective places and gathered around the old man. Gay Jim hopped from one foot to the other, humming to himself until his brother laid a hand on his shoulder.

'Cant take any chances with this setup,' Jacoby said. 'Cabin seems like it's in a high spot—until you take the surrounding mountains into view.' He stopped and chewed his lip for a moment, gazing around the walls of stone and forest surrounding them. 'Dont forget we're in MacKowski territory here. And this Wyrick'—he looked now directly at Norman—'he cant be trusted. Dont let no one see us comin or goin from this cabin. Oz, I want you to take your brother up onto the slope there an find a good perch. Camp out there, but no fires. Raybur, you do the same—close to them, but not too close.'

'Youre takin Norman into the cabin with you then?' Raybur asked. He stared at Norman.

'Norman an Lucas Brown here,' Jacoby said. 'Time he took a part in what we do.'

'Might keep him from warnin that brother of his.'

Jacoby ignored the remark. 'No fires,' he said again. 'No loud noises, no movement if you can help it. You gotta piss come time for the action, you piss your pants. Up on the slopes you'll hear four gunshots in the cabin. Hear more than that an you know we got a problem. Dont come runnin right away—make sure there aint anyone else comin in. If one of you's got to run down here shootin, it's Oz.'

Oz nodded solemnly.

Jacoby smiled and clapped his hands. 'Everybody take your places. Now we wait.'

The supplies had been evenly divided—the dried game, canteen, ammunition, and a bag of sunflower seeds. Inside the cabin the air hung stagnant and stuffy. The three men sat on the floor, clear of the windows like Jacoby instructed. Every once in a while the old man would crawl to a knothole he found beside the door and peer out. After checking it the first few times and stating that all was clear, he had now resigned to shrugging.

'You aint never killed anybody,' Lucas Brown said. He stared at Norman.

'No.' Norman could barely speak—his throat had grown too dry. He looked to Jacoby but the old man cleaned his gun and hummed quietly to himself.

Lucas Brown smirked. 'Think you can do it? Think you can shoot Abner the Wyrick?'

All Norman had to do was lie, say yes he could do it. But he felt compelled to tell the truth, admit that he did not know if he could kill Abner, kill the brother he so long believed dead.

'Youre not for sure?' Lucas Brown asked. He repeated the question, this time more directed at Jacoby.

The old man clapped the chamber of his revolver back together and squinted down the sights. 'Norman here is not as green as you might think him to be,' he said.

Lucas Brown snorted. 'Why? Cause he done raped some girls back where he was from?'

A flash of cold shot through Norman's spine, followed by a surge of heat prickling across the back of his neck. 'I didnt—'

'You did, Norman.' Jacoby held up a hand to silence both of them. He turned his gaze to Lucas Brown. 'Killin a man is a sacred thing; lets not cheapen it by comparin the act to other crimes. What we do is holy work.'

Lucas Brown spat and addressed Norman directly. 'You think youre smarter than the rest of us cause you done committed a crime an got away with it, cause you done went to school. Murders different an I dont think you got it in you.'

Unable to formulate a retort, Norman sat open-mouthed. Instead Jacoby spoke. 'Normans smart enough to realize the different shapes murder can take,' he said. 'We've not discussed why you came back like you did, what your intentions were.'

'He done wanted us killed. Wanted to leave the clan behind,' Lucas Brown said.

They both stared at Norman, each trying to read his reaction.

'When Norman here left, he had every intention of leavin for good, of tryin to save his brother. But it didnt work out like that, did it?'

'No.' Norman's voice remained weak.

'You found out the world became a different place while you were gone, that civilization as you knew it had ended. You found out you were different.' Now Jacoby turned to Lucas Brown. 'Some men change their nature, some men in name only, some in both regards.'

'Could be some men dont change,' Lucas Brown said. 'Norman aint never killed nobody before, an he hasnt done it since comin back.'

'Aye,' Jacoby said. 'Theres more than one way to kill a man. Lead a man—two men—back into the desert, to a place that means death an let nature run its course.'

'Youre talkin about those two hunters?'

Norman began to protest. 'I never meant for that to happen.'

'Of course you did,' Jacoby said. 'You knew something followed you an you brought it back to Jacobyville, where only one thing could happen.' Jacoby shifted to face Lucas Brown directly. 'Leadin men into certain death, thats murder, yes?'

'Their fault for follerin him.'

This answer amused Jacoby. 'What Norman possesses is a secret mind—a brain that works unbeknownst to even him at times. He does things he cant understand; he doesnt see the consequence during the action, but knows the outcome. The question as to why I saved him has bothered you an Raybur, I know. Youre both too simple to understand.'

Lucas Brown flushed. He began to stammer—almost pleading for Jacoby to shut up. But the old man kept talking. 'Norman has changed his nature—he's let his secret mind guide his decisions. He's come a long way from rapist to Jacobyite.'

Now came Norman's turn to protest. He spoke up, weak and without resolve. 'I—this cant be—'

'We dont judge you,' Jacoby said. 'We took you in an freed your secret mind. It's other kind of men we have to worry about—the men who change in name only.'

Finally, Norman found the words he wanted Jacoby to hear and understand. 'I aint a murderer.'

The smile parting Jacoby's ancient lips exposed his rotten teeth. 'What we do isnt murder—you know that—it's our profession.' He sat for a moment contemplating. When he looked to Lucas Brown the younger man smirked and Jacoby asked for his pistol. At first he balked, but Jacoby asked again, more kindly this time, and Lucas Brown handed it over. 'Need your boot knife too,' Jacoby said and the man unsheathed the knife, passing it over handle first.

'Now, lets try a little experiment.' Jacoby turned his full attention to Norman. 'Could you kill Lucas Brown?' The question came with an air of politeness, as if asking Norman to fetch a tool or offer an opinion.

Lucas Brown glowered and Norman failed to respond. Jacoby handed him the knife. 'Youve got to do it quietly,' he said. 'Noise carries in these mountains. Slit his throat.'

The room suddenly felt smaller, the air stale and hot and ripe with the men's odor. 'I cant,' Norman said.

Lucas Brown sniffed, his eyes darting between Norman and Jacoby. 'Good test, Jacoby. Looks like Norman failed.' He held out his hand for the knife and gun. But Jacoby would not address the man; he kept looking into Norman's face. 'No one will ever know. After the Wyrick action tomorrow, we'll concoct a story an give Lucas here a proper Jacoby clan burial. We'll return to Jacobyville with our spoils of war—each of our shares just a little larger.'

'He aint gonna do it,' Lucas Brown said. 'This boy here aint got a secret mind or whatever youre tryin to tell him. He aint special. He aint part of somethin bigger. He aint any more special than me.' He snorted and stuck his hand back out for his weapons.

'I suppose youre right,' Jacoby said. He slumped against the wall. After a measured pause he said Lucas Brown must be the one with the secret mind, a man who changes in name only. 'Youve learned more than youve let on,' Jacoby said. 'Norman, on the other hand, pretends to know more than he does.'

All three watched each other for a long time, each trying to untangle the riddle unfolding before them. 'Lucas Brown.' Jacoby turned the name over in his mouth. 'A Jacoby man in name only. We saved you, took you in. You father two children with Martha. Then comes this setup, this mission into MacKowski territory...' His voice trailed off, but his eyes remained steadily on Lucas Brown. 'The thought occurred to me: This mission is different. I laid down in my house puzzlin out how you as Lucas Brown or the man you were before—the boy you were before—could have broken away from the clan for long enough to put a plan like this in action. I decided it was not possible.'

Lucas Brown sighed and said, 'Alright then. Aint possible. Lets get ready for tomorrow then.'

But Jacoby continued. 'And I was certain this mission just signaled a change in the Wyrick system—that clans would be pitted one against the other—another way to perpetuate war. Then I saw you handle that rifle earlier today.'

Lucas Brown's face darkened and Norman knew Jacoby drove at the truth. 'Wait a minute—' Lucas Brown started.

'Slung that rifle cross your shoulders while standin guard in an elevated spot.' Jacoby shook his head woefully. 'I thought of shootin you down then an there.'

'Why didnt you?'

'I want truth.'

—

In the end Norman did the deed. Lucas Brown gave himself over, admitting he had left notes for the Buchanan brothers when they went into his territory, hoping they would pass along his message.

'What did you ask them for?' Jacoby wanted to know.

'I wanted to rejoin the MacKowskis,' he had said. 'In one of the Buchanan setups they would pass along the message to the Wyricks—an if it was agreed, they would give me the signal I asked for at the setup.'

'And what signal was that?'

'A blond Wyrick. You already know how I showed them who I was.'

'So theyre watchin us right now?' Norman asked.

Lucas Brown spat. 'You really think this old man here has all the universe figured out?' He smiled wickedly. 'You think he knows everything? Havent you seen us sleepin through his lectures night after night?' Jacoby sat stone-faced. Lucas Brown did not abate. 'Tomorrow the MacKowskis will wipe you all out. Theyve been watchin you since we first come into the mountains. An by next week the Buchanan brothers, as payment for helping set this up, will go into Jacobyville an they will take turns rapin Martha an the Madonna an the children. Then they will chop them up—'

'You fucking animal.' Norman started toward Lucas Brown before Jacoby stopped him.

'We have to do this right,' Jacoby said. He scooted around Lucas Brown and coddled him like a hurt child, bringing one of Lucas Brown's hands up to his mouth. 'When you feel pain, bite down on your hand,' Jacoby instructed.

Lucas Brown tried not to cry, but his eyes glassed over and his bottom lip quivered. He whimpered a plea, but Jacoby was deaf to it. He forced the hand between his teeth. The breath escaping through his nostrils grew louder. Norman took the boot knife and started toward them. At first Lucas Brown kicked, then Jacoby wrapped his leg over Lucas Brown's and Norman held down the other leg.

'Cut up and in,' Jacoby said.

Norman nodded, not daring to look either man in the face. He guided the blade up Lucas Brown's leg, toward his crotch, stopping four inches from the groin. Lucas's body twitched and his breathing escalated into hyperventilation. Jacoby restrained him, pressing the hand deeper into his mouth. A trickle of blood ran down Lucas Brown's chin and the whites of his eyes were wiry with veins. First the blade cut through the cloth and then it sank into flesh. Norman worked the blade back and forth and blood surged out, hot and sticky, stinking of copper. A second later, another wave of warmth spilled out, smelling of urine.

Lucas Brown let out a long cry, stifled only by Jacoby pressing the hand harder into his mouth. The younger man coughed and began to go limp. The floorboards beneath them pooled with fresh, wet stains. His chest rose and fell in one final sigh. Jacoby released his grip and the hand fell from Lucas Brown's mouth—the web between the index and middle fingers bit open halfway to the wrist.

They left his body on the floor, a formless heap of rags and flesh, a mop of hair. Night fell and the cabin became engulfed in a darkness so absolute Norman felt as if space around him—the dimensions of the world—ceased to exist.

4.

Jacoby shook Norman awake, saying they needed to get ready.

'You stay back there.' He pointed to the stone fireplace. 'Safest spot in all of Clawson.' They broke the legs off the chair and set it on its side as an extra layer of protection for Norman at the mouth of the hearth. Next Jacoby took the table and broke the legs along one side, making a lean-to. He put Lucas Brown's corpse along the empty side as an additional shield.

'While you were dreamin last night, I was thinkin,' Jacoby said. 'More than likely, Wyrick an our target are gonna walk through that door an theyre gonna expect there to be a few shots—shots meant for you an me.'

'Yeah?' Norman took note of their inventory: a shotgun, four pistols—including the one Wyrick had given them, and a rifle.

'Well, we could take out the Wyrick an the target still pretty easy.'

Norman looked up from the guns. 'Thats your plan?'

The old man shrugged, saying he didnt have much to work with. 'Theyre expectin Lucas Brown to be alive in here. Ready to tell them where my boys an Raybur are. With any luck, Oz will see what a mess this is an hightail it back to Jacobyville.'

Both men knew such a scenario to be a false hope and they started loading the weapons. 'I told you before, Norman, leadin the perfect life means dyin at the end.'

As he divvied up guns, Jacoby stopped at the semiautomatic pistol. He crawled over to Lucas Brown's corpse. He took the hand nearly bitten through and broke the fingers, then wrapped them carefully around the gun. 'That should confuse the hell out of them after we're dead.'

'Arent we gonna need that?' Norman asked.

Jacoby clucked disapproval. 'Givin us a gun with only two bullets,' he said. 'I would guess it to not even work. Cant squeeze off practice rounds to calibrate it. Probably got the barrel rigged so it'll pop apart the second you try an use it.'

They ate the last of their dried game and split the sunflower seeds before retreating to their respective cover locations. Outside the sun climbed above the peaks until all color washed out of the sky and the world appeared blank and white. The cabin lay quiet. Neither of them spoke or stirred or thought. Norman kept the double-barrel of the shotgun propped across the seat of the chair, aimed at the door. They waited.

Sometime later—minutes or hours—the subtle crunch of footsteps on gravel. Jacoby crawled from his hiding spot. He peered out the knothole and turned to Norman, signaling that two men were approaching. Norman did his best to shallow his breathing. Footsteps fell on the porch planks. He could hear the men conversing in low tones. The rusty hinges on the door moaned as it swung open, cut short by the shotgun blast. Smoke instantly filled the cabin. Both of the men stumbled backward in a bloodied heap. The edge of the door splintered and swung. One of the men—blond with a beard—struggled to his feet. 'Norm,' he said. And the voice cut Norman to the bone. 'Norm, it's Abner. Jesus.'

Abner raised his hands above his head and where his suit jacket pulled apart, Norman could see a pistol on his hip. Jacoby looked back at Norman and nodded.

'Norman, are you in there?'

'I am,' Norman said after clearing his throat.

'Come on out,' Abner said.

'Youre a Wyrick.'

'An youre part of a ghost town clan.' He nearly laughed as he said it. 'Come on out.'

A prolonged silence followed. Norman stayed obscured in the fireplace and, though he felt the eyes of Jacoby staring at him, he did not look away from his brother the Wyrick.

'Clans are the only thing holding back the end of the world,' Norman said.

His brother laughed. 'Thats what they told you, I'm sure. Walk out here with me, would you?'

'How come you never came home?' The question originated from a part of Norman's brain he did not recognize. His brother's arms began to falter and Norman readied the shotgun.

'I couldnt,' Abner said. 'Not after seein what I did in Nam. Changes a person.'

'You changed in nature and in name.'

The Wyrick's brow wrinkled in confusion. The roar of the shotgun seemed to echo forever, continuing on as white noise. The Wyrick jerked backward as if pulled by an invisible force. A red blossom appeared on his chest and he fell dead.

All was quiet and Jacoby crawled out from under the table to secure the door again. 'You did good,' Jacoby said. Norman nodded in acknowledgment and reloaded the shotgun.

At first it sounded like hailstones pelting the house, just a couple knocks on the heavy shingles of the roof and nothing more. But then the gunmen must have moved into a better position and the bullets began to pop through the slatwood siding. Beams of light appeared where each hole was knocked. And their number increased quickly. The windowpane on that side of the cabin popped apart, leaving a jag of glass. But that also shattered a moment later. The staccato blasts of the guns drew nearer, louder, until they crescendoed into a constant roar of fury.

Norman pulled his knees up to his chest and dragged the chair in close. He clutched the shotgun. A few bullets bounced off the stone face of the fireplace, ringing and releasing dust as they went. The bullets only entered through one broad side of the cabin. They were not surrounded. Oz and Gay Jim and Raybur must have been holding the MacKowskis off. Jacoby appeared to notice the same thing. He buffered the side of the table with Lucas Brown's body and scooted, inch by inch, across the floor toward the fireplace—where the hearth protruded from the wall and formed a cubby in the corner of the room.

The gunshots stopped. Dust and smoke swirled in the air. Chips of wood mulched by gunfire lay strewn across the floor. Light poured through holes chewed in the side of the cabin.

A voice called out. 'Jacoby!'

Norman did not recognize it. Jacoby cursed under his breath. 'Smitty, goddamnit.'

Smitty called his name a second time, but did not wait for a reply. 'We got yer gunner put out there on yonder slope. Sure shot he was. Took some of my own goodest men, he did.' He cackled, high pitched and wheezing. 'But we got him, by God. Took him out with a brainer of a shot.' He waited for a beat before making an offer. 'Whyn't you come out of that there cabin, Jacoby-boy?'

'They got Raybur,' Jacoby whispered.

Smitty's voice drew closer to the side of the cabin. 'I know youre still alive in there. My boys asked if I thunk we done killed you.' He laughed. 'An I says, An old coot like Jacoby-boy? Man who blowed my man an a Wyrick right out the door? Naw, no he aint dead.'

Smitty stood not far from the cabin wall and Norman heard him ratchet a pump-action shotgun. Norman winced in the anticipation. Then a distant gunshot sounded. Smitty grunted and other voices called out in panic.

'Yup,' Jacoby said. He stood up from behind the table and pointed both pistols at the wall of the cabin and fired. His arms pumped back and forth, his teeth gritted and eyes squinted. Norman couldnt tell if he could see through the perforation of the wall or if he fired blindly with the hopes of hitting something. Whatever the intent, Norman mustered the courage to load two more charges into the shotgun. He leaned out of the hearth, awkwardly angling the barrel of the gun without exposing himself, and fired. The concussion of the blast seemed to silence all other gunfire and a hole as big as a window appeared in the wall. An anguished cry went up in the wake of the blast and Norman knew he had cut some-one down.

The gunfire from Oz and Gay Jim forced the MacKowski gang further down the slope in an effort to use the cabin as a blind. The volleys coming from inside the cabin quickly neu-tralized any safe ground and all descended into chaos.

Jacoby exhausted his last round and ducked into the cubby to reload.

'Fire the other chamber!' he barked at Norman.

Norman leaned out of the fireplace—a little farther this time—and blew a second hole in the wall. He saw a figure run past the aperture and then he looked to the doorway where a man appeared a second later. Norman fumbled for the pistol in his waistband. The man leveled a rifle toward the fireplace and Jacoby stood up again, letting two rounds fly. The assailant's head crooked, blood running out along the neck where he had been shot. Keeping one gun trained on the doorway, Jacoby emptied the other through the side of the building. A renewed blaze of gunfire filled the air. The window on the opposite side of the building finally popped and a glass shard caught Jacoby in the eye. The old man cried out. Blood streamed from where the glass flayed him to the bone. He dropped one pistol in front of the table and slumped back into his cubby. Norman fired his pistol at the wall indiscriminately.

'Jacoby!' Norman called. From inside the hearth he couldn't see the old man any longer.

Jacoby grunted a response.

'I'm comin back there,' Norman said.

Jacoby kicked the table aside to create a gap wide enough for Norman to enter. 'Bring the shotgun,' he said.

In the distance Gay Jim whooped and Norman imagined another MacKowski had just met his demise. Crammed back into the corner, Norman looked Jacoby over. It was worse than he thought. The old man bled from several wounds in addition to his eye. While the hardwood of the tabletop did protect him, a few spots from closer-range bullets cut through. Lucas Brown's body had been turned to a purpled pulp of flesh and bone and hair and rags. The wooden floorboards slimed over with the grease of blood.

'Give me that,' Jacoby grunted. He took the shotgun from Norman's hands and breached it open. He plopped in two charges. 'Cover fire,' he ordered.

Norman squatted, pointing his pistol over the table, and released a couple of rounds. As he let a third round loose, the shotgun roared behind him. Wood splinters and hot air gusted up around him and he collapsed, coughing and swearing.

Jacoby had blown a hole in the lower wall, where the slatwood met the floor. He kicked at the remaining scraps of lumber. 'Theres your escape, boy.'

Everything sounded quiet now in the wake of the shotgun blast.

'What?' Norman asked. But it wasnt deafness prompting Norman to ask for clarification.

'Get out of here an make a beeline for the mountain where Oz an Gay Jim are,' Jacoby said.

'But—' Norman started.

Jacoby thrust a pistol into Norman's hand. 'Run zigzag—makes it harder to draw a bead on you.' The old man stood and bellowed a war cry like a crusader of old. The shotgun spewed fire and dust and smoke and death.

The hole was just big enough for Norman to slide out. A stray splint of wood raked at the scar in his armpit and the pain it caused squelched anything else at the moment. He squatted, darting glances back and forth, holding the pistol at ready. Up farther on the slope, he spied a gray cloud he assumed marked Oz and Gay Jim's perch. He ran.

For the first fifty yards it seemed like no one had noticed him. He figured the MacKowskis must still be gathered on the other side of the cabin. Then a bullet landed in the dust just ahead of him. Though now inert, Norman stepped around the spot and began to run, head down, changing course every few steps. Shouts went up behind him and more bullets pelted down around him.

He reached the tree line at the edge of the slope and straightened his path. Above him Gay Jim and Oz rained down cover fire enough to stave off any accurate shooting on the MacKowskis' part. He stumbled over small boulders, grabbing at the trunks of the pines. Twice he fell hard, smashing his left forearm against the rocks. A bullet ricocheted off a nearby stone, sending out a long whine in its new trajectory. The cabin behind him remained sieged, the gunfire inside alternating pistol and shotgun—the MacKowskis clueless as to which instrument would be used next.

Norman made it to a flat spot where the trees parted for an outcropping of large boulders and the brothers lay on their bellies, rifle barrels lain flat across the stone.

'Dont shoot!' Norman said. He ran for cover just as a shot rang out from the opposite slope.

'Dumb bastard,' Oz said. 'They got us pinned down—sharp shooters trained on us up here. Youre lucky you didnt catch no fire.'

Norman began to apologize, but stopped when he saw Oz's condition. His hair matted to one side of his head with blood. Crusts of dried blood flaked off the back of his neck and stained his shirt. On his left hand his little finger hung perpendicular to his hand, swollen and black.

'Jesus, Oz,' Norman said.

'Piece a rock jumped up an got me,' he said. 'Tad to the right an it'd be through my eye.'

Gay Jim peered out from behind a boulder and squeezed off three more shots in rapid succession. No sooner had he rolled back into the cover of the rock than a half dozen shots dusted the place where he stood a moment ago.

'Cant shoot from the same place twice in a row,' Oz said. MacKowskis wont give you that chance.'

He stood abruptly and fired a single shot across the valley, dropping back to the ground immediately. A few bullets whizzed overhead.

'Jacoby dead?' Oz asked.

'No,' Norman said. 'Told me to get up here—for us to get on back to Jacobyville. Buchanans are going to raid the place.'

Oz kept his sights on the nether slope, only nodding to acknowledge the news. 'What the hell happened?' he asked.

'Lucas Brown sold us out—the whole thing was a setup.'

Still Oz did not look at Norman. 'You an the old man couldnt talk your way out of this one,' he said. 'Cant talk your nonsense to each other an dream up a way to keep from dyin.' He shook his head, then beckoned Norman to come close. 'From here you can look down to the cabin without them takin a shot at you.'

The boulders came together and made a V-shaped channel facing the cabin at an angle. A person would have to stand in proximity to the building to have a clear shot. From the soot stains on the stone, Norman knew this was where the kill shot of Smitty MacKowski originated.

Gay Jim fired two shots, ducked behind the boulder and, in the midst of the return fire, popped up to let one more round loose. He let out a triumphant yell Norman knew meant a confirmed kill.

'Shit,' Oz said.

Norman followed his gaze through the stone channel down to the cabin. Three men, guns at ready, darted under the porch roof. A moment later a smattering of gunfire erupted from inside the building. Some yells and then silence. Gay Jim hunkered down next to Norman, watching the cabin sit idle in the gauzy cloud of gunsmoke.

A man stepped off the front porch with a companion. Together they dragged Jacoby by the pant leg. Oz shouldered his rifle, the stock holding steady next to Norman's ear. Gay Jim whimpered. As Jacoby's body slid past Norman's kill, his arm moved and seized the long gun by its barrel. Jacoby sat up, swung the rifle, catching one of his tormentors full in the jaw. The companion dropped Jacoby's leg and kicked him. Yowls of pain emanated up the slope. Jacoby's assailant knelt next to him. All the gunfire had ceased and all sets of eyes in Clawson focused on these two figures. Jacoby swatted futilely. Then the man stood up and brought his leg up quickly with the intent to stomp on Jacoby's head.

Norman would never know if Oz missed the first time or if he was really that good a marksman. Jacoby's body absorbed the first bullet and he was dead. The second shot left little mystery as to Oz's intent. With his leg still raised, poised to stomp on Jacoby, the man fell backward, clutching at his stomach. With these two shots Oz betrayed their vantage point and a half dozen men came around the cabin, firing up the slope—first without any aim, then with deadly accuracy. Bullets careened off the rocks around them and the sharpshooters on the opposite slope renewed their barrage.

The three remaining of the Jacoby clan pressed themselves flat to the ground, waiting for a break in the onslaught. But there was none. Gay Jim raised his hand and fired blindly in the general direction of the gunfire. But the MacKowskis continued, undeterred. Oz drew out his boot knife and began to dig at the graveled soil near the base of the boulder. Gay Jim kept shooting blindly.

Finally Oz gasped. He had augured out a small hole where dirt and pebbles filled a crack between the larger rocks. The opening allowed him a limited cone of vision into the valley below.

'Shit,' he said a second time. And hearing it like that again, Norman expected the worst. Oz rolled away from the hole. He reached into his pockets and frantically loaded the rifle and the carbine before tossing it to Gay Jim. 'How many shots you got in that pistol?'

'Three,' Norman said.

Oz swore again. 'Give it here.' He took the pistol from Norman, trading it for a revolver that matched Jacoby's. 'Six in this one,' He reached into his shirt pocket, cursing all the while and drew out four more bullets. 'Use them wisely.'

'What do you want me to do?'

When Oz looked at Norman, his eyes were dark, sorrowful, reddened and irritated with sweat. 'You an Gay Jim get the hell out of here—straight up an over that peak there. I'll give you some cover fire, take them out as they come up the slope.'

The instructions stupefied Norman. 'You want me to go? How will I get back there?'

'Everyone of us has said it at one point or another: You cant get away from Jacobyville; you'll find your way back. Get there before the Buchanans trample Martha and the kids. Save our Madonna, alright?' He paused. Then, without ceremony, he told Norman to go on and get. He leaned out alongside the rock and fired into the trees below. For a second, it seemed the MacKowskis had disappeared. But then gunfire erupted again—this time much closer. Shots rang out from across the valley.

Norman and Gay Jim ran zigzagging back from the out-cropping of rock, bullets clipping around them. The path to the peak was shorter than from the cabin to the perch, but it also proved more hazardous. There were fewer handholds, less tree coverage, the steepness of the slope exposed them to sniper fire. Norman tucked the revolver into his waistband to free up his hands and he climbed on all fours. Gay Jim bumbled along, his pistol in one hand, the carbine in the other, walking upright.

Behind them Norman could hear the shots growing closer and more frequent. For the moment their escape must have been successful, though—their climb putting them out of range from the sharpshooters. They emerged from the sparse tree cover to the summit of the small mount and Norman could see down to the perch and farther down to the cabin, now just a toy-sized object laying in the valley. Oz fired, ducked and shot again on the perch. He reloaded, his back to the rock. He rolled across the ground, let off one random round, then stood to take aim and pressed the trigger again. He squatted and stood again and a cloud of misty red emanated from his chest and he staggered sideways, dropping his rifle. From where Norman watched, the events did not look real—they were muted and small and distant. Often the dealings of men are.

Three men emerged from the trees near Oz and began firing their pistols, each of them double fisted. Oz lay supine behind a boulder, the pistol with three shots in his hand. As the men approached, Oz rose.

He squeezed off a single shot before the pistols cut him low.

Both Norman and Gay Jim witnessed it. They stood at the peak and watched the MacKowskis strip Oz of all but his shirt. Down in the valley a lick of orange flame sprouted from the cabin and a pillar of black smoke billowed through the fog of gray gunsmoke. More men came out of the trees to the perch and stood over Oz's body. One man prodded it with his toe.

Then a man turned, pointing to the bald peak where Norman and Gay Jim stood and all the other men turned to look. Norman grabbed Gay Jim by the elbow and they ran over the crest of the mountain just as a single rifle shot called out a salvo in the open air.

5.

They ran. Tumbling over rocks and roots, skittering through the dusted patches where scrags offered no shade, through thick pine woods where needles reduced their footsteps to dampened patting, across creek and ridgeline and trail, Gay Jim and Norman ran. All precaution usually taken for long-term preservation vanished and all that remained was panic. The need to go farther, run faster, get away. At first Norman stayed paced with Gay Jim, trees cutting between them, their paths diverging then colliding. Behind them muted shouts called out taunts. A gunshot clipped through the undergrowth flicking at leaves and snapping twigs as it went. Norman's stamina surged and he pulled ahead of Gay Jim.

Gay Jim fell in line behind Norman, huffing as he loped along. Their pace had slowed, but so had their pursuers. Eventually someone would tire and give out and Norman vowed it would not be him. He would keep running—and right now it felt like he could. His legs stretched out, touching the ground for only a moment before bringing his next leg in stride. His arms pumped back and forth. His chest heaved rhythmically. Two shots barked out in quick succession—each from a slightly different vector. Their pursuers came at them from more than one direction.

'Come on,' Norman called over his shoulder, waving for Gay Jim to follow. They turned through another grove of trees and made a steeper descent. Running here was less of an option and they leapt from one embankment to the ledge of another, using saplings to balance themselves. As they descended to the point where they could once again run, they heard confused shouts. Not long after there were more shots.

The inside of Norman's mouth gummed over with sticky saliva and his nose burned hot and dry. As they wound their way through the low passes in the folds of the mountains, their gait became more than a shuffled walk. The occasional shout or distant gunshot propelled them along without respite or break for water. They passed by a creek and Norman only stooped to plunge his hand in the liquid, sucking the droplets from his fingers as they continued on.

Twilight fell and the forest lost dimension, the trunks of the conifers seeming to form into a picket, their boughs like low-hanging clouds. Whatever their destination—whatever lay ahead—became obscured in the premature mountain darkness. Norman reached his hands out in front of himself, feeling from one tree trunk to the next. Gay Jim disappeared into the opaque, his presence only denoted by his panting. The whooping and gunshots fired into the air by the MacKowskis continued on, until Norman noticed with more distance that the sound had faded.

Finally he stopped. He clung to a low bare branch of a pine and he slowed his breathing. He heard Gay Jim navigate his way through the darkness to where he stood.

'Should hunker down here for the night,' Norman said. 'Cant keep runnin like this.'

Gay Jim warbled a sound of agreement.

'But we both cant sleep,' Norman said. 'If you can stay up for a while, I'll get some rest and you can wake me up. Then we'll switch.'

They didnt bother searching for a decent spot to sleep. Instead they collapsed where they had been standing.

Sometime in the night Norman awoke. He heard a twig snap. At first he told himself it was a woodland creature—maybe a ground squirrel or an owl. Unsure of his own reasoning, he lay awake listening. For a long time only the sound of Gay Jim snoring sounded in the night. Then another footfall crunched down on a pinecone. What starlight shone through the thick canopy of pine illuminated the world as black on black. Norman crawled toward the snoring and shook Gay Jim awake.

'Someones out here,' he whispered.

Gay Jim mumbled and drew in a sharp breath.

'We gotta go,' Norman said.

Then there were voices—two, maybe three, distinctly male. They called back and forth to each other like they were spread out, trying to net a wider path. Gay Jim rose to his feet and they set off.

Without much light to see by, they trundled along slowly, hands outstretched to feel their way forward. They couldnt help but make noise—and in a moment of quietness, their pursuers heard them. A gunshot cracked out across the night. Norman immediately recognized this as a scare tactic and he took a few more steps when he realized Gay Jim had stopped. Before he could say anything a flash of white and a pop resounded behind him. Gay Jim had returned fire.

'Goddamnit,' Norman said and pulled at the idiot's sleeve. 'You just told em where we are.'

Already running, a hail of gunfire whipped through the trees where they had stood just a moment ago. With barely any light to see by, their strides remained tentative and confined to short bursts. A low-hanging branch caught Norman around the neck and he fell on his back in a fit of coughing. Gay Jim pulled him up and took the lead until he tripped over a rock or root.

Finally the first light of dawn came. They ran through the faded murk of morning without the vigor of the day before. Keeping to the low passes, they could reserve some energy and possibly put some distance between themselves and the MacKowskis.

Even after they ran for several hours and any hint of morning had disappeared into the bluster and sunshine of midday, they continued on. Gay Jim by pure chance stepped on a mouse. He backtracked three steps to retrieve the rodent. Picking up its crushed body, Gay Jim broke it and gave part of it to Norman who stomached his portion, blood and fur and all, before spitting out some of the thicker bones.

In their exhaustion they slowed to a walk, casting backward glances as they went. A few times they paused by a trickle coming off one of the foothills and they drank. Gay Jim picked some chive growing beside a stream and they ate it while Norman used this downtime to calculate their course. He figured they could just head south toward the state route. Once they found the state route, he would know from the mile markers which vector to follow through the desert to arrive at Jacobyville. The thought of seeing Martha tightened his chest. They would be out there alone now—only an idiot, children, and the Madonna for companions. He would have to provide for them. He thought of growing old, to Jacoby's age. He thought of the stories he would tell the children.

A shot echoed out through the pass. Gay Jim howled and hopped on one foot. Norman stood dumbfounded until a second shot buried itself in the trunk of a nearby tree.

As they took cover, Gay Jim continued crying out in pain. He sat on the ground, kicking his leg until his boot shook free. Blood dribbled off his heel and Norman could see the damage—a bullet caught several inches above the heel, slicing the tendon. Gay Jim's foot flapped about without control.

Another gunshot landed between their respective hiding places, sending a poof of pine needles up in the air.

'Can you walk on it?' Norman asked. He already knew the answer.

Gay Jim nodded. He was milky white, his features sallow. Using the tree trunk for support, he stood. His injured leg bent at the knee, the foot dripping blood. He used his free hand to break off a dead limb. This would be his crutch.

'Alright,' Norman said. He was interrupted by more gunfire. Bullets landed around them. 'We gotta head up this slope. Theyre probably circlin round to close off the pass.'

Gay Jim nodded again. Then he threw up. Norman ignored this. 'Lets go,' he said. He began to dart from one tree to the next. Gay Jim took a few steps and collapsed, screeching out in agony. He cried like a hurt child, rolling on the ground clutching at the leg just above the wound. A MacKowski bullet found him and his cries redoubled. Blood flowed down his back from a small hole in his shoulder. Norman stayed behind a tree watching as another shot grazed Gay Jim's hip, leaving a long red streak in his jeans. Norman pulled out his pistol. Then, running from one tree to the next, he passed by Gay Jim and put a bullet through his head. As he did so, he stooped to grab the dead man's pistol. Gunshots—too many to count—dotted his path. He stopped behind the next tree and cast one last look back at Gay Jim, the side of his face now bloodied, his eyes staring out at nothing. Flecks of flesh flipped up into the air as the MacKowskis used the corpse for target practice. Norman swallowed hard, then ran to the next tree, listening to the gunshots growing fainter.

Halfway up the slope, Norman realized his options for running had become more limited. The MacKowskis fired at him from two directions, forcing him to climb higher along the backbone of the mountain. His plan to crest the foothill and continue running had been foiled. If he continued on this path, he knew they would encircle him at the mount, where the trees provided no cover. He would be executed like the rest of the Jacobys. Every time he paused to consider his predicament another rash of gunfire spurred him on.

Looking over his shoulder while he ran as fast as his legs allowed, Norman turned only to catch the splintered end of a tree branch full in the face. Pain radiated like a hot fork through his nose, eyes, and mouth. He staggered, hands clamped to his face. He felt the warmth of blood seep out between his fingers. He forced his eyes open and saw the world blurry and spotted and red. He took a few steps and tripped. He imagined the MacKowski men watching through their sights, now dropping their long guns and drawing their pistols, charging up the hill to kill him slowly. Using his legs to push against the ground, Norman scooted to a broken pine with a wide trunk. There he opened the chamber to the revolver and checked the shots left. Five. The pistol he picked up from Gay Jim held a magazine. He tried to check the clip, but his hands were slick with blood and he fumbled with it. In his mind he resolved to use the revolver, take out four of the MacKowskis then turn the gun on himself. He used his other hand to probe the wounds on his face. His nostril had been punctured through and a gash ran from just below his eye down across his cheek. The skin at the end of the cut hung loose and ragged. He pulled a splinter of wood from the open cut. For a long time, he studied the gun. He listened for their footfalls, but heard none. Then he lifted his head to gauge the sun. If the MacKowski men were coming, they were taking their time.

In the side of the mountain, obscured by some pines, an oblong dark spot peeked out from the tree trunks. At first Norman mistook it for a shadow. Then he saw it for what it actually was—a mineshaft.

The coolness of the stagnant moldered mineshaft air washed over Norman's body. Hikers, Boy Scout troops, and hunters were always stumbling across these abandoned claims. Every once in a while Norman would catch a story about a kid or a foolish hunter who decided to crawl into a shaft looking for shelter or fortune or adventure. These people it seemed never considered the claim had become abandoned because it was without value. Any riches thought to reside within did not exist, and any promise of shelter remained blighted by the tunnel's insecurity. They might become entrapped, or the mine—already in poor repair—would cave in. But more often than not, people who entered the mines would end up dying of asphyxiation.

Norman stayed close to the entrance. He planned to shoot the MacKowskis as they entered the mine. With any luck he could pick off one for each bullet. He set the pistol on the stone floor—a grooved surface worked over by chisels and spudbars. He began ratcheting the chamber of the revolver, each click echoing in the cavern of the mine. He stopped, then crouched low. Air circulated through here. At the same moment, Norman heard shouts and a shrill whistle. He imagined one of the MacKowski men had spotted the mine entrance. Caught between making a stand and going further into the darkness, Norman chose the latter.

He secured the guns, tucking one into his waistband and keeping the other in hand. Then, ducking his head, he began crawling deeper into the shaft. The daylight behind him faded as the mine veered downward and to the left. Soon shadow cloaked everything completely and light gave shape to nothing. He closed his eyes and that soothed the pain somewhat. The construction of the tunnel grew less uniform and Norman stumbled, his knuckles scraping against the walls, his head knocking against the stone ceiling. The deeper he went the more he could feel the air rushing through the shaft. Behind him he could hear men making catcalls, whooping, throwing stones that clattered down the length of the chamber. From what Norman could tell, no one actually dared to follow him in here.

He progressed slowly, stooped nearly to half his height, hands waving back and forth to feel out a path. Each step taken more gingerly than the last as a twisted ankle was a death sentence. He stumbled and caught himself, the metal of his gun clacking against stone. The echo continued downward in front of him ad infinitum, but he also heard the same echoing continue to his left. The path of the mineshaft forked.

Weighing his options, he did not see virtue in either decision. He continued forward, descending at a steep angle. He sat on the floor, the seat of his pants wet with rock sweat, and he began crabwalking. His hand brushed something that felt like hair and he jerked it away. Then, after another moment to consider, he felt it again and realized it was rope. Keeping the rope in hand he scooted ever farther, ever downward. Sand, rough in grain, began scrunching under the canvas of his trousers, rubbing his legs and buttocks raw. He stopped and listened, then began to scoot forward again when he felt water on his feet. Blindly groping with one hand, he felt out the path ahead. Stagnant water blocked his path.

For a long time Norman sat by the edge of the water in this cavern thinking. Mainly he thought of dying, his mind harkening back to myths of an underground river where the dead entered into the afterlife—how a thing of fiction and belief was, in this small space, a reality. But death means so little after a time and Norman began drinking his fill of the rancid water.

He cleaned his wounds—the ones on his face scorching anew when he splashed the water into them. Then, keeping the rope in hand, he climbed back up the incline.

Once he cleared the top, where the tunnels converged and the rope was tethered to a metal bracket, Norman smelled smoke. Little more than a faint wafting of smoke, but he smelled it just the same. For a few minutes he sat at the intersection of tunnels and pondered his course of action. But only one course of action remained and he was resigned to the fact that it was death.

He took the other tunnel.

It cut at a lesser grade in an upward angle. The girth of the tunnel fluctuated, going from barely wide enough to crawl into pockets large enough for him to halfway stand. Gravel, rough cut and uneven, began to litter the floor and Norman recognized this as a sign he was nearing the tunnel's end. Moisture caused his hands to soften and they tore open easily from the rock. His knees received similar treatment. A spot on the top of his head he knocked several times knotted up, the skin broken and a trickle of blood mixing with sweat.

As he continued crawling, he stopped. Something had changed. Fifty, sixty—maybe even a hundred—feet ago, something had changed. Since he had entered the mine, the air drew from the mouth of the tunnel, remaining at his back. But now—as when he took the wrong path—the air hardly moved at all. It dawned on him: he must have crawled past the ventilation shaft.

Because the passageway was so narrow here, Norman slid backward until he found a spot to turn around. Then he progressed slowly, pausing every few seconds to gauge the air, listen, feel the rock around him.

When he finally came upon the ventilation shaft he couldnt figure how he missed it the first time. It formed an alcove between two wooden tresses. He squirmed into the cubby and felt above him. Nothing but space. Wind rushed around him, almost at a constant howl now. His back scraped along the shaft as he stood. Craning his neck back, he expected to see some glimmer of daylight. Instead there was only more darkness.

He resolved to climb. Tucking both guns into his pants, he used both hands to pull at the rough cuts in the shaft. But more often than not, his hands bore less of the burden while his elbows took the toll. The vertical shaft was never intended for a human to pass through it, making it so tight in places that Norman had to turn his head, hold his breath, use whatever body parts had a range of motion—toes, chin, shoulders—to gain an extra fraction of an inch. At some points he became so securely lodged in place he could let everything go and remain jammed within the fissure of rock. He'd exhale, relax some muscles, then begin digging his toes in, flexing his feet up and down until it felt as if the toenails would break free of their beds.

While fitting through one particularly tight spot one of the pistols caught on a rock and fell free of Norman's waistband. Moving his leg quickly, he pinned the gun against the wall. But without his arms to grab a gun he had no choice but to let it fall the rest of the way. It rattled dully and a faded thump resounded as it hit the bottom. And there the gun remains, neglected beyond use, the bullets fused into their chambers with rust.

After some time Norman began smelling something different. He didnt recognize it until his head knocked against the side of the shaft and the impact did not hurt as much. He had climbed beyond the stone—this was clay. The air around him smelled of earth, of soil. What seemed impossible now seemed likely—he would reach the surface.

He kicked more furiously now. Determined to make it to the surface, he used the last of his strength. Tufts of dried grass and dusty topsoil obscured the top of the shaft. He felt them break loose as he pushed through. His hands grasped at the grasses and he heaved the trunk of his body from the hole. Rolling onto his back, he began to gasp for air. The sky above was dark, a few faint stars winking in the firmament. After he caught his breath, he smelled smoke again. The thin stream of it screened the stars as if it rose upward.

Voices, as if carried toward where the rounded top of the mount fell away and became a rocky barren cliff. He peered over. Down below, no more than a few hundred feet, a campfire burned, figures passing back and forth in front of the flames. The fire threw out light in all directions, save the shadowed hole where Norman had disappeared hours ago. All of his work, stumbling through the darkness, and he had only gained a hundred feet.

Morning would come soon enough and these men would navigate the mine, taking torches with them. Once they entered, they would notice the tongues of flames pulling long in the draft of the mine. They would locate the ventilation shaft and find Norman's pistol, his route of escape. He couldn't rest here tonight. Using the heel of his hand, he pushed back from the slope. In the process of doing so, he knocked a stone loose. It tumbled down the slope—silently at first. Then it hit another rock and the few tumbling stones turned into a cascade of loose gravel and dirt.

The shadowed figures stopped moving around the fire, staring out into the darkness where the sound came from. One by one, they lit torches and came to the base of the slope. Norman didnt stay long enough for them to see the spillage and figure out where he stood upslope from them. He ran.

6.

They followed him out of the mountain steppes, always just a couple miles behind. The smoke from their fires always faint in the air; their catcalls and heckling echoing in the passes. When Norman came to the boundary line between the mountains and the desert—the state highway—he walked along the pavement. The wreck of the bread truck had been hauled away, but a scorch mark sooty and black marred the ground where it had exploded. It was the mark he had been searching for. He turned into the desert, trotting across the open expanse. Somewhere behind him the MacKowskis followed into whatever lay ahead.

In the night he woke, swearing he heard Martha's voice. Above the sky swirled two tones of indigo and black, stars banding across space. A speck streaked from the center of the sky and curved down toward the mountains until it blipped out of existence. His eyes tracking the path of the shooting star caught sight of a different light, yellow and pulsing. A campfire—not more than two miles from him. It flickered in and out—and Norman knew too well those flickers denoted a human walking before the flames. He rose and began running through the flats. The air around him neither hot nor cold. He could not feel his legs. And his feet, though blistered and bloodied, felt no pain. He thought of Martha, of the children of the town, of the Madonna in her jam closet. He thought of the Buchanans and the MacKowskis and the life of the world to come and he kept running.

During the daytime Norman stopped and scanned the flats behind him. No one followed, but he knew they were there—his vision diminished by the dust and harsh sunlight. In his mind, though not in his sight, the MacKowskis followed him. The snow had long melted and there was no water to be found. Whatever plants Norman came across he pulled up by the roots and gnawed. He put a stone in his cheek to sate his thirst. He slowed to a walk.

Days passed this way.

In the night, the fire of the MacKowski gang burned brighter, closer than it had previously. He was losing ground and he kept walking. One morning as he pulled himself up from behind a flat low stone, he looked into the darkness of the west and spied a cloud brewing there. The form stretched to the ground, skirts of silk dragging beneath a bubbling cumulus. He set off at a trot.

As the storm approached and daylight blared into the east, Norman noticed something strange. The clouds were not gray with gunmetal underbellies like a thunderhead. Indeed there were no flashes of light, no peals of thunder—no sound at all. The storm washed brown and tan, the tops of the clouds wispy with dust. Under their muted shades of clouds there were streaks of red and they rained down like blood.

—

The storm swept over Norman suddenly, as if he had run full force into a wall. Dust cascaded over him, whipping through his clothing, blasting his skin. He scrunched his eyes shut, but granules still embedded themselves in his eyelids. Debris of sticks and twigs and dirt clods, sagebrush and cheat grass swirled around him, accosted him. Noise engulfed him as a constant relentless howling. He pressed on.

He trudged forward as a blind man or a leper might—arms outstretched and each step tentative and resigned. He coughed and the stone in his cheek lurched into the back of his mouth, blocking his air, and he fell to the ground on all fours and the stone dislodged from the back of his throat. Around him the dust whipped violently—a tumbleweed rolled over him. He covered his face and prayed for perdition.

He woke and figured it to be the next morning. Loose tufts of grass idled across the open range. A thick layer of grit covered everything. Out toward the east, where the sun broke just over the mountaintops, the storm had vanished. He stirred, shaking off the dust. Blinking rapidly to clear the dirt from his eyes, he began to study his surroundings. Then he saw it—a jut of rock, a range of wayward mountains shaped like a shipwreck. He began to run.

The mountains and Jacobyville were still miles off. But their appearance on the horizon gave him renewed strength and he redoubled his effort. Then, a single long gunshot called out across the pan. Just by virtue of hearing it, Norman knew the bullet had not found him. Several strides later another shot ran out. They were distant—maybe out of range—but they saw him now. And they followed, gunfire marking how close they were. Norman allowed himself one look over his shoulder and he could make out a smudge he figured to be the whole of the MacKowski gang. When he stumbled, he resolved not to look back anymore.

Once the sun beamed down from directly overhead, Norman's pace slowed to a shuffle. His pursuers must have been equally exhausted for they did not gain ground. Using what little remained of his rational mind, Norman figured the MacKowskis, in their stopping to shoot, actually must have lost ground. The thought provided only a modicum of comfort. By late afternoon, when the sun cooked down its most unforgiving on them, Norman reached the outer edge of Jacobyville. He considered hiding in one of the beehive kilns, but knew the MacKowskis would simply send a barrage of bullets into the darkness. And Martha would still be left unprotected.

A bullet glanced off a rock behind him, sending out a long whine. He'd slowed too much; now he was in rifle range. Trundling through the outskirts of Jacobyville, he stepped over broken bottles and loose stones, the occasional driftwood timber. He reached the gulley running up the side of the mount, where the bulk of Jacobyville sat. He summoned what strength he had and called out for Martha.

He put his hands around his mouth and licked his lips. 'Martha!' he called a second time. His voice carried up the slope. More gunshots rang out and spurred him on. As he climbed the slope, navigating between the piles of till, bullets began flying. A few pelted the ground just behind him. Then one bit his arm. Like an involuntary twitch, his arm jerked to the side and he fell over. Pain ravaged his body. Blood smeared out from where he gripped the wound. He rolled over and sat on his butt, taking the pistol in his good hand, and he aimed lazily at the men clambering up the slope—nearly a dozen of them. He squeezed the trigger and the men climbing after him took cover. When he exhausted the chambers, the MacKowskis emerged again. Now he could see their grizzled beards, their lean bodies, and leathered faces. The one leading them had a tall hat with a broken brim.

Somewhere above them all, higher up on the slope, a gunshot clapped out. Norman looked back and saw Martha standing at the edge of the till, rifle to her shoulder. She fired again and again and again. The MacKowski men dove for cover.

Seizing the opportunity, Norman began ascending the slope again. His arm felt heavy and dull with ache. Blood dripped from his fingertips. He rounded the slope of the till and came up behind Martha. She nodded and fired again.

'Theres a good dozen of them,' Norman said. 'The kids an the Madonna safe?'

'Up in Jacobys house.' She fired again, then stooped to pick up a rifle laying next to her feet. 'Load this one up,' she said, dropping the spent weapon. A box of rifle bullets lay on the ground and Norman did as instructed. The task pained him and he was clumsy without the dexterity of both hands.

'We cant hold them off forever,' Norman said.

Martha dropped the rifle and took the one Norman reloaded. The break in the gunfire was enough. A hail of bullets flew up the slope as the MacKowskis emerged from their cover spots calling out profanities and running headlong up the slope.

Martha left the empty rifle in the till, pulled Norman to his feet and they began to retreat. The angle of the mount and how the till broke flat across the top gave them a minute's respite from direct gunfire.

On the porch of the Jacoby homestead the boy waited. He jumped up and down, clapping his hands. From a distance he looked like any child might. As Norman and Martha ran zigzag toward the cottage a shot belted out and the boy's body folded in on itself and he lay dead on the porch. Martha's scream came out as an unnatural sound—a wailing erupting from her lungs loud enough to shake the air. Norman stopped running. He turned, leveled the pistol, firing at the men who had just came over the edge of the till. He fired all but one of his bullets. All were misses.

When they reached the porch he had to push Martha away from the boy's body. Yoking her under one shoulder with his good arm, he dragged her through the door. Inside the cabin, the girl stood at the window, watching as the MacKowskis drew closer. Martha heaved sobs.

'Get me a gun,' Norman said and the girl ran to the corner where a shotgun sat propped on its butt.

The muzzle broke through the windowpane and Norman did his best to fire it one-handed. The kick almost knocked him over. Splinters of pain radiated from the wound and he staggered backward.

'A pistol,' he said. 'I need a pistol.'

Martha took the shotgun from him and fired the second barrel through the window. Outside a yowl went up and Norman knew she had hit someone. The girl put a six-shooter in Norman's hand and he turned sideways and peered out of a dusty, still-intact windowpane. The MacKowskis came closer, each man firing then taking a few steps forward. Both Norman and Martha fired.

'Go sit in the closet with the Madonna,' Martha told the girl. 'Dont come out no matter what.'

For a moment, the girl stood dumb. Then Norman said, 'Go on, now.'

The girl went to the jam closet and opened the door. The stink of the old woman wafted from the opening and the girl looked sidelong at them before shutting the door. Bullets knocked at the wooden slats of the building; windows popped and broke and sent shards of glass across the floor. The walls dotted with holes. As the MacKowskis advanced Martha crouched to reload the shotgun, then moved to another window and stood to fire. Norman watched as the blast pushed against her body and her breasts shook. The muscles in her arm tensed, her teeth gritted. He watched as a tuft of fabric sprouted from across her stomach and a well of purple blood spouted from underneath and she staggered backward and coughed.

Norman tried to call out her name, but his voice became lost in the volley of gunfire that followed. Before her body hit the floor, flecks of flesh flew from her body. When she finally lay still, she was unrecognizable. Norman fired his pistol blindly through the wall until the chamber clicked.

A bottle with a bright orange tail came sailing through the broken window and broke into a pool of fire on the floor. Heat emanated from the spot immediately and Martha's body—such as it was—became engulfed in fire. A second bottle launched onto the roof of the structure and droplets of fire fell through the tarpaper ceiling. Amidst the roar of the flames, gunshots continued popping. Through the smoke and the haze, Norman could see the MacKowski men standing just off the porch, their guns at their hips, throwing unguided potshots into the flaming structure. His skin prickled from the heat and a few beads of sweat dragged down his spine. He backed toward the jam closet, the swaths of orange flames sweeping across the floorboards. The table and chairs outlined in licks of orange and yellow. The tarpaper above peeled away, leaving blackened rafters outlined by more flame. Norman covered his mouth and continued backing into the rear of the building.

He reached up and pulled the door open, the metal knob searing the palm of his hand. Inside, the girl sat by the Madonna crying silently. The candle lantern swung back and forth, throwing strange shadows in the small room. Norman pulled the door shut and gasped. Though stagnant and stale, the air in this small room was fresher than the choking furnace air of the fire. The crack beneath the door glowed and he took his shirt from his body. Already soaked with blood and sweat, he stuffed it into the crack.

'We gonna die, aint we?' the girl asked.

Norman nodded. He could not imagine an end to this story where they could live.

The Madonna rocked back and forth, wheezing. Her one giant eye rolled around in its socket, wide with fear. There was a sound like paper crumpling and Norman knew the door itself must now be on fire. The Madonna continued rocking, the lantern swayed more violently until the whole room seemed to sway. Norman watched as the little girl disappeared in shadow and then emerged, her knees tucked to her chest, tear stains running down from her puffy eyes. The IV bottles hanging from the hooks refracted the light and clinked together and a loud pop resounded that Norman took for a gunshot at first. Then he realized the wood of the door had begun to split from the sheer heat of the fire. Sliding his back up along the interior wall, he searched for a way out. He knew better—this closet was dug into the side of the mountain. The only way out was through the door.

A single finger of fire poked through a fissure in the door. The girl jumped back and whimpered. The Madonna made a choking sound and her eye went wide, blinked once, long and slow. Norman batted at the flame with his bare hand. The fissures began to widen and he could see the inferno just beyond here.

He stopped swatting at the flames and turned. He took one of the bottles from the hook in the ceiling and ripped the hose from its mouth. Liquid poured out. He poured it over the girl, then disconnected another bottle and began to drench himself. The old woman began breathing heavily, a grunt of dismay resounding from deep in her throat. The third bottle's hose wouldn't break free from the mouth and he smashed it on the door, flinging its contents on them all—flecks of glass too.

Norman had to shout over the roar of the fire. 'When I say to, we run.'

The girl did not respond. He cradled her face with his hand.

'Look at me,' he said. 'I'll go first and you follow me.'

He tucked her wet hair into the back of her tunic and his hand lingered on her back.

'Hold up your skirt so you dont trip an fall,' he said. Then he looked at the door. It warped in its frame and the crack now bisected it vertically. He kicked and coals slagged off it in a show of sparks. He kicked a second time and the door cracked further. The girl cried while the Madonna grunted. The third kick broke the door in half—one side falling across the floor, the other swinging out on its hinges. He took the girl by the hand and took his first step out into the blaze.

The heat was unreal, sucking the air from his lungs, blistering his skin. Tongues of flame lapped at his legs as he ran. He squinted until he could barely see. He held his breath. Running full force through the flames without regard for anything between him and fresh air. It was no matter—the slatwood walls were gone, only the exposed studs left holding up the skeleton roof. His footsteps carried him through, the girl just a step behind. They came off the porch, the scorch of the flames radiating from their bodies, and there were gunshots. Smoke still blinded him and he swatted at the air in a futile attempt to fight his foes. He let out a long yell—half cry, half curse. Suddenly his arm jerked and the girl's hand fell away from his. Instinctively he turned to look at her, but the world was a blur of smoke and heat and carnage. He heard men whooping and the whoosh of the homestead collapsing. He heard all of this as he was falling, falling, falling.

FIVE

V W

Many who encounter death, who straddle this world and the world to come, claim to see a light at the end of a tunnel. This is exactly what Norman saw. The world around him was black, without depth or dimension. And the light appeared as a square of white. He blinked and the edges of the square became hazy. Aware of the mythos surrounding one's demise, Norman wondered if this was death, if he could make it to the light.

But he wasnt dead. The whiteness of the light in front of him came into focus and the expanse was blue—a single wisp of cloud drifting by. He wiggled his toe, inhaled like it was his first breath, tried to lift his head. A creak—long and metallic—echoed and the surface beneath him moved. He had fallen into the mineshaft, landing on the metal cart suspended by the chain. From here it was hard to gauge how far down he was, but he knew from standing at the top that it was far enough to cloak him completely in shadow. If the MacKowskis did bother to look down the shaft, they would not have seen him without a light.

He lay listening for a long time—long enough for another cloud to drift by his window into the world. Everything remained silent save his breathing. As he lifted his head and tried to roll onto his side, pain raked over his entire body. His injured arm felt afire and he made himself flex his fingers before moving his wrist and elbow. Using his good arm, he pulled the injured one over his stomach and propped himself up. A sharp stab of pain shot through his back. He leaned forward and the metal platform groaned and tilted at a dangerous angle. He braced himself with his heels and felt his back. Just to the side of the shoulder blade his middle finger grazed over a foreign object. The pressure of his fingertip brushing it was enough; the cry he let out echoed around him.

The object was a shard of glass. He stretched his arm to pick at the shard in his back. Each time it moved, he grunted and screamed and the metal platform rocked. Whether it gave out and plummeted into nothingness didnt matter to Norman anymore. With one final twist at the shard, he felt his back go cold and heard the glass clink when it fell onto the metal platform. He sighed and leaned backward, the platform swaying and groaning, flakes of rust from its ancient chains sifting down on him like snow.

Some time passed and he opened his eyes. He lay in a puddle of his own sweat. He shivered. The wound on his back had crusted over with dried blood and he knew he had slept through at least one day. He resolved to climb out of the mine.

He struggled to sit up, the platform again tilting and creaking, Norman's head swimming. Something—a nail or a rock or a fleck of glass—slid off the platform and resounded beneath with a distant plop.

The metal platform hung suspended by a single chain with two A-shaped arms on either side, meeting where the chain divided into two lengths. A great metal triangle brought the three chains together. Norman studied his surroundings, blinking to clear the cobwebs from his mind. He spoke aloud in an effort to make sure he made sense.

'If I stand in the center of the cart here,' he rasped, 'I can just climb straight up the chain, yeah?'

The echo of his voice seemed to answer him with the same question and he had to think about it. He looked up again, the outline of the rigging black against the blue.

'How in the hell did I end up in here?' he asked. This time the echo just seemed like his question repeated and fading into nothing.

He stood, panting, his hands clutching first at the support arms of the platform, then the chains overhead and then finally at the base of the metal triangle. As his hands groped over the links of the chain, he realized his feet would have a much harder time with his boots on. He crouched and the platform tilted. He braced himself with one hand and used the other to tug at the heels of the boots.

At first he tried to toss one of the boots up to the surface, but he missed and lost it to the abyss as it plummeted back past him. He left the remaining boot on the platform. Standing again, he summoned all his strength and hoisted himself up. Beneath him, the metal squeaked and teetered back and forth. Kicking at the air with a renewed burst of energy, he swung his leg out and caught one of the support chains. One hand rested in front of the other. His toes dug into the links and he grunted. The entire rig began to shift back and forth. As he let go only to reach one hand in front of the other, the corroded metal began to grate and burn his palms.

The mouth of the shaft was not as far as it appeared from inside. Once Norman grabbed hold of the timber arm at the top, he could better survey how far he had climbed. No more than thirty feet. Still, exhaustion consumed him. His bones ached. He fought the urge to collapse once again. And the urge left him once he saw the devastation of Jacobyville.

The girl lay as a half-naked heap of skin and hair and bones by the shaft opening, most of her clothes burnt away from her body. Her face pressed hard into the ground, and for that Norman was grateful. The homestead just beyond the shaft opening was reduced to a crater of black ash and lumps of coal. Wisps of smoke still eddied from mounds of char in the occasional breeze.

Being barefoot he took his first steps into the coals timidly—but they had cooled enough and he paced through the remains. Not a single plank of wood—a timber or floorboard—had been left unburnt. He came to where the back wall of the structure used to butt up against the cut bank of the cliff. He found the cubby where the jam closet used to be. The space held a heap of coals, the arcs of glass from broken bottles and the bones of the Madonna. For a long time he stared. Then he took a couple bones and peeled strips of leathered meat off them. He chewed the sinews thoughtfully.

He turned to look down the mountain slope, out into the desert pan. A black scorch mark with a trail of light gray smoke hanging above it stained where his cabin used to sit. Another patch marked the place of the meetinghouse. He followed the MacKowskis' path of destruction to the outer reaches of what was once called Jacobyville. Even the beehive kilns had been knocked in, their bricks scattered. They had effectively erased this place from all but a few men's history—and they had nearly eliminated those men. Norman was the last of them.

His path canted wide—out into the open and under the desert sun. He limped and rubbed his eyes, turned his mouth up at the sun as if to drink its light. An hour later he found himself at the entrance to Jacoby's underground lair. He crawled in and sat in the dark, waiting to die.

But death is a hard thing to think into existence. The two—thought and thing—run contrary to each other. Norman hadnt learned this yet.

Insects roved over his supine body and he caught them, ate them. As soon as he swallowed the bugs and sustenance filled his stomach he renewed his promise to die. Some nights, like a dispossessed somnambulist, he wandered out, searching for food and water, finding a saving grace in the form of a dry-skinned toad hopping toward a trough of muck hidden in a shadowed space. He licked the dew from the walls of mines and ate reptiles and insects and grass. As daylight crept over the horizon, he absconded back into his hideaway.

Then he heard voices. At first they were muted and he believed them to be the whisperings of his broken mind. Perhaps a dream had overstayed its welcome and plagued him now in his waking hours. Neither case was so. The voices came from outside.

Thinking it was the MacKowskis, Norman fumbled in the darkened space for the pistol Jacoby kept stashed in the crate. He found it and checked the chamber—all but one slot loaded and ready. He trained his sights on the hole, where the dusty light of day still shone down. A shadow passed above and he thumbed back the hammer. More muted conversation preceded a pair of feet sliding down into the hole. Any daylight vanished and Norman held his breath and pressed the trigger.

Inside the small space the flash and the bang temporarily blinded him and his ears rang. Above the ringing he heard someone screaming. The body slumped and the neck fell back so the light illuminated his face. He was clean shaven, wearing a T shirt. Norman crawled over his corpse and up into the desert flat. A woman ran toward a short rectangular VW van. Norman cursed as he tried to spur himself into a sprint, but all he could manage was a hurried gait. The woman ran around the far side of the van, opening the driver's door. Once inside she shrieked and Norman figured the man he shot still had the vehicle's keys. As he approached, the woman screamed for him to stay back as she locked the doors.

'Ive got a gun in here!' she yelled. 'I'm getting it out right now.'

She used the palm of her hand to push down the pin locks on the doors. Then she crawled toward the rear of the van to lock the back door.

'Stay back or I'll shoot!' she called.

Norman approached anyway.

He came to the side of the van and, peering through the window, he saw her sitting on the floor, clutching a pocket-knife. For a long time he just looked at her through the glass. Then he walked to the front tire and let the air out by pressing on the valve. Over the hissing, he could hear the woman sobbing. Then he walked to the next tire and did the same. When all the tires sat flat on the ground, Norman pulled on the door handle.

The woman renewed her threats, but Norman used the butt of his gun to break the window. He reached in and unlocked the door, pulled it open and climbed inside. He crouched between the driver and passenger seats and looked into the back of the van where the woman sat crying. The rear of the van was a kitchenette, complete with a sink and mini oven. There were drapes on the windows.

'Youre going to rape me and kill me, arent you?' the woman asked.

Norman considered the question a long time—long enough for the woman to lapse in and out of several crying fits.

'If you are, just do it already,' she said. Her eyes scrunched shut. 'Maybe you could do it the other way around—kill me, then rape me.'

She dropped the pocketknife and cried out for God several times. Norman recognized the incantation, but it held no more meaning for him than the formless sobs that came in between. He lowered the muzzle of the gun.

'You dont recognize me, do you?' The sound of his voice startled him as much as it did the woman. It had been some time since he heard it. 'It's like a dream now—when I last had you.'

'I dont know you from Adam,' the woman said.

'You an me.' Norman used the gun to gesture to himself and her. She flinched. 'We've had a life together.' His voice rose in amazement. 'The world is a miraculous place to bring us together again—it's the nature of the universe that you an me be here like this.'

The woman shook her head, trying to formulate her disagreement.

'Theres a grand design to everything,' Norman said.

The woman lunged forward and flung the side door open. She tumbled out and began running through the open desert.

Norman shook his head and watched her grow distant. Methodically he searched through the kitchenette of the bus. Amongst other supplies he found food and drinks. He loaded them into an empty milk crate he found under the sink. A lighter lay in an ashtray on the counter next to a bag of marijuana. For a moment he considered it—considered the many gospels of Jacoby. Then he lit the van on fire and began carrying his crate of goods back to his lair.

She sat next to the body of the man Norman shot. She must have pulled him up from the hole herself. Dusk fell now and dyed the world deep blue and sanguine and all the shades between. Norman came up on her. He cast one look over his shoulder. In the distance the yellow orb of flame burned, a pillar of black smoke rising from it and disappearing into the falling night.

He set the crate down and pulled out a bottle of milk, which needed to be drunk first since it was already warm. He levered the metal cap from the glass mouth and took three deep swallows. Involuntarily he sighed with relief. He sat facing the woman, her grief isolating her from all else.

Finally she spoke. 'I dont know what you are or why youre here,' she said. 'But this is evil.' She stroked the dead man's hair.

Norman sipped the milk.

'You killed him,' she said. 'We were going to get married when we reached California. He wanted to stop out here after he heard some locals talking about ghost towns—old mining camps. He said he'd find a gold nugget and make me a proper wedding ring.'

She lapsed back into sobs.

'You watch too much TV,' Norman said. He chuckled ruefully. 'A gold nugget. Proper wedding ring. Heading to California.' He began to hum a song he remembered from his life before, a song about going to San Francisco.

'Youre crazy,' she said. She did not mean it as an insult, Norman could tell. There was genuine surprise in her voice.

Again, Norman chuckled. 'I was once as stupid as you are now.' He sighed wistfully. 'What I'd give to be stupid again.'

He gathered his crate of supplies and descended into the lair, humming as he went.

The next morning she was gone. Her fiancé still lay in the dirt, his shirt stained brown with blood, a small puncture in his stomach. When he had lived he must have been an attractive man.

At first Norman followed her tracks, but he soon lost interest. Out here she would either return or perish—such is the way of the desert. He tramped out toward where the buildings of Jacobyville lay now as little more than scorch marks on the earth. During the days he had taken to sifting through the ashes, looking for anything of use or value—a nail or a cut of glass, a bullet or bone. It kept him busy.

As he squatted in the rubble, he held up a bottle neck to examine it in the sunlight. A movement in the distance, out in the pan, caught his attention. A lone figure traipsed and fell, brought herself to her feet and walked a few more steps before falling again. He ran down the mountain.

When he arrived she lay panting shallowly, her eyes fluttering. As he knelt next to her, he bit his lip, cracked his knuckles, pressed at the crotch of his pants. Finally he picked her up the best he could. Her skin clammed to the touch and she murmured incoherently. It took some time, but he eventually brought her back to his lair. He laid her down inside and dragged her fiancé's bloated body farther away. He nursed her with the goods he took from the van: He mashed an apple into pulp and placed dabs of it on her tongue, then bits of white bread. Several days later, as he crumbled granules of Ovaltine onto her tongue, she emerged from her delirium and shuddered at the sight of him.

He spoke first. 'You walked out of here. You must have been headin back when you collapsed. You nearly died.'

She looked away and said she wished she had died.

Norman said he knew what she meant, but the body knows better. 'Your mind lies to you, tells you death is better. Your body only knows one thing, though, an you keep on livin.' He laughed. 'Divorce the mind from the body an you'll do things you never thought possible.'

The woman's eyes glassed over either with exhaustion or the sadness that comes with trepidation.

'Here,' Norman said and he scooted across the floor and pulled out the dictionary. 'This book here is the human mind unbridled.'

Her brow wrinkled. 'It's a fucking dictionary.'

Words failed Norman now. He started a response, but he was too late—she had lapsed back into a fevered slumber.

Over the next couple days she fell in and out of lucidity, each time surprised and sickened by the realization she was not living a dream. Whether she remained conscious or not did nothing to stop Norman from narrating his life out in the desert. He stroked her hair, placed bits of food on her tongue, cleaned and dressed her wounds. When she fell into the deepest of sleeps, he lightly placed one hand where her legs joined together and he began to rub until her eyelids fluttered.

He told her of the sacred trade of the desert—the trade of corpses and drugs and guns. The Wyrick, as Norman explained him, came back each time as a different man. 'And each time, in whatever form the Wyrick took, we had to barter for our life out here. And each time he asked for us to make a sacrifice out of someone—someone he brought with him.' He laughed and wagged his finger, though the woman lay sleeping. 'But you know what it is like to deal with these gods of the desert—always trickery and sorcery and smoke and mirrors. When he came back, we killed them both. Once it was my very own brother.' If she lay awake, she studied him warily through half-closed eyes, her countenance stony. Norman felt compelled to tell her more.

'There are higher powers than the Wyrick,' he said. 'Unseen powers. In order to stay alive we have to know what they want, what their motivations are. And all we have out here'—his voice rose and he pointed at the earth—'all we have is tradition. That is our protection. A sacred rite. We learn the way of the desert in the same way I am teaching you now.'

A measured pause passed as Norman waited for the woman to thank him. No such gratitude passed from her lips. Instead she lay her wrist across her eyes and asked him for death.

'You wont die,' Norman said. The idea of death shocked him. 'The desert is about preservation, not destruction.'

'We came out here looking for a gold nugget,' she snapped, her eyes still covered.

'To melt down and make into a ring,' Norman said. 'I know. You told me. A ring to serve as a symbol of matrimony—a way to preserve your relationship.'

'Youre crazy.'

'Youre dumb.'

The woman's upper lip curled. 'Why wont you kill me?' Her voice broke and Norman recognized the inflection as being a genuine question.

He considered all of the possible answers—and there were many. He sorted through them one by one, taking long enough that the woman uncovered her eyes and stared at him. Finally he settled on an answer he felt satisfied her inquiry. 'Because we are all thats left,' he said. 'After us, this way of living dies.'

'Good,' she said. 'Kill me then.'

He reached out and stroked her hair, the strands now rough and ropey. She shuddered at his touch. 'This way of life is sacred,' he said, his voice cooing like a parent telling a bedtime story. 'We see all. We know all. We are not beholden to the petty laws of men, but we enforce them. What happens out here is a miraculous thing.'

Under his hand the woman's body began to writhe as she sobbed uncontrollably. He shushed her and stroked her hair more gently—from what he could recall coming to terms with this world was the hardest part.

'How long have you all lived like this?' she asked.

Some days had passed since her fever broke and she sat awake and captive.

Norman scratched at his hairline. He had been philosophizing, imagining what Jacoby would have said, then giving voice to it. The question interrupted his musings and he pondered it for a few seconds.

'Life has always been like this,' he said.

The woman shook her head defiantly. 'No,' she said. 'How long have you lived like this? You havent always been this way, have you?'

The inquiry seemed simple enough, yet Norman spent a while contemplating the question. 'Yes,' he finally said. 'Ive always been like this.'

Again, the woman shook her head. 'Theres no way. No one can live like this. You aint from this place.'

Norman insisted, saying everything that came before this place was death and everything outside of this place is death.

'And this is living?' she asked.

Norman leaned forward, knowing how a shaft of light would fall directly across his face. He allowed a pause and began to launch into a speech about the desert way of life, how scant of food and water one really needs, what the human body really is. She interrupted.

'It's just that I think I know you,' she said. 'Like maybe I saw you somewheres outside of here—somewhere dead, I guess.'

Norman searched her countenance for guile, but her eyes remained steadfast. If he did know her from before, he could not recollect how.

At night he slept across the threshold of the lair in case the woman tried to escape, but no attempt was ever made. Once the sun reached a point in the sky where the rays directed down into the hole, he woke. As it continued to rise and bake down on the pan with greater fury, he would leave to scavenge.

He caught bugs, slew a bird, killed a snake. He scraped dew from mineshaft walls and collected a measly half-cup of water from a sill he devised on the slope. When he returned to the lair, she waited. They ate in silence, save for her gagging.

'I tried to cook the snake in his skin a little,' Norman said. 'Used a strip of glass I found and a flat rock, sandwiched the meat between so it might heat up enough.'

She nodded once and ate a pinch of the meat. Her stomach lurched and she held her hand up to her face.

'Hold on,' Norman said. He set his portion down and scrambled out of the hole.

Since the woman, Norman had been keeping a slop bucket outside—a shallow cast iron pan he salvaged. Whenever the woman vomited or shat, he could take the pan and transport the refuse outside. In situations like this, he had to scrape the emissions into the pan.

As he stooped to pick up the pan, he caught sight of something distant—a faint rising cloud of dust. Behind it, two more clouds rose. He stood frozen. Perhaps the sheriffs or some law enforcement had come looking for this woman.

Inside, the woman retched and asked if he was bringing the pan.

The clouds drew nearer, the vehicles kicking up the dust becoming evident. Only luck would lead a sheriff to Jacobyville. The other ghost town families—what was left of them at this point—would be on foot, he reasoned. The only other beings that knew of Jacobyville were the Wyricks and their higher-ups. And they would never send three vehicles to set up a mission.

The woman called again.

'Stay in there,' Norman said. Then he ran toward the slope.

From where he squatted on a jut of rock, Norman could see the jeeps rumbling in a line across the flat of the desert, fins of dust rising and fading into beige clouds in their wake. They slowed and stopped and inspected the burnt wreckage of the VW van before changing course and heading toward Jacobyville. As he predicted, the woman climbed out of the lair, flailing her arms and crying. The jeeps stopped again and men dressed in hunting garb and uniforms piled out of the vehicles. One of the them held a pair of binoculars to his face and scanned the mountainside. Norman did not move. With the sun at his back, up here at the peak of the mount, he himself would look a part of the landscape—a silhouetted rock. He watched the woman, she pointed at the remains of the town, then down at the lair where he had left her. Two men descended into the hole while a third stood with his rifle trained on the opening.

They re-emerged from the hole and dropped the artifacts they found on the ground. Amongst them was the dictionary. The woman kept talking, pointing toward the mountain. A man with a metal tank strapped to his back came from one of the other jeeps. In his hand he held a wand with a lick of fire lapping at the end. The man with the binoculars fixed his gaze right where Norman squatted and he was not distracted when the man with the flamethrower set Norman's only possessions aflame. Norman closed his eyes and exhaled long and slow. Next, one of the men took the woman by the arm as if to guide her. She took a single step forward and he pointed his pistol at the back of her head and with a single shot dropped her to the ground. Still, Norman did not flinch.

They stuffed her body down into the hole. Then the man with the flamethrower stepped forward and set the place ablaze. Now, Norman moved. He ran crouched low to the ground. Distant gunshots rang out, but he did not bother to look, knowing they were out of range. He passed by a screen of oak scrub and into the square opening of a horizontal mineshaft. The blackness engulfed him and the sounds of the world were taken over by a screaming silence.

He wandered in and out of the mineshaft for an indeterminate amount of time, staggering out of a smaller opening at sunrise or sunset, only to turn and walk back into the darkness. He learned the routes by touch, by smell, and committed them to memory. When he found himself back out in the light of day, he squinted hard trying to recognize his place in the world. Each time he went back in he plumbed deeper and deeper yet, finding adjoining caves with pools of freshwater teeming with albino fish, supplies left from miners and explorers. The body needs so little to survive; it can live on out of habit.

Eventually the clothes rotted off his frame and he went blind. He ate bats plucked from the rafters like overripe fruits. As he grew older and older yet, his back bowed from living in these shadowed places and he ran through the tunnels—up and down and crosswise—only to poke his head out and turn his whitened eyes toward a sun he could no longer see. And he listened to a world that sounded like a strange symphony of car horns and diesel engines, steam whistles and jets soaring overhead.

In the dark he dreamt of dying, of the promise that is granted to us all. Laying in the tunnels, he imagined how the earth would move, the mines collapsing beneath the pressure, his body crushed and ground into meal. He imagined his fragments of bone tumbling across the floors of distant seas, tumbled into sand and washed ashore where children might build sandcastles and defend them from the tides.

Leabharlanna Poiblí Chathair Bhaile Átha Cliath
Dublin City Public Libraries